Winds Of The Goshi

Winds Of The Goshi

Gary McConville

The Winds Series by Lagomorph Publishing LLC
Suite 420-328
855 Woodstock Road
Roswell, GA 30075

ISBN: 978-1-6653-1095-6 - Paperback
eISBN: 978-1-6653-1096-3 - eBook

Library of Congress Control Number: 2025921169

♾This paper meets the requirements of ANSI/NISO Z39.48-1992 (Permanence of Paper)

Grammatical edits:
    Nancy Ford McConville

Final storyline edits:
    Misty Parker of Dallas, GA

Cover art and interior graphics:
    Devin Maupin (devinmaupin@gmail.com)

092325

This book is dedicated to three people who breathed life into my life and the lives of countless others:

Charles 'Thom' Odette - Nov 25, 1951 - July 6, 2024
Thom and I were close friends since junior high. Growing up in strange times, he frequently offered enlightened opinions. Thom's absence creates a genuine emptiness.

Leslie 'Gene' Lewis, W5LE - July 28, 1948 - March 23, 2024
Gene was a fellow ham radio operator and a jovial optimist who soon became a cherished friend. He had the skill of turning bad situations into favorable ones, often finding good things others had overlooked. His friendship is missed as well as his voice and spirit on the airwaves.

Heather Stephenson Greene - January 11, 1975 - January 28, 2025
Heather was a special friend. As a vet-tech, kindred spirit, and animal whisperer extraordinaire, you gave to us and our bunnies from your heart and soul. Your knowledge and love of all animals will forever live as your legacy.

CONTENTS

PART 1
Awareness

CHAPTER 1
The Reoccurring Nightmare
ANDORF

Returning to his cabin with breakfast in hand, Andorf finds his beloved Serin sprawled across the floor in a bloodied robe. Through a series of jerky movements and gasping with labored breath, she peers up. "Something's terribly wrong. My water broke and … I—I can't stand up."

Andorf wraps a blanket around Serin and gently gathers her in his arms. Running through the hallway, he screams for everyone to get out of his way. Serin clutches his neck so tightly he can hardly breathe, squeezing tighter with every contraction. "Hurry," she squeals. "This baby wants out."

Bearing scratches across his arms, neck and face, Andorf bursts through sickbay doors. He carefully places her on a clean gurney. He turns to summon help but Serin refuses to relinquish her death-grip on his arm. "For the first time in my life, I'm scared," she whimpers between breaths. "Don't leave me, Andorf."

Pulling the sheets from Serin's weak grip, he grasps her cold, clammy hand. Encircled by complex-looking devices with blinking lights and colored probes running everywhere, Andorf feels lost. He cannot place it, but things are not quite right.

"Your wife's lost an awful lot of blood," an assistant says, wiping away tears dripping down her cheeks. "If only you had arrived sooner."

Andorf jumps onto a gurney. He rips off his shirt and uses it to tie a crude tourniquet around his bicep. "Give Serin my blood—all of it if you must. Do whatever it takes. You must save her."

"What the hell are you doing?" a nurse yells, entering the room. She stares at Andorf as if he has gone mad. After removing the tourniquet and ordering him out, she hits one of the wall-mounted panic buttons.

A heavy orderly appears from nowhere. Steaming mad, he wheels Andorf and the gurney out of the surgical area.

Andorf leaps up, jogs around the orderly, and then bolts back inside. Dropping to his knees, he stares up at the nurse with cupped hands. "I'm begging you, please. Give Serin my blood. Do it now. Do it right now, while she still has life."

"Impossible," the nurse says. "Your blood will need to be cleansed and run through a series of complex tests. Only then could we—"

"Forget your damn tests," Andorf yells. "We are of the same blood type, I swear. Hurry! Give Serin my blood. It will save her life." Reading the nurse's nametag, Andorf leaps to his feet. He firmly grabs the nurse's arm. "You must believe me, Jasmine. Whole blood transfusions become common place by year's end."

Growling even louder than her empty stomach, Jasmine reaches for her belt-pouch and waves the shiny device in Andorf's face. "You want me to zap you with this stunner? That's what I'll do if you don't release me. You'll be lying face down on the floor in five seconds, gasping for breath." Counting, Jasmine's eyes narrow. "Four … three … two …"

Despite her weakness, Andorf feels Serin reaching out for him. Her faint thoughts unnerve him. *The old man at the Cos warned … I'll never see my baby.*

Andorf stares hypnotized at Serin's convulsing body beneath the blood-stained sheets. Somewhere between all the machine's strobing lights, multi-colored mini-probes attached to his wife's arms, and the beet-red bedsheets, reality smacks him in the face. He jogs around the gurney. Taking hold of

Serin's cold, clammy hand, he whispers. "I shall come back for you, Serin. As many times as it takes, I swear I will never quit. Until I never lose you."

Serin leans her head to face him. A hard-pressed smile appears on her face. Her eyes then darken, losing their ever-present glimmer as she exhales her last breath.

With nothing making sense, Andorf collapses onto the cold floor. "No!" he yells out. "Serin is my life. How can I accept her in past tense? How? How?"

"Daddy! Daddy! Wake up! You're having those nightmares again."

Feeling himself lying on damp bedsheets, Andorf's eyes flash open. He flinches at the sight of eight-year-old Mila hovering above. He jumps up and then mumbles while washing his face. "How many times? How many more times must I relive this nightmare?"

Mila shrugs her shoulders.

After collecting Mila, the twins, and their toys, Andorf exits the cabin. "Come on kids. A visit with an old friend is long overdue."

CHAPTER 2

A Whole Lot Of Shakin'
ANDORF

ndorf and clan enter a private room deep within the *S.S. Aegean's* infirmary. The kids assume spots on the floor to play with their toys while he takes a seat on Brutus' bed.

Brutus struggles to turn his head to one side. "Why the long face, Andorf? What's troubling you now?"

"Uh … uh," Andorf stutters, not knowing where to begin.

"It's those dreams again, isn't it?"

Mila quits playing long enough to peer up at her Papa. "Daddy's been having nightmares, Papa. He sweats a lot and calls out Serin's name in his sleep."

Brutus knee-nudges Andorf. "It's been two years already. You must face the facts, my friend, our wife's never coming back."

Andorf shakes his head. "Damn, Brutus. Do you think I have not tried to clear my mind of her? Short of dating, I don't know what else to do."

The nurse peers at Andorf and then at her own ringless fingers. Before she can comment, the floor begins to shudder. Everything vibrates violently.

Many vanishing items vanish reappear elsewhere in the room. Even the Goshi finds himself sitting beside the nurse on the cold vinyl floor, staring bewildered up at Brutus.

Brutus' eyes narrow. "You did that, didn't you, Mr. Goshi?"

"I—I don't think so," Andorf takes his time looking around the room. "At least not *this* time."

"If it wasn't you, then what the hell just happened?" the nurse yells above the twin toddlers' giggles. Steadying herself against the bed, she adjusts her white smock and cummerbund before rising to her feet.

"Some visionary you are, Andorf," Brutus snarls his best out a corner of his contorted mouth. "How could you have missed anything this large? I thought you had everything in the near future mapped out."

"Obviously, there are minor variations," Andorf mumbles, finding his feet.

A handful of nurses stream into the room, shuffling about and wiping with sanitary wipes whatever they dare pick up off the floor.

Andorf turns about a full three-sixty. "Mila! Where's Mila?" he yells, beginning to panic.

All peer about the room shaking their heads. Even the toddlers throw up their tiny hands.

Hearing screams emanating from somewhere out in the hallway, Andorf dashes out of the room. The most-recent nurses chase after, wiping everything in their path.

Listening for Mila's screams, the Goshi runs full speed. He leans around a corner, then the next. Approaching a seven-foot-tall pantry closet labeled as low-gravity suits and fire retardants storage, he applies the brakes. Opening the narrow door, he finds medical supplies scattered about and poor little Mila wound in a nest of flexible three-inch hoses. He untangles the frightened girl and scoops her into his arms.

One nurse catches up, gasping. Peering at the medical supplies scattered about the floor, she breaks into an endless rant.

"Hell with the mess," Andorf barks. "What about my daughter? She could have been injured. Quit your bitching and check her out."

A second nurse arrives, only to bend down to rewind strings of red tapes back onto their spools. "Look at all medical supplies. They don't belong here. Oh, the Dribbles will have a field day writing up *this* one. Wait! Don't touch anything. I must contact management. They'll need to file a detailed report."

Holding Mila tightly in his arms, Andorf sidesteps the befuddled nurses knee-deep in red-tape chaos.

"Hey! Where are you going with that little girl?" the first nurse yells. "She's evidence. This mess didn't just happen by itself."

Back in sickbay, Andorf lowers Mila to the floor. He checks in with Brutus and the twins before turning for the exit. Holding Mila's hand, he winks at the attending nurse. "Keep an eye on the twins, will you? I'm hopping the next shuttle back to the *Atlantis*. Surely, someone there will have answers."

CHAPTER 3
A Mingus Amongst Us
ANDORF

pproaching the *Atlantis'* floating steps, Andorf finds Mila's arms wrapped tightly around his waist, clinging onto him in a near-death grip. He tries to peel her off but the girl won't have any part of it. Andorf breaks line to carry Mila into a quiet nook.

"Whatever this fear is, young lady, you must get over it. You are nearly eight years old. It is time you start acting your age."

Mila stares at him like a little lost lamb, unable to speak.

"The floating steps are main passages between decks. You cannot be using the ship's emergency stairs. They are not well-lit and you never know who will …" Andorf peers back at the crowd bunching around the floating-step landing who appear to show interest.

Mila maintains her stranglehold.

Getting nowhere, Andorf gazes deep into the youngster's eyes, analyzes her thoughts. "I see the floating steps remind you of Freedom Day, when you were standing in line to board the *Atlantis.*"

Wiping her eyes, Mila whimpers. "They shot daddy …I mean my *other* daddy. And … and they were dragging mommy away by her arms."

"Ah! The starship ramp was where you saw your father shot and your mother being hauled off."

Mila wipes at tears streaming down her face as she nods. "They had no identification other than the number 666."

"Ah yes, 666."

"What were they hiding? Their faces were all covered up."

Andorf's eyes widen. "Like clansmen." Holding Mila snug against his chest, he takes the floating steps up five flights from the transport deck. The moment his feet are planted firmly on the landing, Mila wiggles loose. She bounds down the G-deck hallway, only to wait patiently for her adopted father at the bridge door.

With Mila boldly dashing past, Andorf enters the bridge. After acknowledging the bridge crew, he freezes at sight of a non-crew member with his back turned. The man is not dressed in white satin so he cannot be one of the intrusive beanos of whom Captain Murray had frequently complained.

Andorf approaches the man. "Excuse me, sir. The bridge is off limits. How did you—?"

As the man turns about, Andorf cracks a smile. "George? George Harrison, I presume?"

Gregory smiles back. "Goo goo kachoo."

Andorf is dismayed by Mila running with hands fanning out toward her uncle's open arms. "Huh?" is all he can muster, watching Gregory jubilantly scooping her into his chest.

"My sweet lord, Andorf. Don't you know anything about George Harrison? Why, he was a most famous British musician of the mid-twentieth century."

Acting Captain Jobriah Cates looks strange at Andorf. "Everyone knows that. What's gotten into you?"

"It took three rides just to get us back to the Atlantis." Andorf wipes his brow. "Do you know how many express shuttles are out there?"

"I'll bet. But later we'll have time to discuss such pleasantries." Cates ushers his visitors to Peter's navigation screen. "I assume you are both here for the same reason."

"Mila and I were aboard the Aegean when—" Andorf says, before Cates hushes him.

"Perhaps my navigator won't mind explaining a second time now that Andorf has finally arrived."

Peter rehashes the lengthy explanation, using pointed sticks on his navigational console display to demonstrate. "And such, the armada has entered one finger of this inverted spatial rift. Crews of the *Phoenix* and the *Truffle* have verified this as factual."

Andorf appears lost in the details. Peter clears his throat as if preparing to play his spiel for a third time.

Gregory graciously interjects. "In layman terms, Andorf, the incursion we experienced is called a Mingus Inversion. Named after the British theorist, Charlie Mingus, no one really knew if such an oddity really existed."

"Until now." Jobi laughs. "And here we fly smack dab into the middle of one of the suckers. But fear not. There's been no reported casualties, no ship damage other than a few displaced items here and there."

Glaring at Jobi, Andorf wants nothing more than to grab the acting captain by his shoulders and shake some sense into him. "Are you kidding me, Jobi? My daughter rematerialized inside a storage pantry some forty-feet away. We were aboard the *S.S. Aegean* but—"

Mila begins to dance about the Atlantis' small bridge. "I was tangled up inside heaps of hoses and medical stuff."

"And you say there we have nothing to fear?" Andorf's eyes narrow. "My daughter could have re-formed inside a wall or—"

"Out in space … holding my breath." Puffing her cheeks, Mila wraps both arms around her torso, pretending to shiver. "Brrr! It's freezing cold out in space."

All but Andorf chuckles at the youngster's dramatics. After a knock on the bridge door, Gregory steps aside to allow a serving cart to push past. The waiter places a bib over Peter's chest as he sits and proceeds to spoon-feed the navigator a full three-course meal. Looking embarrassed, Peter dismisses the waiter before lifting his spork. He pauses to grin at the other's stunned faces.

Pol's face sours. "Guess who won the high-odds bet against ex-councilwoman Rita."

Peter swallows a bite-sized portion of dinner. "You think it's been easy? I've got 'Do Not Disturb' signs legibly posted on my new C-deck suite door and women still come around knocking at all hours. I'm getting little sleep."

Jobi raises a brow. "Space can be such a dangerous place."

"Especially for starship captains," Andorf adds. "You know, Jobi … you being our third bridge captain in as many years."

Jobi nervously shuffles in place. He looks about the bridge before clearing his throat loudly and turning back to Andorf. "We shall study this anomaly further while we are stuck inside its belly. Hopefully we'll know more it by the time we exit the other far end which I'm told will occur in another—"

Andorf squints hard, eyeing the timepiece dangling from a lanyard around the acting captain's neck. "Fifty-six days, eight hours, and three minutes to be precise. And you can uncross your fingers from behind your back, Jobi. I sense countless unreported injuries and missing passengers throughout the armada's forty-four starships resulting from this anomaly."

Mila's small fingers tug on the acting captain's shirt. Her voice rises by octaves. "Don't worry, Mr. Jobi, sir. Daddy does this all the time. Everyone thinks he's crazy but he's—"

Spotting Andorf's fingers held to his lips, Mila abruptly hushes.

Jobi's eyes dart between Mila and Andorf. "Wait. Which part are you referring to, little lady?" he says, choking out words. "Are you telling me your daddy is our infamous prophet, the Goshi himself?"

Being called a Goshi, Andorf looks suspiciously at the acting captain. "None other," he says, stretching the words. "So, this anomaly you call a Mingus Wave … the one which is amongst us."

"To be more precise," Peter offers between chews. "It is *we*, the armada, who are adrift amongst the Mingus."

"Uh oh. Here he goes," Gregory mumbles, catching his best friend winking at Mila.

"So, let me get this straight." Andorf begins to pace about the small bridge while rubbing his furry chin. "Before the incursion of this so-called Mingus Inversion, there was a Mingus adrift amongst us. And now with the armada adrift inside this anomaly, it is we who are amongst this Mingus, if you catch my drift."

Mila and Gregory begin to howl in laughter. Jobi pats Mila's head as she skips past. "I suspected all along your daddy might be insane, young lady. Now that I've met the guy, I'm totally convinced."

Gregory takes a pause between chuckles. "You should be glad, Jobi. You caught my friend on an off-day."

Andorf winces. "One definition of insanity is taking life less seriously than anyone else."

Jobi plops his butt into the captain's chair. He again clears his throat. "So, what's the latest on captain Murray? Last I heard he's been in an induced coma ever since The Incident."

Pol winces. "I wouldn't bet on the captain pulling through."

Peter wipes his mouth after polishing off the second course of the catered dinner. "Ole nine-finger Murray is tough."

Fanning Andorf's animosity toward the acting captain, Gregory approaches the over-stuffed chair. "Murray and his predecessor, Thom Mallory, both sat in that captain's chair, Jobi. I suspect that seat may be jinxed."

Sweat dripping off his forehead, Jobi quickly rises. As if rethinking his recent assignment, he circles the captain's chair, toe-kicking the three screws now securing it to the floor.

Andorf leans his head to one side. "I advise you to make peace with that chair, Acting Captain. You may become the *Atlantis'* captain sooner than expected. A nurse aboard the *Aegean* gives Murray less than a ten percent chance of recovery."

Gregory fiddles with one of many devices implanted in his forearm. He abruptly stares at the others. "Murray's chances of recovery are not looking good. They've been downgraded to three percent."

"Not looking good," Jobi mumbles, glancing suspiciously at the reconstructed chair. "Not good at all."

Pol drops his headphones. "Word just in from the *S.S. Calypso*. Concentrations of hydrite compounds have been detected outlining the inversion's well-defined edges."

"I would expect a repeat performance upon our exit from this rift," Peter adds between chews.

Pol nods. "They've also discovered multiple rifts such as this one directly in our flight path."

Gregory grabs the acting captain's arm. His voice narrows as well as his brow. "We've got to circumnavigate these atrocities, Jobi. I can't be resetting my tic-tocs all the time. It takes days to get all the eyes in sync. There must be some way to avoid these things. Can we possibly change course?"

Jobi stares hard at Gregory as if he has lost his mind. "Everyone knows the armada's flight path is fixed. Even if we *could* re-route, we left our fifteen percent fuel margin back on Titan. And thus, being in the hole, our pending sling around Neptune remains in question. We may never reach Nero."

Peter drops his spork on the fiber tray. "If our mission fails our home world will run out of energy. Earth will forever remain in darkness."

Vivid images intruding Andorf's thoughts leave him shivering shivers at the mere mention of Planet Nero. He envisions hungry pterodactyls circling overhead and three-legged natives taunting miners by vanishing and reappearing. Arms folded tight and sighing, he peers out one of the reinforced front portals. "Ah yes, our destiny," Andorf smirks. "The foreboding planet Nero."

CHAPTER 4

Winds Of The Goshi
ANDORF

Face cloaked within the confines of a hoodie, Andorf battles his way through the starship's crowded hallways. Even with fingers pressed in his ears, surrounding voices lunge at him like daggers.

"The Goshi never dies, you know. He just lives his life over and over."

"Must be how he knows things. The guy hears everything … even words yet to stain our tongues."

"He reads our thoughts, all without us knowing. I'll bet he's listening to us at this moment."

"It must be what's driving him crazy."

"Hush! Not so loud, my friend. You never know what he hears."

"If I were not in right mind," Andorf grumbles. "I would show you what crazy is."

A stranger suddenly bumps Andorf, sliding the hoodie off his head. People fall back, gasping at sight of the Goshi's elongated ears. Many point and call out 'Goshi.' A few boldly reach out to stroke the Andorf's ratty, graying beard.

Andorf pulls the hoodie back over his head as he hustles through the thickening crowd. Not soon enough, he stumbles into Gregory's B-deck cabin. Turning about, he finds his eight-year-old daughter and his best friend ready to lay into him. He stares back, standing arms crossed. Both are trying to speaking above the other.

Andorf raises a hand and silences the pair before either has a chance to get in the first word. "Those people in the hallways … you should hear what they are saying about me. Some call me a mysterious wizard. Others … well they say I have gone totally bonkers. And what about this Goshi thing? How long has everyone been calling me a Goshi?"

Gregory shrugs his shoulders.

Mila smiles awkwardly. "Forever."

"I suppose it began years ago with that troubled gypsy in the breakfast line." Andorf grumbles. "What was his name? Oh, yes, Atlas. Atlas was first to call me a Goshi."

Gregory chuckles. "You must admit, the name fits you well. Besides, it sounds trendy."

"It sounds grippy," Mila adds.

Gregory smiles at his niece. "Yeah, grippy."

Peering at Mila, then Gregory, Andorf throws both hands over his head. "And what's that other thing everyone's calling me? Oh yes … an old man who wanders aimlessly through life."

Gregory covers his mouth, as if trying not to laugh. "Well, what do you expect, Andorf, walking around out there dressed in a black, hooded robe like some crazed Jim Butcher wizard? Shall I find a pointed hat to complete your ensemble?"

"What?" Andorf yells. "The so-called story wizard of whom you refer requires devices and assistance to perform his magic. Does he have the ability to read minds like me?"

Mila and Gregory shake their heads.

"And what about putting thoughts into people's heads? Can this Butcher fella do that?"

Gregory winces as he takes a sip of his cannabis tea. "Perhaps you are mistaking such powers with—"

Andorf raises two fingers, points them at his friend, and then lowers them.

Gregory lowers his teacup and pries his mouth open with both hands. "Well perhaps not."

"It's these, isn't it?" Andorf pulls at his elongated ears. "Why have they grown like this?"

Mila snickers. "Better to hear with."

"What do these people want from me? Why are they so afraid of my visions? Half of them treat me like their savior, someone to magically rescue them from their many woes. Others believe I should be locked away for my own good."

Gregory takes a seat in a comfy recliner. "No one is saying such things, buddy. You're merely reading everyone's thoughts. Unless I'm wrong, people are still allowed to have their own thoughts, aren't they?"

"Best they heed my warnings." Andorf begins to pace about, pausing to scratch his itchy chin. "If they only knew what is in store for them. There must be some way to lay my visions out there for everyone to see." He peers down the wall leading into Gregory's bedroom, squints at the array of focal lights illuminating framed sets of one-inch paper squares with descriptive label below. Lining the wall beneath are a half-dozen tic-tocs with animated eyes. Unlike displayed times, their sweeping eyes move in perfect unison.

Waving her hands back and forth in sync with the tic-tocs' animated eyes, three-year-old Ayla wanders into the hallway to greet her father. Her hands stop and for a brief moment, as do the six pair of animated eyes. She then climbs into Uncle Gregory's lap only to touch his mouth and demand he recite one of his tall tales.

Andorf glances at the tic-tocs and then at Ayla in wonder. He halfway smiles, knowing there is no place she would rather be than sitting in Gregory's lap, listening to his endless stories.

Twin brother, Sarak, appears quite content playing in Gregory's living area, hiding toys and making them reappear in other places. His favorite toy, the plasma-like plio-blocks are known to reclaim their shapes around whatever solid form they contact. He cackles, watching the pieces bend around chair legs as if they were large centipedes.

Tiring of the child play, Mila steals her brother's plio-blocks. She places them atop a shelf high beyond his reach. Sarak patiently gazes upward, waiting with outstretched hands. Seconds later, the blocks ooze off the shelf and reform into blocks in the lad's awaiting hands. Playing again with his plio-blocks, Sarak yelps in contempt at his big sister.

Though Mila can at times be troublesome, she is one-hundred percent daddy's girl. Peering about Gregory's living quarters, Andorf spots a miniature hologram of his late wife, great Serin Gray, his best friend's sister. He wipes at the dampness of tearing eyes. "My sweet Serin, I would do anything to have you back in my arms," he mumbles to himself before Gregory interrupts.

"Captain Jobi is certainly a nervous chap, don't you think?"

Andorf peers back at his best friend. "Don't you mean acting captain Jobi?"

"Guess you didn't hear about Murray's passing."

Andorf's face saddens.

"What I meant was he seemed a bit edgy the other day?"

"Ed—gy," Ayla repeats.

"Edgy?"

"Yes, edgy. Much more than usual, I'd say." Gregory winces. "One worries too much about what others think."

Andorf stares at Gregory's face, eyes volleying between his best friend's left and right eyes. "We are not talking about Jobi here, are we?"

Gregory releases Ayla and rises to grasp Andorf's arm. "Look at you Andorf. You've quit shaving. You've been trapesing around the starship walls with your head covered in a hoodie. I'm beginning to worry about you."

Andorf takes a step back. "There are only two things to worry about. Broken things beyond our means of repair and …"

Gregory winces. "And what?"

"Things we longer worry about."

Sharoobed
ANDORF

Viewing displayed holograms of his late wife leaves Andorf teary-eyed. He blows his drippy nose on a fiber cloth as Mila sits on his lap peering intensely at the images.

"What was Serin like, Daddy? I only remember her lying on the bedroom floor the day you brought me home."

Gathering thought, a smile puffs Andorf's flush cheeks. "Well, Serin was pushy, I can tell you that. Never was a time when she had not gotten her way. And talk about persuasive … why she could talk a cheeseburger into giving up its cheese."

Mila stares at him bewildered. "What's a cheeseburger?"

Andorf chuckles for a brief moment. "Well, when I was your age, we ate animal byproducts stuffed between hinged layers of bread."

Mila squinches her face.

"Over the years it morphed into some sort of veggie compound within the bread. Burgers eventually became genetically-modified soy extracts pumped full of hydrogenated fats to give it flavor. Then it was injected into fiber wafers."

Mila covers her mouth and dashes off. She returns moments later, wiping her face with a damp hand towel. "Why would anyone in their right mind eat such garbage?"

"You do not understand, sweetie. Like those before us, my generation grew up never questioning where *anything* came from or where it went. Who would have guessed the food industry became the primary source of our diseases?" Andorf shuts off the display, removes his wedding band, and then drops the ring in a top drawer. "For my own sanity I must put that woman out of my mind," he mumbles, heading to the bathroom to shave off weeks of chin whiskers.

"But you can't do that," Mila calls out, appearing suddenly at the bathroom door. "Serin's inside all of us."

Andorf hugs Mila and then wipes shaving cream off her face. "I agree. Every last person aboard these starships is indebted to her. She is the reason we are out here on our energy quest. You can say Serin is in our souls."

"No, Daddy. Serin was in our food. We ate her!"

"Ouch," Andorf yells, after gouging his chin with the hand-held shaver. Wiping his bleeding chin with a damp towel, his eyes focus on the girl. "I cannot believe what you are telling me, Mila. Who the hell is filling your head with such rubbish?"

"My teacher, Ms. Wells. She's real smart. She knows everything."

"Looks like we need to have a little talk with this Ms. Wells."

*

With the child-keeper watching the twins, Andorf takes Mila's hand and leads her through the crowded A-deck hallway. At sight of the floating steps, Mila reaches up and clings tightly to her daddy's chest. Holding Mila, he pauses. Feeling her fear, he carries her away from the crowd.

"You are too old, for this little lady. We have been through all this. The floating steps may be crowded but they are much faster than using the main stairwell."

With Mila clinging tightly against his chest, Andorf hikes down two levels of floating steps. Mila releases to drop onto the landing and run ahead. The C-deck hallway eventually terminates at an observation area repurposed into clusters of classrooms. More than one instructor pauses their lecture to observe the father/daughter as they breeze past. Andorf scans the names above the fourth-grade classroom doors and following Mila, he enters Ms. Wells' classroom.

A woman of early thirties gazes up at the unannounced visitors. Face glowing as bright as the iridescent nameplate on her desk, she flashes a smile at her favorite student. "Why, hello, Mila. I see you've brought your Father."

"Hi, Ms. Wells," Mila sings out. "Andorf Johnson is my Daddy. I picked him out when I was five years old."

The teacher chuckles. "By the way you phrased that, my dear, one would believe you plucked him off a tree like an apple."

"Or in a damp, moldy storage room," Andorf mumbles. With a tilted head, he attempts to coax Ms. Wells into a corner away from the nosey ears of associate teachers.

"The team and I are prepping for our next session. Now's not a good time for a private …" Ms. Wells gazes at Andorf's clean face and then into his inviting eyes. She stumbles for words as if lost in the Goshi's baby blues.

Andorf's eyes sharpen as does his voice. "I do not approve what you have been teaching the nine-year-olds, especially my highly-impressionable daughter. I believe you may have broken Tenulian guidelines in teaching personal edicts of what occurs after death."

With eyes volleying between Andorf and Mila, Ms. Wells appears confused. "I—I assure you, Mr. Johnson, I am doing nothing of the sort. I merely teach them about what becomes of people after they pass … how the deceased are introduced into terrarium soil to nourish the next generation of Tenulians."

"Wait a minute," Andorf says. "Perhaps Mila and her classmates are being introduced to death much too early."

"Not at all. Most of my kids have already experienced the loss of a pet or a family member's departing."

Peering down, Andorf shuffles in place. "Well …"

"Everyone is eventually returned to the soil. Now, if you feel I'm presenting this material improperly, you are free to bring it up at the next meeting."

"Not my wife. Her casket was jettisoned into space along with captain Thom in absentia. You may remember the elaborate ceremony with the simulated bugles four years ago."

"Yes. I do recall the late captain Murray's long-winded eulogies. Wait! Are you saying your wife was the great Serin Gray?"

Andorf nods.

Ms. Wells bends down to address Mila. "Your Father really doesn't know, does he?"

Mila shakes her head.

"Well, I hate to break it to you, Mr. Johnson, but your wife's casket was as empty as captain Thom's."

"You mean …?"

Ms. Wells nods. "Like everyone else, her body was placed in a soilenator and converted into soil."

Red-faced, Andorf breathes deep as he falls back a few steps. After long moments, he apologizes for his rash behavior and then turns toward the exit holding Mila's hand. At the doorway, he abruptly turns about.

"Is there something I can help you with, Mr. Johnson?" Gazing at Andorf's bare ring finger, her voice softens. "May I call you Andorf?"

"Well, there *is* one thing."

She flashes her un-ringed left hand at the single father. "I'm certainly available. Ask me anything you'd like."

"What is this sharoob I hear people talking about? I have heard the phrase quite frequently accompanied by bouts of laughter."

Appearing disappointed, the teacher's posture tightens. "I'm surprised how you could have missed the recently created Tenulian word. Sharoob implies a deliberate act of hiding something behind another's back."

"Like a little white lie?"

"Bigger," Ms. Wells says. "Think much bigger."

Andorf peers deep into the teacher's widening eyes, sifts through her thoughts. Recalling Serin's ceremonious funeral, he suddenly covers his mouth. "The two pall-bearers … they easily lifted Serin's casket with a single hand … like it was—"

Ms. Wells raises a brow. "Empty?"

"And all this time, everyone has been smirking behind my back?"

The teacher shrugs her shoulders. "Sorry but the recycling process I teach readies young their minds for the inevitable."

Andorf's mouth suddenly sours. "I find the idea of my wife decomposing in terrarium soil quite disheartening."

Mrs. Wells smiles at Mila. "I believe it was a large man with greasy hands who placed your wife in the soilenator."

"Papa Brutus converted her into soil!" Mila yells out. "She was added to the Atlantis' terranium."

Ms. Well corrects. "Terrarium."

Andorf wipes a lone tear escaping down his cheek. "All that time, I was led to believe my beloved Serin was in a casket, drifting in space."

Mila touches her daddy's arm. "Papa told everyone you weren't ready to accept reality."

"Oh, he did, did he?"

Ms. Wells again shrugs her shoulders. "What can I say, Andorf? You've been sharoobed. Now if you're free next—"

Grabbing Mila's hand, Andorf quickly exits the classroom. He storms down the C-deck hallway. With Mila clinging to him tightly, he hikes down the floating steps to the lowest level. A series of steps in the main stairwell direct them down to the dreaded engineering deck in the bowels of the starship. With each step, the clankity machinery noises grow louder. Exiting the stairwell, the racket becomes nearly unbearable.

Opening the mechanical room's huge door, he and Mila cover their ears at the deafening noise. Milling noises bark at them as if they were yelling trespass warnings. The clicks and clanks morph into song with each machine's unique voice adding harmony to a common work tune.

"Listen, Daddy. Can you hear the machines? They're all singing."

With techs paying them little attention, Andorf and Mila side-step what-nots spewed across the grease-ridden floor. They breeze past air handlers which appear to be sucking dust, grit, and hair into their casing cracks. Holding onto their clothing to keep them from being sucked into the machines as well, the visitors tromp down a half-level of perforated steps. They walk hand-in-hand, daring themselves not to slip on the greasy floor. Approaching rows of humming gravity generators, Andorf spots the collection of eight-foot-tall replicating printers in a rear corner. Weaving between machines, he sees what appears to be the back half of his childhood rival protruding out the rear cabinet of replicator #6.

Andorf pauses to cast an open palm. "Stay put, Mila. Do not go any-where." Suspicious of the busy machines surrounding him, he takes time scanning the busy mechanical room. "Whatever you do, absolutely do not touch *anything*. One never knows what any of these hungry beasts do or …" Andorf sucks wind between his teeth. "Who they have recently consumed."

"D—do you mean eaten?" Eyes enlarging, Mila wraps both arms tightly against her torso. She looks around the oil-smelling room, staring at one machine and then another as if wondering which monster will be the first to attack.

Feeling the floor vibrating around them, Andorf has second thoughts. He turns back and takes Mila's hand. In slow, deliberate steps, he leads her across the slick floor. Mila's eyes scan the immediate vicinity as if expecting someone … something to leap out at them without notice. Nearing the replicating printers, Andorf yells above the loud machine noise.

"I need a word with you, Brutus."

Through a series of animated body jerks, Brutus extracts himself from the filthy innards of replicator #6. It takes the better part of a minute for the chief engineer's eyes to focus on his guests as #6 emits clicks and loud ticking noises as if she was running low on grease.

"Good gosh, Andorf! What happened to your ears? Why have they grown so long?" His brow narrows. "What's got a bug up your uh—?" he says, pausing at the sight of Mila's disapproving glare.

Mila leans closer, away from the raging machines. Her voice jitters. "Papa Brutus, be nice." Arms crossed, she and Andorf stare in silence.

Brutus' eyes bounce between Andorf's scowl and Mila's cringing face. "Damn," he mumbles. "I've been ratted out by a six-year-old."

Mila's eyes narrow. "Nine—and a half. I'm almost ten, Papa."

Andorf's hones in on his old friend's arms, one in a splint and the other appearing to require serious medical attention. Both limbs are covered in grease. "Take a good look at your papa, sweating his life away in this greasy dungeon, Mila. You may not be as anxious to grow up."

Mila eyes the slime oozing down her Papa Brutus' face and his filthy hands wiping it off. "Nine," she yells out.

"Mila's teacher has been teaching fourth-graders how we recycle our dead. What a marvelous way to discover Serin's casket was actually—"

"Empty!" Mila shouts.

Andorf leans against the nearest gravity generator. After feeling parts of his inner-self vibrating, he steps away. "Tell me it isn't so, Brutus," he yells. "Tell me you have not been advising everyone to hide the truth from me ... that Serin was transformed into soil."

Brutus nods. "You know as well as I, starship food supplies require a closed system. We feed plants. Plants feed us."

"I heard it in people's thoughts but I—I guess I refused to believe." Andorf slaps his head. "And so, all this time I have been the joke of the *Atlantis*?"

Brutus grins. "Face it, Poo. You've been sharoobed. Look, Serin was a great leader. I know what she meant to you."

Despite being twice Andorf's size, Brutus finds his back hard-pressed against one of the vibrating gravitation generators staring at the Goshi's outcast hands. Words vibrate out of his mouth. "W—what t—the h—hell?"

"Don't hurt papa," Mila yells, tugging urgently on her father's arms.

"What did Serin ever see in you?" Andorf releases the chief engineer only to stare him down. "One day that grease box you passionately call #6 will swallow you alive. She will digitize you ... spit out Brutus replicas by the dozens."

"Ah," Brutus growls, dismissing Andorf with sweeping hand motions. He worms a path around gravity generators only to reenter the rear of his troublesome machine. Replicator #6s rough mechanical noise mellows to that of a chirping sparrow.

Mila glares at Andorf with folded arms. "That's an awful thing to tell Papa. I don't care if he deserved it. You should never say such things."

"Trust me," Andorf says, snarling. "There is truth in my words. As your Papa reminds us before, space is a terrifying place. We must all wear fear in our hearts."

Mila's hands take refuge on her hips. "And what about you? What do you fear?"

Andorf's face turns pale as he listens to the rhythm of the busy machines surrounding them. "Spending the rest of my life without Serin," he sighs beneath his breath.

Mila runs over and wraps both arms around Andorf's waist. "Don't worry. I'll never leave you." She flashes emerald-green eyes up at him and then squints. "And I can't wait to eat you too, Daddy."

Andorf unpeels Mila and takes her hand. "Let's get home, Mila," he yells above the raging machines. "We need to have a long talk."

Stomping her feet, Mila slides on the grease-ridden floor. Andorf grabs her arm just in time to prevent a fall. "Don't be mad. No one could tell you about sharoob. It wasn't even an official word until last week."

Gazing at the innocent girl standing before him with outstretched arms, Andorf's eyes dampen. He bends down and scoops her into his arm. "What would I ever do without you, my precious Mila?"

C H A P T E R   6
Growing Pains
ANDORF

eep within the bowels of the *Atlantis*, the now five-year-old Sarak chats with whichever half of Brutus protrudes from equally chatty machines, all vying for the chief engineer's attention. Sarak loves leaning against the humming air handlers, marveling at how everything not secured down gets sucked into their casing cracks. When time comes to advance filters, he assists techs with rehoming items wedged within the filth-ridden air filters. Instead of sorting them into their designated bins, he frequently runs off with choice parts and stashes them in a special workshop adjacent to the mechanical room. Techs sent to recover pillaged items spend humorless hours trying to outwit the chief engineer's son's increasing ingenuity. From years of pestering Brutus' techs, the young lad knows more about the inner workings of the starship than most adults outside of engineering.

Twin Ayla, makes a sport of out-gaming her best friend, Emin. Nine months younger than Turk's only child, she toys with the boy without even his slightest knowledge. But as much fun as it seems, she'd gladly give it up to spend time in her uncle's lap, begging a recital of yet another rendition of the never-the-same tales. With his questionable memory, Gregory's narrations are often shaded by exaggeration and lofty ad-libbing.

Meanwhile, Mila spends most of her day in class dreaming she were elsewhere. She paws at the medallion time-piece Andorf slipped around her neck on her eleventh birthday, grateful of time away from domestic chores and picking up after a sloppy father.

*

Andorf looks about the shared living area, noting the many rearranged items. He lifts an orphaned chess piece off the shelf and returns it to the dresser's slick surface. After examining the piece, he glares back at the hovering youngster. "We need to talk about your obsessive cleaning binges, young lady. Will they ever cease?"

"But, Daddy …," Mila cries out.

"Your Uncle Gregory is a neat-freak and look what has become of him. Have you seen his face and all the lines settling into it? Have you? Huh? It would not surprise me if his days are numbered."

"That's a terrible thing to say. Ayla absolutely adores her uncle Gregory. Imagine what would happen to her."

"I did not mean to sound derogatory. I only meant he does not appear well."

Mila reaches past her father to lift the queen and wipe the shelf before returning the queen. "If I didn't clean up after you this place would look like the storage closet where you found me."

"Ah, yes. Back in the dark, dreaded bowels of the starship."

"There' was dust lingering everywhere." Smirking, Mila throws her arms outwardly. "Even more than what's here."

Andorf picks up the queen and then stares at the lone piece gripped firmly in his hand. "Dust has purpose, I want you to know. Without dust, how would I ever know where my queen belongs or for such matter … where any of us really belong?"

Mila rolls her eyes.

"There is a certain familiar comfort in dust. It will outlive us all … be here through the end of time. No matter how badly we treat dust, our faithful friend always returns. I dare you to name any friend who would do the same. Go ahead. I dare you to name one."

Eyeing the lone chess piece being massaged between her father's long fingers, Mila sighs. She snatches the piece and returns it to the shelf. "I know you miss your queen terribly, Daddy. If Serin were here, still alive, she'd be the luckiest—"

The cabin speaker awakens to the captain's harsh voice. "Your attention. Your attention please. This is Captain Cates speaking. We are scheduled to exit the current Murray Disturbance in twelve … no … make it eleven minutes. Take refuge in your designated safe locations. If you do not have a designated safe …"

Mocking Jobi's words, Andorf quiets the speaker. He gathers up the twins and straps them in their safe seats. He then straps himself in, facing Mila. "Jobi lags by twelve seconds this time."

Mila winces. "Are you sure I'll be safe? I recall the time I rematerialized in an overstuffed pantry closet. It wasn't much fun."

"We should all be perfectly safe this time. I have checked out weak areas in this cabin. Most every fault area along the *Atlantis'* outer hull has been mapped. Your papa's techs have had ample time to reinforce the starship's critical areas."

Binky shifts his eyes left and then right before homing in on the hay-filled litterbox, secured beneath Andorf's desk. After a series of hops, the aging pet rabbit lands inside and burrows beneath the excessive layers of hay.

Peering at Mila's timepiece, Andorf counts down from thirty. Mila counts along with him while Binky's wide-eyes peek above the litterbox. When the timepiece reaches ten, Andorf and Mila grab hold of their harnesses. The twins hold onto their seats. Binky's paws firmly grip the litterbox edges.

The room vibrates violently for ten seconds before abruptly ceasing. The smell of smoke and a gurgling sound of gas rushing through overhead pipes has everyone peering up at the ceiling. Andorf and Mila unstrap themselves and then the twins before rushing everyone outside. Binky hops after them. The closing cabin door brushes his tail.

An overzealous horn wailing in the hallway competes with a flashing red overdoor light. Binky attempts to leap into Andorf's arms but his hind legs are not what they were years earlier. Andorf bends down and scoops his furry pal into his chest as he distances himself from inquisitive neighbors asking if everyone is safe.

The moment the horn silences and the red light extinguishes, Andorf and the kids dart back inside. Binky leaps from Andorf's arms and hops ahead, checking out the cabin.

With the twins returning to play with their toys, Mila pauses to watch Binky investigating each room. "Look, Daddy. Your bunny thinks he's protecting us."

"Much better than this middle-age Goshi," Andorf snorts.

Binky kicks both hind legs high in the air, as if granting the all-clear. He turns his head slowly and winks before hopping for the bedroom.

Mila's eyes widen. "Did you see him wink? It's as if Binky knows what we're saying."

Andorf chuckles. "Oh, the stories I could tell, Mila. The stories I could tell."

CHAPTER 7
That Damn Dust
GREGORY

Fraught by nightmares and despair, Gregory sits, gazing out a portal on the *Atlantis'* starboard bow. He feels caged inside the darkened room, millions of miles from home. Wallowing in self-doubt, his hands tremble likes those of someone well beyond his late thirties. With diminished vision, he squints at stars drifting lazily past. His head suddenly jerks, twisting back to view the row of empty vials lining the dresser.

"Blasted pill lady," he calls out. "Why is she never around when I need her?"

The troubled man thinks about his chair position, relinquished, so as not to frighten those on the Council any further. Between his collection of metalized appendages and his failing health, guests rarely visit the isolated cabin.

Gazing down, Gregory opens the ivory box on his lap and then smiles at captain Thom's parting gift. His shaky hands examine the fine craftsmanship of the hand-carved shofar within. Pressing it against his lips, he recalls scores of masked rebels back on Earth, perched high atop the many summits overlooking the launch plateau on Jake's Mountain. There, a female choir was poised, arms stretched upward. Their sweet voices harmonized with hand-carved woodwinds of their male counterparts, all singing songs of distaste for the Empire and its prized *Starship Atlantis*, perched below.

His heart flutters in remembrance of Rena's voice, echoing above the others in the dew-kissed, pre-dawn morning. Her fiery words … her almighty plan … the twenty-third of November. Rena's rebellious acts burn through his memory. *If only she hadn't been swallowed up into the darkness of the night. If only I could be with her again. If only I had kept away from that damn dust.*

A disturbance in the hallway disrupts his thoughts. He drops the shofar inside its protective sleeve in the felt-lined case and then slides it across the room. As it finds safe haven beneath the single bed, his gaze returns to the starboard portal and the impersonal blackness beyond.

The patter of small feet scampering across the cold, linoleum floor draws a rare smile. Without hesitation, five-year-old Ayla climbs into her uncle's familiar lap and wraps both arms around his neck. Overlooking her uncle's metallic-appearance and his losing battle with Tourette-related tics, Ayla fails to accept the mechanized man as other than perfect. Staring past his similar long nose, she bats dark-brown eyes at him.

"Tell me a story, Uncle Greg. Make it something about Mommy."

Gregory brushes hair from his niece's eyes, as he once did with his kid sister. "Doesn't your dad—?"

"Every time I ask him about mother, Father gets really quiet … like he's seen a ghost or something."

"What about …?"

"Oh, him? Papa always pats my head and sends me off to play. Then he disappears behind one of his slimy machines." Ayla's lower lip swells. "They never have time for me. Even Binky no longer wants to play."

Watching Ayla shake her shoulder-length blonde hair as she squirms in his lap, a tear gathers on Gregory's cheek. With visions of his kid sister running through his thoughts, he pauses for a brief moment.

"Well, Binky *is* getting old. Rabbits rarely live beyond twelve or fourteen years. As for your father and papa, they really loved your mother. I can tell you this, my kid sister was one special girl."

Ayla wipes at her uncle's tears. She reaches deep in her pocket and then shoves a graphene bunny in his face. "You can have this, Uncle Greg. Papa made it for me." She watches as Gregory takes it in his hand and grins before setting it on the floor at his feet. "Father said they locked you in a crazy place … gave you carrot symptoms."

"Tourette's Syndrome." Gregory pats her head as his niece settles in. He clears his throat, loudly. "Now, how about that story?"

Ayla buries her head in his lap. "Please! Please!"

"Now, promise me you'll stay awake this time, Ayla." Feeling her nod, he begins to spin his tale. "You must understand, sweetie, things were not always like this. Why, your great Grampa James—"

"I remember him."

Gregory chuckles. "I was merely your age when he … departed. There have been many changes since his time, none for the better. I remember sitting on *his* lap, listening to *him* carrying on about endless wars over stupid—"

"What are wars, Uncle Greg?" she asks, raising her head.

Arms beginning to twitch, Gregory scans the room looking for answers. After a minute, he regains control of his 'mind of their own' hands. Taking a deep breath, he grins at his niece.

"Hush now, Ayla. Let me finish." Gregory's hands again tremble. Taking deep breaths, he grins at the full yawn devouring Ayla's face as she returns it to his lap. "As I was saying, your mom was different. She was one member of a special triad that was like … three of a perfect pair. Each of them filled me in on details of what happened from their own perspective after I … uh … was away."

"Like you're filling me in now?"

Gregory nods. He marvels at Ayla's soft innocence as she lies in his lap. His eyes dampen as he turns to gaze out the starboard portal. "If only we hadn't disturbed that damn dust. Things would have been way different. Oh, it all began with a rugby game. I remember like it was yesterday," he mumbles, coughing, very shallow, so as not to stir his niece. He feels Ayla squirming in his lap, struggling to sit up. "Things would have been different, very different … if not for what took place at that fateful evening."

At Gregory's softening voice, Ayla's eyes open to peer at the storyteller. "Uncle Greg, why's your face all white? And your lips … they're turning blue."

Struggling to breathe, Gregory's hands tremble uncontrollably. He squints at Ayla's small hands tugging on his shoulders. "If only we hadn't disturbed that damn dust," he wheezes in fading breath. Slumping into the chair, his eyes turn inward. He struggles to understand Ayla's frantic words between her erratic sobs.

"Uncle Greg! Uncle Greg!"

Gregory fights to remain in the fading world if only for one breath longer. He reaches for Ayla but she is no longer on his lap. All he hears is the fading patter of bare feet running across the cold floor and her scream as he shuts his eyes a last time.

"SOMEONE … ANYONE … HELP ME!"

CHAPTER 8

An Untimely Parting
ANDORF

Andorf cradles Binky in his arms close to his chest, listening to the furry confidant gasp his last breaths. As if losing Gregory was not enough, he feels robbed, run over by a freight train and dragged miles along its tracks. Sweet memories of his furry friend saturate his thoughts. He recalls Serin awakening to Binky licking her feet as if welcoming her into the fold. And the time Binky scared off those detectives, biting their legs after they roughed up his human. And how miserable it was when Binky disappeared that horrid night before the starship launch.

"Be free, my old friend. Let nothing weigh you down," Andorf whispers, gently rocking his companion of fifteen years. "I give you permission to dance amongst the butterscotch fields of grain on your journey to the Rainbow Bridge."

An out-of-place smile appears on Binky's face as he seems to gaze beyond the depth of Andorf's blue eyes. For a last time, the rabbit's linked thoughts hint at what lies ahead.

"M—me?" Andorf stutters. "A Master Goshi?"

Yes. Lest you forget to take good care of Lavendar. The girl really adores you.
Without questioning, Andorf nods.

A special someone awaits you at your journey's end.

"But without my Binkers, how will I ever find my way?"

An old acquaintance resurfaces. A grieving widow … a starving artist … a mad stitcher. They shall briefly enter your life. Assemble the pieces, my dear friend. Act outside your—

Binky lets out a shallow breath, his last.

Wiping tears streaming down his cheeks, he places Binky in a self-sealing argon disposition bag, destined for the final resting place. Staring at the opaque bag, he breaks down sobbing.

It takes every grain of strength to deliver his best friend to the Soilenator. Andorf finds it the most painful thing he has ever done. He places Binky onto the perpetual conveyor belt and then follows the bag until a solid wall blocks his passage. As Binky enters the swinging flap door, his heart sinks, feeling he has somehow betrayed their fifteen-year bond.

"To the soil you return," Andorf chants. "Until my final breath, you will live in my heart. May your soul inspire every last one of us."

As the passionate of Mila's voice rings between his ears, Andorf finally understands. He half-smiles.

"I cannot wait to eat you, my friend."

CHAPTER 9

A Somber Gathering
ANDORF

Andorf takes the reserved front row seat between his daughters. He gathers Mila's reluctant hand.

Mila winces at his red face and damp, swollen cheeks. "You can't be showing up looking like this, Daddy," she quietly scowls. "It's a funeral for gosh sakes—Uncle Greg's funeral."

Lowering his head, Andorf sniffles. "Binky is gone. He took his last breath in my arms."

Mila squeezes his hand. She turns away to hide her own tears before peering back. "I suppose Binky gave you final instructions?"

"Indeed," Andorf says, looking strangely at Mila. *How could Mila know of mine and Binky's telepathic link? How can she be aware of my furry friend's last-minute guidance?*

Andorf clenches Ayla's wadded up hand but squeezing a wet tissue, she refuses to reciprocate. He cannot blame her. Gregory was more of a father to her than he could ever hope to be. Andorf has come to accept this reality. Taking a moment, he reflects on how gatherings such as this not only finalize a parting but reshuffles alliances within the family like a deck of cards at a high-stakes poker tournament. He then grimaces at the sight of Brutus' bulky arm resting upon Sarak's shoulder.

Mila removes her father's hand off Ayla's unresponsive hand and squeezes it tight as she scans the many empty seats. "Why are there so few people?" she whispers. "Where are Uncle Gregory's friends?" She follows Andorf's eyes past cameras monitoring the memorial and the man panning across the many cardboard cutouts filling the seats.

Dressed in black from head to toe, a slightly intoxicated preacher staggers into the room. smiling sarcastically at the life-like cutouts filling floor space between the speckling of curious spectators. The last-minute fill-in finds his place behind the portable pulpit. He suddenly raises his sharp voice. "Unlike those attending this memorial service, I did not know Gregory well. But judging by the size of this gathering, I can tell he had many friends."

Once again, the cameraman pans across the many expressionless cardboard faces filling the seats and lining the walls. He then focuses on the inebriated preacher.

"We are born into this world to leave our mark," the preacher calls out. "Like treasures, we are remembered by the friends we accumulate along life's twisted path. Through Gregory's brief time in this world, his life has surely intertwined with many here today. And like those before him, Gregory Gray has returned to the soil."

The preacher reaches into his pocket and then sprinkles dust on the empty coffin. "Hashish to ashes, dope to dust. If the good Lord won't take you, then his devil brother must."

Andorf leans into Brutus and whispers. "Where the hell did you find this clown? "Did you snag him from the rear of some food line?"

"Easy there," Brutus whispers back. "I was lucky to find anyone on such short notice. And with Gregory's metal appendages and his twitching, what did you expect? Most everyone's scared of the mechanical man."

Andorf growls. "I'm just saying you could have done better. Gregory was Serin's brother for gosh sakes. Don't you have feelings about that? I would bet if it were one of your fellow gypsies, preachers would be lining up … real ones, not like this … this bozo. You gypsies have some sort of union, do you not?"

"It's more of a fellowship." Brutus clears his throat. "Look, Andorf, I know Gregory was your best pal but you must admit, the guy's been awfully sick for quite some time. His arms were twitching all the time from that terrible disease he contracted at the Cos. The guy was scary. Hell, he even scared me."

"Uncle Greg never scared me," Ayla says, pouting her lips and folding her arms.

Mila offers her baby sister a rare sisterly smile. "Me neither."

"Well, Uncle Greg scared *me*," Sarak adds, clinging to his papa's shoulder. "I never liked any of his made-up stories."

Brutus pats his loyalist son's head. "At least not everyone has turned against me."

Ayla snarls at her twin. "Most of the stories were true … but I'm not sure which ones."

Sensing a family feud brewing before his eyes, the preacher hushes everyone with fingers to his lips. He turns to address the cardboard cutouts encompassing the room. "Anyone wishing to give their final words of respect, please rise."

Breaking free of Mila's tight grasp, Andorf is the only one to rise. The preacher acknowledges Andorf's approach and steps aside.

Homing in on Ayla's tears, Andorf makes his way to the pulpit. He feels her heart breaking. She is falling apart right in front of him and there is not a damn thing he can do to lessen her pain. He longs to take Ayla in his arms, comfort her, but knows she will have no part of it. And now, with both of his best friends now gone, Andorf feels drained. Turning to peer toward the others in the small gathering, he wipes his eyes.

"As most everyone knows, Gregory and I were best friends. Back in the day, long before he became known as Metal Man, he and I …"

Andorf touches on his and Gregory's wild exploits, spinning new twists on his friend's over-spun tales. Closing eyes, he details their night at the Archives, where huge rats scurrying around them and nibbling on their shoes. He describes the aftermath of mad pounding on Gregory's apartment door … how he and his best friend hid shivering beneath a bed. And how he awoke the next morning to find not only Gregory's apartment had not only been vandalized but his best friend was gone.

"And despite everyone telling me to give up searching for Gregory, I never quit … never quit looking for my best friend. He made me promise …"

Andorf opens his eyes to see a vacated room. Only he, Mila, and the cardboard cutouts remain. Shaking her head, Mila grasps his cold hand.

"Well, Daddy, you certainly have a way of clearing a room."

PART 2
Discovery

CHAPTER 10

A Quantum Of Pebbles
ANDORF

With both of his best friends being only memories, Andorf's life has become bland, colorless at best. Months are sifting through between his fingers like water, leaving but a wash of spent pebbles. Years seem like strings of dulled pearls strung together by moments of time.

Living with a Goshi most of her life has honed Mila's intuition. Weeks shy of her twenty-eighth birthday she has become a highly-valued member of the armada's ruling Third Council.

At twenty-two, sister Ayla had married her childhood playmate, Emin. Much to Admiral Turk's only son's displeasure, he finds his wife still keeps steps ahead of him with each endeavor.

Twin-brother Sarak spends more time working in his lab tinkering with one particularly promising project than tending to his expectant wife's cravings. To spite her husband's absence, she often toys with the idea of changing the selected baby name to something more appropriate than Gorin. Perhaps it should be David or Walter or even Kyle. Yes Kyle, the cousin who awoke one morning to find himself incarcerated, not knowing how he got there. Naming their son after Kyle would certainly drive the point home.

Wondering where it all went, not a single day passes without Andorf wishing his beloved Serin was still alive. He would leap at any chance to save her, even traveling back in time if only such a thing was possible. Serin would have cherished how their family has grown.

CHAPTER 11

The Breakthrough
ANDORF

Andorf wanders through the bowels of the *Atlantis*, covering his ears at obnoxious milling sounds spewing from the greasy mechanical room. The virtually unknown science lab's door opens at his outstretched hand. He smiles briefly at twenty-two-year-old Sarak and then Brutus who is oddly positioned in the rear of the lab. "What in charred tilapia is going on down here, Sarak? I could not make out what you were fussing about on my undersized comm-box speaker."

Sarak stares back bewildered. "Charred tilapia?"

"There's a story about tilapia, Son," Brutus says, grinning at Sarak as a wad of drool drips onto his work boots. He runs a greasy rag over his salivating lips. "Your mother would always burn the fish."

Andorf winces. "Even soapy-tasting fish would be more palatable than anything *Atlantis'* cafeteria dishes out."

"I couldn't agree more," Sarak says in a muffled voice, head stuck inside his equipment rack.

Andorf's nose twitches as if reliving the unnerving moments. "On more than one occasion Serin nearly burned down the apartment cooking tilapia."

He steps closer to find Brutus standing beside their son at one of the floor-to-ceiling racks stuffed with knob-centric pieces. He examines intertwined wires running between multiple enclosures. "I haven't seen a mess like this since I walked in on those confused installers assembling medical devices destined for sick bay. Did you build all this equipment by yourself, Sarak?"

"Yeah, Sarak." Brutus snarls. "Where'd you find all these parts? Are you still pillaging them out of my mechanical room bins?"

Sarak pokes his head out from one of the racks. "Oh, I've collected things here and there over the years." The young experimenter drags a single finger across a display screen's surface causing strings of multicolored numbers to sweep across the display from top to bottom. A second finger swipe sends a triple-helix holo-image spinning in the space between him and his fathers.

Brutus stares at the full-spectral holo-image spinning before him waist-high above the floor. Eyes widening, Andorf reaches to poke at the image but Brutus knocks his hand out of the way in the nick of time. "I wouldn't do that. Not if you value your fingers."

"But I ..."

Brutus turns to grin at his son. "This is serious stuff, Sarak. I had no idea you've been dabbling in such complex matrices."

Sarak frowns at the triple-helix's imperfect edges. Seconds later, the holo-image collapses upon itself. "Dammit," he yells, side-stepping around both fathers. He dashes to the front of the equipment rack and analyzes the inter-twisted helix on the display. After much head-scratching, he winces back at Brutus. "You may not like what I'm about to say, Papa."

Brutus grumbles. "What'd you lose this time, Sarak?"

"Well ... uh."

"Whatever it is, I'm sure my techs will eventually locate the item and return it to the parts bin."

Sarak gulps. Before he can shut his mouth, slippery words escape his lips. "Your one-hundred-cent coin has gone missing. I—I had it in my hand just moments before you arrived in the lab."

Face reddening, Brutus' grumble morphs into strings of angry growls mixed with incomprehensible swear words. For long, stressful moments, he stares his son down, yelling. "You lost my collectible coin? How … where'd you get that coin?"

Sarak's toggles glances between both fathers. He gasps at words on the tip of his tongue which had best not escape his mouth a second time.

Brutus' fuming eyes fixate on his son. "How many times have I told you to keep your hand off my personal things? But do you ever listen? Papa will never miss his valuables you say. He's never going to miss things when he's never around you say."

Andorf steps between them. He presents a closed hand and then opens it, displaying a shiny-silver coin wedged between his thumb and index finger. "Are you looking for *this* hundred-cent coin?"

Eyes crossed, Brutus stares hard at the coin, presented by Andorf like a magician's trick. He grabs the piece and then examines it beneath the lab's bright overhead lights.

"What the hell are you doing with my collectible coin?" Brutus yells, leaning his head toward Andorf. "How'd you—?"

Andorf smiles. "Relax, Brutus. Your coin appeared on my desk shortly before our son buzzed my comm-box." Andorf winks covertly at their son. "Sarak, you must be more careful with other's belongings."

Rolling his eyes, Brutus snarls as if sensing collusion. He slams a fist down hard onto an adjoining workbench where many devices are located.

A doubloon-size brass trinket suddenly appears on a counter in the rear of the lab, twinkling in the glow of the equipment's now decrementing numbers.

Exchanging glances at the brass piece as does Sarak, Brutus pivots on one foot before taking baby steps toward the piece. Sarak strides closer in wide scissor-steps. Brutus hops twice, like a frog and then pauses, eyes fixated upon Sarak. Then both break into jogs, each trying to push the other off course with flailing hands. Brutus having much longer arms is first to reach the piece. He then freezes at the sight of himself aglow in an iridescent mixture of every color of a rainbow. His eyes widen as his upper torso becomes translucent, transcending downward until he totally disappears.

"Damn!" Sarak yells, dashing for the control panel to shut down the equipment as the lab fills with thick, dark-gray smoke. But it is too late. Papa Brutus is gone.

Smoke continues to pour out of one floor-to-ceiling rack, smothering the lab in a thick carbon-scented fog until overhead fans activate. As the fog thins, Brutus appears in the middle of the lab, standing with an outstretched hand gripping the brass trinket. He looks about the lab bewildered.

Eyes widening, Sarak gulps. "Oh boy!"

"Son, you've got some explaining to do," Andorf mumbles.

"What the hell just happened?" Brutus yells. "One moment I was in the back of your lab over there and now I'm …" He peers at Andorf, then back at their son. "I'm halfway across your lab."

Sarak sprints closer. "Papa! Are you okay?"

Brutus pats himself down. "Except for feeling tingly from my fingertips to my toes, I think I'm all right." His eyes again narrow upon the young experimenter. "Mind explaining what the hell just happened? Tell me I wasn't a subject of one of your risky experiments. How many times have I warned you about—?"

Sarak throws open hands outward. "It's not my fault this time, Papa, I swear. The device somehow triggered by itself. It—it was focused on that trinket, the one you're currently holding."

Andorf flails his hands, warning the lad not to continue.

Sighting his father, Sarak begins to stutter. "Y—you must have entered the absorption field when you grabbed for the piece." Sarak glances back at the flashing readout. "It occurred at the exact moment the field was energized."

"How—when—who gave you this piece?" Brutus yells. He runs a finger across the once festively-colored brass-mascot-engraved piece. "Wait! This was stashed away in my closet … I mean my old closet back at the …" He spins his head about. His voice revs. "Andorf! Why the hell are you giving away my valuables? What gives you the right?"

"Those things were left untouched in my closet over the years. I saw no problem with our son borrowing a few coins for his experiments." Andorf glances over Brutus' shoulder at the brass coin with its imprinted Izzy mascot grinning in a weird twisted-up face. "It's not like Izzy is complaining. And besides, you left the collection behind when you moved out after Serin passed twenty-two years ago. Why do they all of a sudden hold such importance?"

"You guys can't be doing this. This trinket came from the '96 Summer Olympic' collectibles I inherited from Grandpa Brett. It's all I have left of the guy."

Andorf snickers. "Judging how you and Serin stole my entire family flatware to finance the starship hijackings, consider this small payback."

Brutus' facial tone darkens. As if attempting to remain civil, he takes many long, deep breaths before speaking. "It's not the same. We both know it."

"Must I remind you, Brutus, it was a complete setting for twenty, all melted down for the silver. Unlike your trinkets, I'll never get *them* back."

Brutus eyes the brass trinket and then Andorf before mumbling. "And they say a Goshi holds no grudges."

Sarak's eyes again widen. Pointing to the rear of his lab, he taps Brutus' wide shoulder. "It worked, Papa! You've proved my teleportal device actually works. Don't you see? I've instantly teleported your brass trinket from there to over here." Sarak's smile morphs to concern at the sight of Brutus standing, arms folded, staring him down. He swallows hard. "The only problem is you were holding the brass trinket in your hand at that very moment. Thus, you've become the first live person to be teleported."

Judging by his facial expression, if Sarak were not his offspring, the beastly-sized man surely would have ripped Sarak's head off. "But my Izzy medallion," he growls. "Did you know the ghostly character was the first pseudo-Olympic mascot? That was two-and-a-half decades before Andorf and I were even born."

The young inventor eyes the dull brass piece in his papa's open hand. His focus volleys between both fathers. "If you ask me, your Izzy looks more of a Whazzy."

Andorf slaps a hand across Brutus' back. "As our son said, you've just become the first human teleported. You should be proud. You've made history."

Brutus sniffs at the trace of carbon scent of the fog dispersing. "What burned up, son? It smells like I broke your equipment."

Sarak revisits the instrumentation rack. Inspecting the internals, he frets. "If I only knew I'd be teleporting such a large mass, I would've used higher wattage drain resistors. Next time I'll—"

"Next time?" Andorf yells, face twitching at Brutus' scowling face. "You could have killed your papa … or damaged him well beyond repair."

Brutus chuckles. "I'm okay. All three hundred pounds of me."

"You should at least have a bio-parts specialist check you out."

Brutus smirks. "I've experienced a brutal space launch, lost a wife during childbirth, and survived being crushed by magnetic drones. Now I've become the first human teleported. What else can I add to my resume?" He takes a deep breath and lets out a loud sigh. "Next time I'd appreciate a little warning, Son."

Andorf raises a brow. "Don't forget eliminating the fascist dictator, Maximillian Harigados, back on Earth. Remember? You sliced off his head."

Brutus swallows. "Not my finest moment."

Andorf grins slyly at Brutus and then at Sarak. "Did you know your papa played an instrumental role in the starship hijackings?"

Shutting both eyes, Brutus shivers long and hard. "Fat Max."

With Brutus appearing to be on the verge of convulsing, Sarak and Andorf each grab one of the big guy's hefty arms. Brutus casts them aside with a sweeping arm motion and then scratches at his balding crown. "One thing troubles me, Sarak. The very moment I reappeared over here grabbing Izzy, I saw myself still in the rear of your lab."

Sarak cringes. "You may have arrived where you presently stand a split-second before you left. I suspect there was a minor time-displacement … perhaps a side effect caused by cumulative lead impurities in my solder joints. A few grams of impurities could have possibly changed the phase-coupling for you to arrive, say … twenty or thirty milliseconds before you left. But no worries, Papa, I'll have the lead impurities removed on my next version."

"Next version?" Andorf yells. "Wait! You mean you sent Brutus back in time?"

Brutus snorts. "Ha, I guess I can add time-traveler to my growing re-sume."

Sarak sucks wind between his teeth. "As if a sixth of a second will do anyone good. B—but don't worry. I suspect the problem can easily be remedied."

Andorf rubs his chin. He glances at Sarak's floor to ceiling racks and the equipment therein. "A few grams of lead in the solder," he mumbles, exiting the lab while counting his fingers. "A fraction of a second … a three-hundred-pound man. Hmm."

Brutus runs out of the lab after Andorf. He taps his old friend on the back. "Thank you for granting me a moment of glory. You know how the young lad idolizes his papa." He presents both coins as an offering. "Will you forgive me for the silverware?"

Without accepting the gifts, Andorf walk off. "I would not hold my breath."

CHAPTER 12

Word Gets Out
SARAK

Much to Sarak's dismay, life has suddenly become more complicated. With news of his teleportal spreading faster than cropped FaceJive photos, he becomes an overnight sensation. His name seems to be mentioned in every conversation. Everywhere he turns, there are hand-drawn illustrations depicting the young scientist as a wizard's son. Many sketches show him as pulling rabbits out of odd places including an assortment of domed or pointed hats. Other sketches depict Sarak as a circus performer. A few go as far as to paint the Goshi's son as a crazed, lunatic madman.

Sarak paces about his lab in the bowels of the *Starship Atlantis*, rambling on and on to himself about the new-famed notoriety and how neither of his fathers wear hats. It is not long before he faces oddly dressed men asking even odder questions about his experiments.

The strangers abruptly enter his lab without warning. As if he were not present, they take it upon themselves to attach cables to his instruments and jot data into their miniature recorders with plugin pica chips, similar to the one Serin once wore on a lanyard around her neck. Without lifting eyes, they toss unwanted questions at him.

"How did you overcome poly-morphic unbalancing—?"

"What about shielding issues with the—?"

"How much power does this sucker draw?"

The young Sarak can no longer take all the insidious questions. He props the lab door open and one by one, whisks them out using sweeping hand motions.

*

Days later, Sarak has a private discussion with his other father, the starship's chief engineer. Frustrated, the young experimenter again paces about the lab. "And they asked endless questions about how I came up with the concept … whether I constructed the device all by myself … where I obtained parts." With his face reddening, Sarak looks around the lab for anything to throw in disgust but not much remains. "It's not fair, Papa. I create something wonderful and a handful of arrogant men assume it's theirs for the taking. Look around. They took most everything."

Brutus throws both hands up. "I must tell you, Son. There's no such thing as ownership rights out here in space. Anything you create becomes property of the armada. That's the way it's always been."

Again, Sarak looks about his near-empty lab. "But they took everything … even the buckets of aged fruits from failed experiments."

Brutus reaches deep within his pants pocket, pulls out a coin-sized doubloon, and chuckles. "At least we still have my piece from the 96 Summer Olympics inherited from Grandpa Brett. Now, about your visitors, Sarak. How many were there? Did you grab them by their collars and toss them out into the hallway?"

"There were six of them." The young experimenter scratches his chin for a moment. "I simply whisked them outside by the wave of my hands."

"And you never touched them?"

Sarak shakes his head. "No. Why?"

The chief engineer winces. "I believe your other father's Goshi powers may be rubbing off on you."

CHAPTER 13

An Old Friend
SARAK

After several months, teams of engineers have reduced Sarak's rack-sized conglomeration of wires and modules down to a single chip the size of a belt buckle. Cleaning up the design, they not only eliminated all tingling sensation but resolved the undesirable time slippage issue by eliminating every bit of lead in the circuitry. A simplified interface with programmable music interludes has been integrated into the final product. The standardized version of Sarak's teleportal has been retrofitted in each of the armada's forty-four starships.

Mindlessly fingering the single monolithic sample chip encased in clear a poly-carbonate case, Brutus appears dazzled by the pure simplicity of the miniaturized circuit. "And everything has been reduced to this single chip?"

"Follow me, Papa. I'll show you how the friendlier interface works." Sarak leads Brutus along the A-deck hallway. They arrive shortly at a cordoned off area outside the *Atlantis's* last functioning observation deck and pause, staring at the flashing amber lights above the threshold. Sarak enters an access code. In a brief parade of showering color, he steps through the threshold. A split-second later, he appears on the twelve-inch display. Waving hands and speaking into the teleportal's mic, he encourages his papa to step through the threshold to join him.

"Hurry, Papa, before the portal closes. I promise, you won't feel a thing."

Unbeknownst to Brutus, the designers incorporated an array of sounds from their favorite space movies which randomly play as a gag. To the sound of a cheesy digitizer, the chief engineer steps cautiously through the threshold. Brutus blinks and the next moment he finds himself standing beside Sarak, eyeing unfamiliar surroundings of a foreign starship.

"This certainly isn't the *Atlantis*. I can tell you that." Brutus cracks a smile. "Saying I'm proud of you, Son, would be a grave understatement."

Sarak returns his papa's grin. "I only wish my *other* Father were here to give it a try."

Brutus inspects the teleportal's threshold. "Like that'll ever happen. We both know his aversion to technology. Andorf would be of his mind to use such a device." Brutus chuckles. "Just be glad the guy uses the starship's floating steps."

On the twelve-inch touchpad display, they watch Andorf arrive at the *Atlantis'* teleportal. Looking it over suspiciously, he squinches his nose at the tiny camera while tapping it a few times. Sarak and Brutus snicker at the sight of the Goshi flailing his arms as if threatening the device. They turn their heads at the reflection of someone approaching from behind.

"Welcome aboard the *Alliance*, gentlemen." Shaking each of his visitor's hands, the captain smiles at the young inventor before shaking his head at the image of Andorf on the twelve-inch display still flailing his hands. "I take it your engineering skills come from your Papa Brutus' side of the family, Sarak."

Brutus nods.

The captain touches Sarak's arm. "We've successfully teleported fifteen hundred pounds of cargo between starships but I have many questions. Has anyone tested the teleportal's inter-planetary range?"

Sarak rubs his chin for a long moment. "Theoretically there's no limit, but of course you'd need a much larger power supply than what's incorporated in these wall-mounted devices." He begins a lengthy explanation of teleportal theory.

Though Brutus appears to follow Sarak's logical explanation of the device's inner workings in fine detail, the captain shakes his head, appearing confused. He nudges Sarak's arm, if only to interrupt. "But can your teleportal send anyone … anything beyond the range of our armada? Can we safely place someone on a planet's surface?"

Sarak's eyes widen. "A larger version of the device could send someone all the way back to Earth if so desired. But as I had mentioned, it would require much larger power sources such as the one back in my lab."

The captain smirks. "Earth? Good gosh! Last I heard, seven authoritarian empires were running the planet. Who in their right mind would want to return that dastardly place?"

Brutus shrugs his shoulders.

"Earth?" a voice rings through the display's tiny speaker. Andorf butts and eye up against the display's camera. "Earth? Did someone mention traveling back to Earth?"

The captain watches Andorf pace about the *Atlantis'* hallway. "Some Goshi your other father turned out to be, Sarak. Why, the man can't even whisk himself over here."

Sarak winces. "Goshis bend the laws of nature. They cannot break them."

Brutus grins wide. "That's what young inventors are for—right, Sarak?"

"Well, I certain have no time to waste on an indecisive Goshi." The captain shakes his head as he leads his guests away. After riding down the floating steps, the three proceed down the long, winding D-deck hallway. The captain pauses at the last cabin door. He knocks long and hard and then waits.

All wait.

Brutus raises a brow. "I don't understand, Captain. Why'd you bring us here?"

The captain's eyes narrow. "We've been dealing with a sticky situation for some time. I was hoping one of you could possibly—"

Sarak pushes past the captain and begins to knock on the door but instead turns back to face the captain. "I sense someone of a previous generation … someone inside who's old enough to be my grandfather."

The captain leans his head toward the young inventor. "A month ago, we discovered an old man wandering the *Alliance*'s hallways. He was hobbling about with a cane, appearing dazed and confused. We didn't know what to do with the old codger so we put him in our last vacant cabin. It's where we stash broken items destined for eventual repair. He didn't seem to mind."

Brutus reaches past Sarak and knocks on the cabin door.

"I wouldn't be surprised if no one answers," the captain adds. "The old fart appeared to be living out his final days. I only hope we're not too late."

Sarak winces. "I can hear a faint breath. There's definitely someone alive in there."

The captain knocks again. "The guy seemed terribly bothered. It's as though he had an urgent message. But he refused to reveal it to me or my crew."

A weak, jittery voice on the other side of the door finally responds. "Who der?"

The door creaks open, revealing a weathered old man. His translucent skin appears as dry as aged paper and equally as brittle. Attached to a bowing walking cane, he squints at the three visitors gathered in the brightly-lit hallway. Eyes drawn immediately to Sarak's face, he looks the young man over from head to toe, as if trying to place where he had seen him before. Then he nudges his head for all to enter. With the help of his trusty cane and Sarak's arm, he hobbles back inside. After a few steps, the old man pauses. His aging eyes return to Sarak's face.

"Have I met your mudder, son? Your long nose ... brown eyes ... blonde hair, yah, you are definitely her son. Dis I am sure." His shaky hand releases Sarak to point a finger at him. "Sharon, yah. Such gorgeous eyes Sharon had ... eyes dat go deep inside you ... eyes 'ya never forget ... dark brown ones like yours. Yah, you are Sharon's son. Dis I am sure."

Understanding few pre-Tenulian words, Sarak leans his head, peers oddly at the old man. Though they have never met, he feels strangely akin to the crusty guy. He hand-gestures the captain and his papa to interpret the man's elder-speak.

The old man backs up to examine Sarak's perfect stance. "Yah! My friend Andy stood straight up like dat. You know my friend, Andy? Are any of you related to him?"

While Brutus and the captain do their best to translate the heavily-accented words into Tenulian, Sarak fans at the pickled stench of the old man's liquored breath.

"Tell me, young man … what you do in dis place?" The old man eyes Brutus' thinning crown and the captain's full, grey beard. "How you know dese men? Dey are much different den you."

Brutus crowds between Sarak and the old man as if to protect his son. He taps Sarak's shoulder. "My son, Sarak, is an inventor. At twenty-two, he single-handedly invented the teleportal. Now there's one on every armada starship." Brutus grins wide. "I'm Chief Engineer of the *S.S. Atlantis*, the father he most favors."

"Hmm, two fodders," the old man grumbles.

The captain offers an open hand. "And I'm Captain of the *Alliance*. You've been my guest for the better part of a month. I apologize but this cramped cabin was our only vacancy. I take it these sparse accommodations have met your—" The captain pauses to scan the variety of spent travel-sized liquor bottles lining every surface in the small cabin. He clears his throat "— your requirements?"

Trying to piece together the loose translations tossed at him from two different sources, Sarak feels lost. He watches the old man steady himself on the flexing cane while his frail, free hand reaches out to shake the captain's welcoming hand.

"Yah. Dank you, Captain. My friends and I are quite comfy." He pivots toward Sarak. "Two fodders you say? Where is dis *udder* fodder? Perhaps he knows what has become of my Andy."

The captain turns to lead the others into the hallway. "The guy we've been waiting on appears to have been delayed. Perhaps another time, old man."

Before Sarak can take a step toward the door, a feeble hand grabs his arm, preventing an easy escape. "You *must* know my friend, young man. Deh way you stand so vertical like dat. I not see anyone stand as upright in a very long time." He examines Sarak's hands. "Unlike you, Andy has never done a hard day's work in his entire life."

Brutus snickers. "Sounds like Andorf."

As the captain tugs on Sarak's arm, the young man stands firm. Gagging at the foulness of the old man's stale breath, he fixates on all the age lines spanning the old man's face. "Tell me about this friend of yours, old man … the one you call Andy. When did you last see him?"

Brutus steps closer to translate. "My son wants to know more about your friend … the one you call Andy. When did you see him last?"

"Dah last I saw of Andy he was of such terrible mind … walking about in dos stained sneakers of his. You see, dey robbed him … took every ting … even his pet rabbit."

Sarak's ears perk at the word 'rabbit'. He listens hard, picking out a word here and there in the gibberish-sounding old language. "Rabbit? Father had a pet rabbit but that was many years ago." Sarak rubs his chin. "I recall how he loved that bunny more than life itself." With his papa and the captain waving him out of the room, Sarak joins the others in the brightly lit hallway. Without their help, he could not begin to understand what the old man so desperately wanted to convey using elder-speak.

"Why are you even wasting your time on that old man?" Brutus says. "Can't you see he's delusional?"

The captain nods. "If you hadn't noticed, he's highly intoxicated. Why, I've never seen so many spent liquor bottles."

Sarak squints at the captain and then at his papa. "Intoxicated? Liquor bottles? Whatever do you mean?"

The captain stares at Sarak, dumbfounded.

Brutus gazes at the floor as if searching for appropriate answers. He cracks a slow, awkward grin. "You must pardon my son, Captain. Consuming alcohol was well before his years."

"What I meant to say…" The captain raises a brow. "The old codger has overindulged in liquids containing alcohol."

"But alcohol is highly toxic," Sarak says. "Why would anyone in right mind ingest that stuff?"

Brutus steps between Sarak and the captain. "Consuming alcohol was an awful waste of resources. However, it was once used to relax someone, put their mind at ease." He clears his throat. "Isn't that right, Captain?"

"Well, yes."

Sarak's eyes widen. "Ah, like the herb growing freely throughout the starships."

Brutus grins. "Indeed, like the weed."

"I know it sounds strange, but—" Sarak winces. "I somehow feel related to the old guy. The way he so passionately described his lost friend, I can't put a finger on it but I feel like I almost know this friend."

"We've run the name 'Andy' through armada-wide scans." The captain smirks. "There is no one going by such a name. This Andy fellow is obviously someone the old coot has conjured up."

Brutus chuckles. "By the way the old goat described this Andy guy as having never worked, it's as though he's referring to—"

Hearing a disturbance down the hallway, the trio turns about. They spot Andorf appearing from around a corner, babbling nearly incoherent words.

"Father!" Sarak yells out. "What took you so long?"

"Those damn shuttle pilots are on strike again." Andorf pauses to grab the nearest zero-gravity hold. "You know how hard it is to find a non-union pilot? I was about to steal one of the shuttles and pilot it over here myself."

Brutus laughs. "Like that'll fly."

The captain displays an open hand at the Goshi. "All this fine technology and you're still using antiquated shuttles?"

"I like having walls around me when I travel," Andorf says. "They give me something to hang onto."

"Well, come this way," the captain says, shaking his head. "We've got someone you should meet."

"He speaks only the old language," Sarak adds, leading the way. "He seems to have been searching for an old friend."

"Don't get your hopes up," the captain says. "We've run exhausted searches of the armada's personnel logs but have no clue who this Andy fella is, or if he even exists."

Hairs on the back of Andorf's neck rising at the mere mention of the long-forgotten nickname. With a show of his two fingers, the captain quiets. "Oh, Andy exists all right, though it is a name I have not heard in many years."

"But the old man was speaking gibberish," Sarak says.

Brutus nods. "And he sounded awfully confused."

"Don't tell me, Captain. You found the old guy wandering about the halls of the *Alliance*. From what you were able to piece together, he has been shuttling from starship to starship over the past twenty plus years … searching for a friend he calls Andy."

The captain stares at Andorf as if shocked by the Goshi knowing so much about the old man. "As a Goshi, you must have read my mind."

Andorf winces. "Think of it more like recalling a distant memory of a world nearly forgotten."

"Our medics ran thorough evaluations on the guy. Apart from old age and a rotting liver, he seems quite stable, although extremely disoriented. Only two things are certain … the old codger is from Scandinavia and he has no clue where he is."

Brutus snorts. "Not to mention the shuttle charges he's racked up during the past two decades."

"I have no doubt your name searches failed, Captain." Andorf takes a moment to briefly smile. "He is of another time and place. And as for him being Scandinavian, I beg to differ."

The captain throws his hands up. "Well, whoever this old man is, you've got to go in there and speak with him. But don't expect much. He's totally inebriated."

"Speak slowly, as not to confuse the old timer," Brutus adds. "He also appears deranged."

"Come along, Father. We must hurry. If the captain is correct, the old man may be nearing his last—"

The old man waddles out his door. Squinting at the bright overhead lights, he carefully steps into the hallway. Holding the bowing cane in one hand and shading his eyes with the other, he looks Andorf over. A wide grin consumes his swelling face as he recognizes Andorf's perfectly vertical stance and unsoiled hands. Tears streaming down his face, his free hand clasps at his heart. "Oh, Andy! I had feeling I not see you no more. Oh, dis is wonderful. Dank you, everyone! Dank you. Dank you."

Andorf's jaw drops as he looks over the ex-neighbor he has not seen in nearly a quarter century. "Sven," he yells, dashing toward the old man.

The frail old man discards his walking cane to slip a trembling arm over Andorf's shoulder before directing him inside. Waving Brutus and the captain on, Andorf follows Sven into the small cabin. Sarak follows and takes a seat at the kitchen table. For the longest time, he listens to his father and the old man converse in the old language. He extracts key phrase such as escaping the Canine Empire and his mother, Sharon, as the old man calls her, and being hunted by arrest-hungry agents. For reasons unknown, nearly every topic circles back to his mother, Serin.

The old friends carry on, jabbering into the wee hours of the morning, until Sven can no longer keep his head up. Sarak helps tuck the old man into bed. He watches his father pat the old man's shoulder and say goodnight, knowing the friends will most likely never see each other again.

Sven suddenly gasps for air. Twitching violently, he grabs Andorf's shirt, pulling his old friend inches from his face. He whispers raspy words in Andorf's ear.

Sarak overhears many spoken promises. He sees his father's head lower as Sven's arm drops suddenly. Tears stream down Andorf's face as he draws covers over Sven.

Wiping at tears, Andorf gazes at his son. "Binky predicted four random events would soon occur. The first was being reacquainted with an old friend. I am left to ponder about the next three."

"That's nice, Father. But what did the old man make you promise?"

Andorf turns away, wiping his dripping nose. "It is a matter which concerns you. We must discuss it at a more appropriate time."

CHAPTER 14

Emin's Warning
AYLA

Working at her desk, Ayla enjoys time to herself. Between writing training manuals and picking up after a sloppy husband, she finds few peaceful moments. After all, the notoriety of being a Goshi's daughter has never been easy but marrying the admiral's only son heightened the situation. Still, Ayla never regrets tying the knot with the childhood playmate, Emin, on her twenty-second birthday three years ago. Like her father-in-law, Turk, she finds her husband foolish and easily manipulated.

The cabin door suddenly bursts open. Swearing in his father's native Turkish accent, a well-trimmed, bearded man enters. He rips the taps off Ayla's temples and tosses them onto the floor. "Why are you still transcribing that kasar laakin manual? You should be—"

"I know … at my birthday gathering a half hour ago." Ayla pouts her lips in a 'tell me something I don't know' kind of way. "What's wrong with our juice dispenser, Emin? Has another one of our appliances fallen victim to Turkish temper?"

Emin paces the room, throwing his head about at his pregnant wife's condescending words. "Damn it, Hanin! Can't a man bear his own thoughts? I hate this—this never keeping anything to myself. Why are you always in my head, knowing what I'm thinking even before *I* know what I'm thinking?"

"Have you never wondered how I beat you at every game when we were kids?" Ayla asks, mimicking his tightened brow.

"Hey! I won more than my fair share of …" Emin glares at Ayla's biting smirk. "Wait! Are you implying you let me win?"

"Where's the fun in always winning? Yeah, yeah. Go ahead. Blame my father again. I've got his genes, as does my twin brother."

"But, Hanin!"

"Damn it, Emin! When will you start calling me your wife instead of spouting your father's medieval slang?"

Emin's mouth scowls. "You're upset because you cannot—"

"What? Roll 'r's with my tongue like the loose one in your mouth? There's a big difference in cannot and care not, as you may find out later this evening."

"A curse I call it," Emin yells. "And that scientist brother of yours … he locks himself away in his lab for days at a time. Have you seen how he snubs his nose at me? It's hard to imagine him being your twin."

"Give Sarak a break. He not only single-handedly invented the teleportal but I hear he's been working on something much grander." Ayla scratches itchy lines of her enlarged belly. "You should be glad he favors papa more than father."

"Ah yes, your papa Brutus. Yet another face we rarely see. The guy also lives down there in the *Atlantis'* dingy underbelly. Whenever I do see him, he appears half-dead, roaming starship hallways like a robot. But at least *he* doesn't share this damn curse of yours."

"You can give papa a break too. He slaves sixteen-hour days in that greasy sweatshop to keep the *Atlantis* running. And I warn you now, lover … you'd better get used to this not so recessive gene. Medics say there's a ninety-seven percent chance our baby will be reading our thoughts before she's able to crawl."

Emin slaps his head. "Ay, just what I need … another female reading my mind. She'll be bossing me around like you. How'll I ever live through this?"

"Enough of the endless dramatics, Emin. If you only knew how I envy your ability to sleep through the night. What I'd give to turn off these visions."

"Those damn dreams! Every night! It's a disease I tell you. And I blame your father. Why, Andorf's infected a good many women's babies with his seed. In generations, everyone in the entire armada will be carrying this disease."

"So, what if Tenulians become mind readers? What's the worst that could happen?" Ayla looks for something within reach to throw. "Now get out of here!" she yells, prompting him with the back of her hands. "Medics are in desperate need of training material for their new devices. You must allow me to complete my work. Oh, how I wish I was as organized as I've heard mother used to be."

"Calm down, my Ha … wife. Nothing will bring Serin back. She's been dead a quarter century, to this day."

Ayla slips off a sandal and hurls it at Emin.

He ducks and squinches his nose at her on his exit. He pauses at the cabin door. "Nothing good comes from these visions of yours. Absolutely nothing."

"Just leave! I promise I won't forget about my birthday celebration."

Emin grimaces at the sight of temporal taps flying across the room towards his wife's open hand. He watches her mindlessly slip them over her head. "Quit doing this, Ayla!" Avoiding a near strike from Ayla's other sandal, he ducks out the door.

Ayla looks about the cabin. She laughs at Emin's departing thoughts and at the reassurance of diminishing footsteps echoing down the hallway. "Of course, mother's never coming back," she mumbles. "I tell father all the time, but he somehow believes otherwise."

CHAPTER 15
Mila's Threat
ANDORF

More than just family members gather in *Atlantis'* festively decorated shuttle bay to celebrate the twin-siblings twenty-fifth birthdays. Andorf recognizes very few guests. Judging by their facial expressions, neither do the twins. He half-smiles at those introducing themselves for the nth time as they grab groat cakes and then cringe at their first taste of tart pino juice to wash down them down.

Sarak extracts an amethyst locket from his pocket. Maneuvering fingers beneath Ayla's long blonde hair, he places the chain around her neck. She drops the jeweled amulet down the same low-cut lavender peasant blouse her mother, Serin, wore during her own pregnancy.

Smiling at her twin, Ayla offers him a belt-buckle milled from one of papa Brutus' replicating printers. She looks around the room. "I'm well aware of the bad blood between Papa and my father-in-law but ..."

"I know," Sarak says. "It's not like papa to miss such an event."

Andorf steps closer. "Especially when there is food."

Sarak examines the belt buckle engraving commemorating their common birthdate and nods. He returns Ayla's warm smile before rejoining his wife and their rambunctious two-year-old toddler.

Turk appears out of nowhere to greet his Goshi friend and daughter-in-law. "I hear congratulations are in order, young lady." Turk looks about the room. "But where is my son? As a future admiral, Emin should never leave his pregnant wife alone at such a festive event."

Emin's mother, whose proper name Ayla cannot pronounce without spitting, approaches from across the room. The abbreviated name of Anel will never suffice … not from anyone of such youthful appearance and certainly not from an in-law. Bearing an obviously-painful smile, she greets Ayla. Her overly-soft creamy hand slips a tarnished ring from her homeland off her finger and taking Ayla's right hand, places it on her daughter-in-law's other ring finger. It spins freely on Ayla's much smaller finger. "Such petite hands," she exclaims.

"Our daughter-in-law can have it resized," Turk begins to say, but pauses at sight of his wife's lowering her brow. "Or maybe not," he mumbles, watching Ayla slip the ring over her adjacent thumb. Turk quickly excuses himself to go mingle with other guests.

Gazing at the precious ring on her daughter-in-law's thumb, Anel snarls beneath her breath. "Let this ring, passed down generations throughout my family, guide your way on life's journey with Emin and my granddaughter to be. You've reached the age of majority … the age of critical reasoning. I expect you shall make wise decisions, my dear. Madato."

"Madato," Ayla says, returning the madam's brief nod.

Anel's smile melts off her face as she excuses herself to join her husband across the room.

Watching her face sadden, Andorf feels his daughter's thoughts darken as her eyes drift past the vacant chair representing a deceased family member. He recalls Ayla as the once five-year-old who sat on her Uncle Gregory's lap listening to him spin wild tales. Missing his best friend is intensified by watching Ayla stare at the vacant chair mark 'reserved'. He steps closer to wipe her teary eyes.

"I remember quite fondly another pregnant woman wearing this very same lavender peasant blouse, young lady. How my heart melted when your mother wore it on our first date. I could not peel my eyes off her gorgeous brown eyes." Andorf clears his throat. "I recall, this blouse was much smaller before Serin let it out."

Ayla halfway smiles. "And mother surprised you with twins, didn't she?"

Careful not to squeeze her protruding mid-section, Andorf hugs her. "Not much longer until I become a second-time grandpa."

"I'm *so* ready for this to be over, Father." Ayla chuckles at the sight of her approaching husband, cake crumbs decorating his face and strawberry icing coating his beard. He appears to have barely survived a cake-diving incident.

To the crowd's delight and her father's dismay, Ayla doesn't hesitate to lick crumbs encrusting Emin's mouth. "Care not or dare not," she says, licking her lips.

Catching her playful wink, Emin leans into his father-in-law. "Mind if I steal my girl, Mr. Johnson? I believe it's time for me and the birthday gal to have a more private celebration."

Nodding, Andorf spots Sarak, wife and toddler in tow, all heading his direction in swift approach. "I can't believe papa Brutus isn't here," Sarak says.

"Not when there's plenty of food," the wife adds.

"The chief engineer's absence is quite puzzling," Andorf says. "Perhaps something has gone awry downstairs."

"Would you mind watching Gorin while my wife and I grab some cake?" Sarak bends down to address the impatient lad. "Aren't you going to a least say hi to your gramps?"

The rambunctious tot runs off. Within seconds he has disappeared somewhere within the crowd. "Maybe next time," Sarak's wife says, before sprinting after the troublesome lad.

Andorf half-way smiles. "Have you tried a radio leash? I hear they are good for at least fifty yards."

"None of them work." Sarak cringes. "Reading our minds, Gorin knows the codes before we can set them. We've resorted to posting gruesome pictures on the cabin door just to keep him inside."

Andorf cringes.

"I know. Sometimes I awaken in the middle of the night and get scared half to death." He pauses to watch his wife cross the room in hot pursuit of the boy. "I never thought it would be this way. We've been dealing with this behavior since he was able to raise his head."

Andorf drops a hand onto Sarak's shoulder. "You must practice blanking your thoughts, Son."

"Does that work?"

"How do you think I ever kept things from you and Ayla? Now, about my old friend's brief visit. Do you remember Sven?"

"The strange old codger back on the *Alliance*? I recall you and he had lengthy conversations about your times back on Earth. He was interesting but I cannot see how we were related. You know, him being Swedish. What was it he made you promise? You said it concerned me."

"Sven was convinced if there was even the slightest chance I could be with Serin again, I should try."

"Try what? To be with mother again?"

Andorf nods.

Blood suddenly drains from Sarak's face. He falls back several steps. "No! That's insane. I cannot help you."

"Before passing, Binky had warned me of meeting an old friend. Soon afterwards, Sven appeared on the *Alliance*."

"What? Binky told you these things? The bunny actually spoke?"

Andorf nods. "We communicated through linked thoughts. He also mentioned a desperate nurse, a starving artist, and some mad stitcher."

Sarak winces. "Perhaps you should sit, Father. I believe you've had a wee too much pino juice."

Andorf tips his head a bit. "Dare I detect the scent of your sisters' bitter pessimism in your breath?"

Sarak peers right and then left. He leans closer. "The sisters made me swear I'd never entertain your fantasies of reuniting with mother. They went as far as to forbid me from performing further time-leap experiments." Sarak again looks about the room. He lowers his voice to a whisper. "Mila even went so far as to threaten to castration if I dare mention any of this."

Andorf chuckles. "I would expect no less of her."

"It's no joke, Father. What if I want another child someday?" Sarak eyes his own crotch before peering across the room. "Oh no! Look over there at Mila waving her hands. You'd better go see what Mila wants before she turns into a windmill."

Andorf's brow tightens. "Soon you shall come into your own, Son. There will come a day when you no longer fear your sisters."

"I—I beg you not to mention any of this. You and I never had this little—"

The room suddenly goes pitch black. Except for one errant tot, running beneath everyone's feet and his mother chasing after, the crowd quiets, waiting on the lights to return from the suspected power switchover.

"Something's wrong. Switchovers never last more than a few seconds." Sarak taps the timepiece dangling from his belt. He grimaces at the digits projected onto the floor. "Twelve minutes late. I must find papa."

"Let me go!" a young boy screams from across the room. "You're ruining everything."

The lights return, dim at first but brightening. In the twilight, Andorf and Sarak spot Mila dragging a tot behind her and grunting upon her approach. "You ain't seen nothing, kiddo. Stick around for the fireworks when I get done with you."

Sarak bends down to scoop up the boy, rescuing him from the clutches of his wicked Aunt Mila.

"Snip, snip," Mila says, threateningly opening and closing her fingers like scissors.

Watching his son and grandson walk away at a hurried pace, Andorf snarls. "What the hell was that about, Mila? Are you threatening them?"

"Whatever do you mean?" Mila bats her eyes.

Andorf takes Mila's arm and leads her into a corner far away from following ears. "Since when have you become so cynical, little lady? Are you forgetting I hear every word said in this room? How dare you say such nasty things to your brother, let alone to my grandson."

Mila snarls. "Not everyone's cut out for kids. Parents shouldn't leave their kids wandering about like abandoned pets. Besides, the little rat was bothering me."

Andorf glares at her. "Keep in mind Gorin is your nephew."

"Not by blood."

"Look at you, Mila. You are smart, attractive, and a prominent member of the Third Council. You are a ruby amongst the dust. How is it in your thirty years you have not found a mate?"

Mila pulls out a mirror. She puffs her cheeks while brushing hair off her eyes.

"Serin was my everything." Andorf becomes pale. "When she passed, I became empty. You came to me as a lost five-year-old girl and helped lessened the burden. But it is well past time to strike out on your own."

"We've been through this before. Mating is not important to me. Now, I see you and Sarak had a little talk. Did he mention what I'll do if I caught him performing any more of those crazy time experiments?"

Andorf pushes thoughts of Sarak deep within the darkest recesses of his mind, away from Mila's probing reach. "You avoid my question so I repeat. Why are you not looking for a mate? A woman your age should not be living with her father."

"Daddy! If anyone has answers it should be you." At the sight of the room quieting and ears turning in their direction, Mila lowers her voice. "If I moved out, who in the world would take care of you? Have you given it much thought? Huh? Have you?"

Envisioning life without Mila's obsessive cleaning sprees, Andorf smiles. He then remembers, her taking care of the little things he has gladly forgotten over the years. Again, he blocks Mila from his thoughts. *But still, the girl deserves her own life. A small nudge is occasionally required to get us out of our ruts. Mila first, then I shall deal with Sarak.*

PART 3
Shuffling The Deck

Council Act 6146
ANDORF

Zombie-like creatures roam the *Atlantis'* hallways. Andorf quells the swelling crowd's worries with hand gestures as if he was a maestro cueing an orchestra. As their demeanor elevates, he uses hand gestures to appease their fears. The third verse of the nightmarish symphony is interrupted by an insistent pounding on his cabin door.

Andorf awakens. Peering out the cabin door peep hole, he sees captain Jobriah Cates fidgeting in the hallway. Andorf throws a black, hooded jacket over his shoulders and exits the cabin. He follows Jobi down the floating steps a few flights to where a mass of frightened people is gathered. The pair pushes their way through the crowd until happening upon a sobbing woman encircled by many attempting to comfort her.

"The thing's a monster," the woman cries, bursting into tears. She covers her face dramatically with a small embroidered hand cloth. "It's a Frankenstein in the flesh!"

While Jobi stares speechless at the sea of scared faces surrounding him, Andorf's thoughts flash back to Earth … to the drooling, eight-foot snail-like beast known as Fat Max.

A few in the crowd abandon the sobbing woman to yell at the captain. "You're the captain, Jobi. You should know how to handle this."

"Yeah, Look it up in your captain's manual."

Jobi's face contorts as he mumbles. "What? There's a captain's manual?"

Sharing Jobi's angst amongst the crowd's brewing anger, Andorf wedges between the captain and his hecklers. Eyes narrowing upon the crowd, the Goshi slowly lowers his hood.

All pointing at Andorf's elongated ears and grey-bearded face, the crowd gasps. Many stumble backwards onto those behind, causing many to fall like dominos. Dropping to their knees, the remaining refuse to stare directly at Andorf.

"Help us, Mr. Goshi," they chant. "You're our only hope."

Andorf raises open palms and the desperate demands lessens. Blank faces scan each other as if a waiting silently for inspiration from the fabled Goshi now in their presence.

"Rise my friends," Andorf says, raising his hands. He peers at Jobi and then back at the now standing terrified crowd. "Was this beast six-foot-three-inches tall with a nasty temper, an orange-colored spray-on tan, and blaming everyone else for his own shortcomings?"

All freeze, grasping at the Goshi's misplaced humor. One man hesitantly steps forward.

"No, Mr. Goshi, Sir. It wasn't that lying conman. It was an entirely different kind of monster … the likes no one has ever seen before."

"Or care to see again," another adds.

"And it was stumbling forward … swinging its arms as if it was trying to keep its balance."

"Tell him about the monster's face! How it looked malformed."

"The creature's face was dripping," the outspoken man says, shivering like those in the crowd bunching around him.

"Like the thing was made of molten plastic."

"And it smelled of lubricant … like those greasy machines in the bowels of the starship."

Raising both hands, Andorf momentarily silences the raging crowd. "This monster of yours, which way did it go? Surely, someone must know."

Distant screams are heard. Fingers point in the direction of the screams. Andorf locks his fingers together and flexing both hands, stretches the fingers. The crowd scowls at the sound of the Goshi's finger joints snapping in protest as he scans the countless terrified faces lining both sides of the F-deck hallway.

A second man steps from the crowd. "Do something, Mr. Goshi? You're an all-powerful wizard. How about performing one of your chants to make the creature disappear."

"Yeah, Go ahead and chant."

"That's right. Ah-chi the monster away."

Andorf and Jobi push their way through the crowd. Andorf flattens a thumb against the nearest wall-mounted informational display. His credentials flash upon the screen with 'Goshi' appearing as his surname. Against the backdrop of the heckling crowd, he speaks slow and deliberate.

"Locate all non-humanoids aboard the *Starship Atlantis.*"

After a few seconds, the screen displays the *Atlantis'* thirteen deck layouts, stacked one above the other. The crowd closes ranks behind Andorf, gasping at the countless blinking lights scattered about every deck.

"Look at em' all," many cry out. "There must be thousands of them."

Andorf raises two fingers, silencing the crowd. He turns about to speak into the display. "Refine the previous search to all non-humanoid bipeds."

The screen clears. Within seconds, the redisplayed floor plans are overlaid with hundreds of blinking dots, reminiscent of old-fashion air traffic controller screens. Again, the crowd gasps.

For a third time, Andorf leans into the display. After clearing his throat, he speaks slowly. "Refine the search to non-humanoid bipeds without wings or tails and taller than six feet."

The display blanks. After a moment, a dozen blue sprites are blinking on the screen. Appearing like pacmen, the sprites appear to be roaming about the cafeteria, engineering, and lower decks in seemingly random patterns.

Feeling the crowd on the verge of panic, Andorf identifies one particular sprite on the wall-mounted display. "This one is located here on the F-deck … just a few hundred feet behind us."

The crowd immediately quiets. Many focus on the blue dot, sucking wind between their teeth. More than one person yells out in fear.

"Look! The creature's circling back."

"What are we going to do?"

Andorf's turns to face the captain. "We cannot allow this thing to enter the starship's main stairwell."

Jobi nods. "Without surveillance cameras, it could move about the starship undetected." Sweat begins to drip down his face. "I … I never signed up for this when I was thrust into that captain's chair. First Thom and now Murray … I'm *Atlantis'* third captain. What's that tell you?"

Andorf jams his face into Jobi's face. "Captains confront unforetold hazards. It says so in the opening pages of your captain's manual, if you ever bothered to read it."

Backing away, Jobi smirks. "So, there's actually a captain's manual?"

"What have you got to worry about? Your predecessors died in the vacuum of space. We are on the F-deck, practically in the middle of the starship."

The captain's eyes narrow. "I've had nightmares about this very thing. First, the monster jams me into an airlock and jettisons me into space. Then it comes after you, Andorf. With both of us out of the picture, there'll be no one to stop it. And with Council Act 6146 banning photon blasters usage within the confines of a starship, even Turk's warriors won't be able to stop the beast."

Andorf takes a firm grip of Jobi's shoulder, stares into the captain's eyes. "Get a hold of yourself, Jobi. There must be a logical explanation for this so-called monster. We only need to discover what this creature is and what makes it tick." He releases the captain to push his way through the crowd.

Breathing deep, Jobi cautiously follows a few steps behind. The pair wind their way through the *Atlantis'* twisting F-deck, expecting the creature to leap at them any moment from. Instead, they discover screams of terrified people around each turn. All of a sudden, they spot the crowd, all with fingers pointing and watching an animated seven-foot human replica from a perceived safe distance. The creature is poised at the floating steps twenty yards ahead, repetitively places one foot atop a step and then retracts it as if unsure of what to do next.

"Look at the size of the beast," Jobi whispers. "Everyone is counting on us, Andorf … every last one of them. What the hell are we supposed to do?"

The creature's testy foot freezes. Its foot drops onto the stationary section of the floating steps landing in a loud THUNK! In slow mechanized moves, it turns toward the crowd, growling. Everyone backs up.

Andorf focuses on the creature's face. The more he stares, the more the thing favors his old friend, Brutus, but in a drippy, plasticine kind of way. He looks about the crowd, listening to them spewing their fears. He waves his hands and the crowd's jabbering lessens. When he turns back to face the monster, the crowd's clamoring resumes. He stares down the crowd a second time with flailing hands. They again quiet. After the third verse, Andorf feels he has become a maestro.

The creature's eyes widen. It gurgles out words, to the likes of singing. "Momma Mia. Momma Mia."

Jobi leans close and whispers. "What are you waiting for, Andorf? You're a Goshi. Read the creature's mind."

The crowd stirs, continuing to boldly voice their opinions.

"Convince the damn thing to leave, Mr. Goshi."

"And never return!"

Careful not to step beyond the landing onto the floating steps, Andorf walks a full 360 around the frozen seven-foot creature. Taking his time, he evaluates everything about the creature, from its composition to composure before looking back at the captain.

"It's a Gort, Jobi."

"Huh?"

"Have you noticed how its motions have been slow, jerky movements? Obviously, the thing is some form of robot. It has no brain." Andorf surveys the crowd for long moments. "Well, not what anyone normal would call having a brain. It's a replica ... a replica to the likes of someone we all know."

Jobi steps closer to the creature. He pokes at the creature's plastic-like skin and then flicks the goo off his finger. The crowd retreats a few steps. "Surely there's an off-switch hidden somewhere. No sane person would construct such a thing with no way of shutting it down."

When the huge replica looks down and growls, Jobi falls into the crowd. He is quickly propped back onto his feet.

"What if the creature was not built by human hands?" Andorf raises a brow. "What if it was made by another machine? Would it have an off switch then?"

Jobi's eyes widen. "Well, that certainly raises the stakes." He steps closer, dangerously close, sneering at the replica and muttering much too loud. "Klaus Nicto Barcelona."

Lowering its head, the creature's eyes narrow upon the captain. Growling much louder than before, it lifts one leg and then the other, advancing in long strides with beastly-huge fingers reaching out. It wraps one of its large hands around Jobi's neck and squeezes.

Jobi gasps for air. Face turning colors, his fingers claw futilely at the creature's bulky oversized arms as its fingers squeeze ever tighter. His eyes begin to bulge out of their sockets as he chokes out what may be his final words. "Now—would—be—a—good—time—Andorf."

"Save our captain," voices yell.

"Do something, Mr. Goshi. The captain's face ... it's turning blue."

"Last thing we need is another Smurf running around here."

As Jobi's face turns multiple shades of deep purple, a few daring souls rush the creature. A loud, beastly growl quickly sends them retreating.

Andorf scratches his fuzzy chin unsure what to do. A wide grin suddenly consumes his face. He reaches beneath the creature's bulky limbs and extracts a pair of dark sunglasses from the captain's shirt pocket. Standing on tiptoes, he slips the shades over the bridge of the replica's nose and then jumps clear of the plasticine beast.

The replica instantly freezes. Jobi somehow manages to peel the beast's huge fingers off his neck. Breathing hard and stumbling around the crowd, Jobi's hands work his flattened neck back into a tubular shape. After a good minute, he has enough wind to choke out 'thanks' in a dry, hoarse voice.

"How did you do that?" many ask.

Andorf smiles. "Back in the day, Brutus taught me one thing about photo-robots. They need light to operate, plenty of it. Using the captain's sunners, I merely starved the creature of its light source."

Confused faces stare at the Goshi as if wondering if their savior has gone nuts. A man yells above the boisterous crowd.

"Say that again."

"Yeah. In Tenulian this time."

Andorf stares at Jobi and then back at the crowd. "Think of it as me putting our little friend to sleep. Luckily, Captain Jobi happened to have dark sunglasses in his shirt pocket."

"Father warned one day I would be blinded in a flash of brilliance." Jobi grins clueless at the crowd. "I've carried sunglasses in my shirt pocket ever since."

Andorf, like those surrounding him, break into laughter. "Say, Jobi, you never took the captain exam, did you?"

"Wait," Jobi mumbles. "Now you're telling me there's a captain's exam?"

While the crowd ribs Jobi, Andorf walks a second lap around the replica. He scrutinizes its likeness to his old friend, Brutus, right down to its thinning hairline and grease smeared across its face. Poking at the replica and cringing at the cold feel of plastic-like skin, he recalls when his then innocent five-year-old Mila shoved her toy rabbit in captain Murray's face. Her young voice echoes between his ears as clear as it did twenty-five years ago.

Papa said he could replicate people but their glycerin skin would feel like plastic.

Andorf shivers in thought of how replicator #6 spent its mechanical life in disrepair, always demanding Brutus' attention … how her rhythm smoothed at the touch of the chief engineer's skillful hands.

He strolls back to the informational display. A selective search reveals two stationary blue dots within the deep, dark bowels of the *Atlantis*. A finger-tweeze narrows the images down to the mechanical room where the most troublesome replicator resides. Grinning slyly, he scurries past the replica and then hops onto a descending floating step. He calls back to the captain. "You know how to stop these guys, Jobi. Gather a team. Round up the other replicas scattered throughout the *Atlantis*. Shut them down. Shut them all down."

Jobi's eyes widen. "Hey! What am I supposed to do with this one?"

"I am sure the Dribbles will know how to dispose of it. Everyone, set your watches. If I am back not from the mechanical room in an hour, release Turk and his warriors. To hell with Council Act 6146."

CHAPTER 17

Replicator #6
ANDORF

Riding down the floating steps, Andorf prepares for the aftermath of the pending confrontation in *Atlantis'* mechanical room. If things play out as expected, how will he break it to the kids? The girls will take it hard, but Sarak being close to his papa Brutus will never understand.

The moment his feet hit the L-deck's landing Andorf takes off running through the winding passages toward the stairwell door. He projects an open hand and the door flies open. Jogging down the double flight of steps, he pauses at the bottom out of breath. Being over sixty is beginning to take its toll.

Vibrations of roaring machinery rattle his being long before opening the M-deck stairwell door. He exits the stairwell and then hikes across the wide hallway. If his suspicions are correct, the chief engineer's sarcasm will no longer greet him. Nor will the big guy be poking his head out of a replicator to yell at his incompetent techs.

The heavy mechanical-room doors swing open at Andorf's projected hand. His nostrils flare at the stench of grease and oil permeating the thick air. Busy machines everywhere he looks are humming distinct rhythms, all sounding off as if issuing warnings.

"Go no further. Leave right now," the air handlers rattle.

Gravity generators rumble. "Not good for you. Not good for you."

"Get out while you are able," the replicating printers chant through milling noises.

Andorf covers both ears as he takes off running at full speed. Hitting a grease spot, he slides a good ways across the room. Determined to remain vertical, he flails both arms while leaping over parts and tools strewn about the slick floor. At the last moment, he grabs hold of a hand rail and jogs down a half-height of perforated step treads. To the backdrop of machinery clinking and clanking out warnings, he again runs full steam toward a far corner of the noisy mechanical room.

Out of the corner of his eye, he spots a lone bean-counter emerging from behind a seven-foot, carbonized replica. Unable to stop, Andorf plows into the man, knocking both the Dribble and himself onto the filthy floor.

Rising to his feet, the Dribble reviews his wrist-mounted pad and its scribe for damages. Noting his clothes covered in grease, his voice ramps to a level beyond his swearing. "What the hell are you doing down here? Watch where you're going. You nearly killed me."

"It's quite all right," Andorf says, reviewing the man's grease-stained white-satin clothing as well as his own. "It was totally my fault. I was going way over the designated speed-limit."

The man changes the civility of his voice after recognizing Andorf. "It doesn't matter if you *are* the infamous Goshi, I'd write you up if I wasn't tied up inspecting this specimen." The Dribble scans the mechanical room. "I take it you're here about these oversized robots? We've been recording counter numbers. Eleven here appears complete. Behind the gravity generators over there is a half-formed specimen number twelve. Someone is really been cranking these things out. They absolutely cannot be wasting precious material like this."

True to his nature, Andorf cannot resist toying with the strait-laced man. He walks slow circles around replica number eleven, rubbing his chin and wincing at the similarities to his friend, chief engineer Brutus

Bittner. "This is hardly a face anyone could easily forget. I believe I have seen it before."

"Uh-huh." The astute man barely lifts his thick glasses as he scribes notes on the wrist pad. "If a link is made, we can put an end to this malady in a jiffy."

Andorf raises a brow. He continues to rub his chin while circling around number eleven. "You know, this face does look awfully familiar. I may have seen this guy quite recently."

The accountant's grease-stained hand grabs Andorf's shirt collar. He pulls the Goshi inches from his own scowling face. Andorf gags at the stench of the man's peppermint-patolli cologne. "Don't think about withholding information from us, Mr. Goshi. We have ways of making you talk. You have relatives in Smyrna?"

"Huh?"

"Perhaps I haven't made myself perfectly clear. Must I spell it out?"

Andorf's eyes narrow. He snarls and the wiry man immediately releases his grip. "I have little time for such nonsense." He throws out an open hand and the accountant stumbles backward.

With the bean counter cowering behind specimen number eleven, Andorf proceeds toward his target—Brutus' pride and joy—replicator #6. He walks around to the backside of the eight-foot-tall machine, reaches for the replicator's large, red door handle but pauses at the machine's mechanical rhythm morphing into a series of whimpering clickity-clacks. She pounds out milling noises sounding much louder than the other machines' warnings.

"Don't touch me there! No! Whatever you do, don't touch me there."

"Leave her alone!" five other replicators chime in. "If you know what's good for you, you will leave her alone."

Andorf gazes at #6 and the strange electrical aura surrounding her. He notices all ground wires connecting to the replicator's frame have been frayed. Despite the machines' warnings and his own intuition, he grabs the large, red door handle. Suddenly, jagged pain shoots down the length of his arm and into both legs. His hand grasps the handle ever tighter, refusing to release. The machine's mechanical rhythm races, as does Andorf's heart-rate.

Convulsing in pain and unable to detach, he becomes surrounded by the shadows of angry techs crowding around him. The lead-tech shouts from somewhere across the large room. After what seems like a lifetime, a gloved hand clamps around his wrist and jerks him away from the replicator. Boxed in by angry techs and jittering from near electrocution, Andorf does his best to thank his rescuer.

The lead-tech leads Andorf away from the tech-gauntlet only to stare him down. "What the hell were you doing, mister? Can't you read the signs? Didn't you hear the warnings? The mechanical room is a dangerous place. This place is off limits to the general populace."

Replicator #6 abruptly changes her milling noises as if scolding the Goshi as well.

Andorf scans the lead-tech's identification stenciled on his coveralls. While waving a hand in a circular manner above the lead-tech's head, he looks up and yells above the machinery noise.

"As Goshi, Andorf Johnson, I grant Silas Angora full access rights to replicator #6."

Overhead speakers awaken to a voice of the starship's consciousness.

Siros: So noted, Goshi Andorf Johnson.

Andorf half-smiles at the lead tech. "Go ahead, Silas. Open her up."

With dark sweat dripping off his grease-covered face, Silas stares bewildered. "Ah, you're the mysterious Goshi I've heard so much about."

Andorf nods.

Pulling at clumps of lint and animal fur clinging to his sleeve, he stutters. "I—I don't know about this. #6 is the chief engineer's baby. I know you're a powerful Goshi and all that but—"

Andorf's eyes narrow. "But what, Silas?"

"Brutus told us to never to lay a hand on his girl. He went as far as to make threatening demands."

Andorf grabs the rag hanging from Sila's rear pocket and then returns to the red door handle. His hand is blocked, this time by Silas' gloved hand.

"If anyone opens the rear door, it'll be me. But I'm letting you know, Mr. Goshi, I cannot be held responsible for whatever happens here on out. I want you to be aware of this." Silas scans the tech's shocked faces. "My reluctance is to be recorded in the ship's logs."

Peering upward, Andorf yells above the machinery noises. "Siros, note Silas' reluctance to open replicator #6's rear access door."

Siros: So noted, Goshi Andorf Johnson.

Andorf nods at the lead-tech, thirty-years his junior and at the techs gathered around.

Sucking wind between his teeth, Silas gloved hand grasps the replicator's red door handle. He turns the handle ten degrees but pauses when the machine's churning rhythm changes to clicking noises, sounding as though she were running dry, without lubrication. Lights high above the replicator begin to strobe. Alarms throughout the mechanical room echo off the high ceiling.

Silas advances the handle in the counter-clockwise motion. Completing a full quarter-turn, he waits on a consensus from the Goshi and his fellow techs. With their hands prompting him to continue, Silas gives the panel door a stiff tug. As the door reluctantly opens, those packed tightly around the door are sprayed with a mix of machinery oil and human bodily fluids. Everyone's face and clothing become saturated in dark, gooey slime.

Dripping in goo and wiping their eyes, all gasp at the horrendous sight of Brutus wedged inside the clicking machine. All lean in and squint at the unconceivable. They see stepper arms mechanically measuring every last detail of the chief engineer's physical being with micron precision. Spirit's 'Mechanical World' begins to play throughout the room from overhead speakers.

Despite having readied himself to see his old friend encased inside the replicator, tangled up in belts and wires, Andorf was ill-prepared to find Brutus totally consumed with his guts splattered everywhere. Staring at the mess, he is unable to differentiate between blood and gear oil. His jaw drops. He begins to tear, not knowing what to do next.

Silas forces the door shut. With his stomach gurgling loudly, he pushes past everyone to reach a nearby sink. Moments later he returns, wiping his mouth with a filthy rag. He gazes up at the overhead speakers and yells. "Siros, stop!"

Siros: I respond only to Goshi Andorf Johnson and Captain Jobriah Cates.

Andorf catches himself swaying to the catchy. At sight of condescending looks he pauses, clears his throat. "Siros, this music is highly inappropriate. Discontinue the music immediately."

The music continues.

"Siros!" Andorf yells. "Did you hear me? Stop the damn music!"

Siros: But I had promised Chief Engineer Brutus Bittner I would play an appropriate tune after his demise. This near-instrumental tune is most appropriate for a man of few words, don't you think?

"Siros!"

When the music stops, visceral noises are heard percolating from within replicator #6's cabinet. The machine shakes wildly about the floor. When a side chute magically appears, all step back to watch a steaming molded replica of Brutus ooze out the chute. The form solidifies on the floor before their eyes. A bell rings 'ta-da' while the freshly-made replica rubs burs from its newly milled frame with its large hands. The replica then shakes off loose plasticine from its hardening shell like a wet dog. It takes one shaky step forward … then another.

Andorf grabs a rag and standing on his toes, drapes it over the replica's eyes. Replica thirteen instantly halts.

The Goshi runs back to #6. He traces plastic conduit upwards, along the ceiling, and down a wall to a massive kill switch. Red warning lights flash when he wraps rags around his hand and reaches for the switch. As before, techs block his reach.

"We were told never to power-down machinery."

Silas nods. "There would be cumulative production losses to the likes we've never seen. Our parts bins would soon empty. Our shelves would be bare. It's why Brutus demanded we work on everything live."

At a whisk of the Goshi's hand, the tech backs up. Voice ramping above machine noises, he leans his head towards the obstinate replicator.

"Would any of you like to join your boss inside #6? I could make it happen at the wave of one hand."

While #6 whimpers out a series of choppy, drilling sounds, Andorf clears cobwebs off the wall-mounted switch. He tugs hard on the large switch handle, putting his weight into it but the kill switch remains in place. Silas adds his leverage to the switch handle which has been in the 'ON' position for a quarter-century. The high-powered electrical contacts break with a sudden *THUD*. #6 winds down, leaving the replicator quintet singing their operatic sonata of 'I told you so' in one less voice.

Andorf flips Silas' stenciled wrist over to verify the identity matches his uniform tag. "Lead technician, Silas Angora, as Goshi Andorf Johnson, I appoint you the new chief engineer of the *Starship Atlantis*. Siros, did you hear me? You shall now answer to Silas' voice commands."

Siros: Chief Engineer Silas Angora, so noted.

Silas grins at his subordinates as he begins to prance about.

"Have your techs extract the real Brutus out of that damn replicator, Silas." Andorf winces. "Scoop up whatever is left of your predecessor and dump it into a composting recycler."

"You heard the Goshi," Silas yells, in the same demanding voice heard in the past. "Clean out #6 and get her back online. Quit standing around! We're running behind on production schedule."

Andorf turns for the exit but pauses to face Silas. "And clear out #6's memory! The last thing we want is for something like this to ever happen again."

Silas watches his techs change into fresh coveralls. "You heard what the Goshi said," he yells. "Hurry up! Time's a wasting! Let's get this done."

Andorf wipes his face with a slightly-clean rag. Watching the techs break out tools, he senses unspoken resentment toward him and their new boss for being so cold-hearted. A team of Dribbles brushes past. All drop to their knees to inspect the piles of plasticine waste discarded by replica number thirteen. The head Dribble's voice sounds above the machinery orchestra.

"No piece of material wasted… not a single drop of oil goes without recycling. Every pico-gram must be recovered." The wiry man turns to face those behind him. "Dismantle and inventory the specimens. Hey, you over there … mind not stepping on precious material."

Andorf shakes his head in disbelief as he stomps up the perforated treads of the half-steps. Stumbling out into the hallway, he recalls the many times his childhood friend threatened to shove a wrench into his pasty hands. For once in his life, Andorf feels truly alone. With Brutus gone, he is the sole survivor of the old clan. Serin left twenty-six years ago. Five years later, Binky and Gregory took their outs. Then Sven and now Brutus.

With his belly gurgling, Andorf dashes for the stairwell. He pushes through the door barely in time to empty his stomach beneath the lower steps. He removes his shirt and wipes his mouth. After tossing the shirt on top, he stares at the mess for the longest time.

"Oh, how I used to hate your guts, Brutus. You were always scheming behind everyone's back. But I must admit you got things done … from the starship hijackings … to surviving a severe crushing at Titan Outpost … to becoming the first human teleported in our son's wild experiments. You even became a time-traveler for a brief moment. In the end, you were betrayed by the one you truly loved … replicator #6. So, goodbye my old friend. Life on this old collection of welds as you once called it will never be the same."

CHAPTER 18

Farewell Old Friend

ANDORF

The *Atlantis'* auditorium fills to capacity. People spill into the hallways. The immediate family sits front-row center, nodding silently at endless affirmations. There is not a single dry eye in the room, including those belonging to Andorf. Listening to the funeral music, he ponders about how the deceased was never a true confidant … nor trust-worthy for that matter. And how the big ox always appeared at the most inopportune moments.

Andorf goes over a prepared speech in his head. He cannot believe how he truly misses his old friend. Perhaps the shock of finding Brutus' remains wedged inside a replicator haunts him. Or maybe it's knowing his claustrophobic friend would never be caught dead in a small enclosure such as the empty casket. Or perhaps it's his bad knee resulting from ascending those fourteen flights of stairs in grief.

Everyone is expecting me to speak warmly of dramatic events leading up to the starship hijackings. That I can do. They'll expect to hear details of Brutus barely surviving being flattened during the Titan refueling incident. That I can do. They'll even want me to rave about him single-handedly saving the

Atlantis *after the bridge implosion. I can lie about that one. But how can everyone be so oblivious to Brutus' dark side ... all those things he has done behind their backs.*

"Stop it, Daddy," Mila snaps, squeezing her father's hand uncomfortably hard. "Now isn't the time to expose callous truths about the man everyone admires. Leave them remembering papa Brutus for all the good things he's accomplished."

Ayla winces at Andorf from his other side. "For once, I agree with sis. You need to be more positive about papa."

Grumblings over Dribbles disassembling his thirteen uncles and scrapping them for material, Sarak sits two seats beyond Ayla. After staring long and hard at his father, he refuses to face anyone else in the immediate family. Ayla reaches across Emin and slugs her twin brother hard on his shoulder.

"Ouch!"

"Now's not the time for that either, Sarak. Why are men in our family always so ...?"

A gypsy taps Andorf's shoulder from behind. "I've heard you and Brother Brutus were quite close—even shared a wife. My condolences go out to you and your fine family."

Andorf turns about to see an aging gypsy, clothes covered in animal fur and sandwiched between two voluptuous women clinging to his arms. He barely recalls counseling the once troubled man, advising how finding a furry friend could improve his social life.

"Atlas?"

The bulky man grins. "Yes, my friend. It is me, Atlas. I took your advice many years ago." He looks to his left and then his right. "As you can see, adopting animals has really changed my social life. I cannot thank you enough."

Andorf nods.

"And by the way," Atlas whispers. "My condolences on your rabbit as well."

Eyes dampening, Andorf turns back around.

Ayla wipes a tear off her father's eyes. She leans in. "Ah ha! I knew it. You *do* have deep feelings for papa."

The background music finally ends. Positioned over the symbolic casket and holding his hands high in the air, a man dressed in traditional priestly garb waits patiently for the room to settle. He then summons all to rise.

"We are gathered here to pay our respects to a working man ... a commoner ... a fellow gypsy. I am frequently reminded how there is nothing more joyous than the sound of a gypsy's laugh—"

The floor suddenly vibrates. Everyone in the auditoriums grabs their bolted down seat and watch the priest lie atop the casket and ride it across the floor.

"Ah, the humor of space life," Atlas says, between bouts of laughter.

The tremors diminish nearly as quickly as they began. As the priest reclaims footing, Atlas and a few others assist in reseating the casket at the pulpit. While the priest completes his sermon and proceeds onto chanting well-known fables from his dossier, a woman on the raised delicately plucks her harp.

Afterwards, a chorus crowds onto the small stage. Their well-rehearsed rendition of 'The Wind Cries Mary' leaves many mourners sobbing aloud.

Maintenance techs take turns approaching the microphone to read handwritten tributes praising their former boss.

"Brutus was always in our faces, ensuring repairs were performed prompt and proper. Like that control arm I found impossible to install. I was getting nowhere, trying to decipher the grease-stained blueprint. Calling me a toad, he grabbed the replacement part out of my hand, flipped it over, and then held it next to the wet sprocket until I understood. That's what kind of a guy he was." The tech sniffs. "Brutus was the father I never had."

"He was always doing things like that," another tech says, taking the mic. "Many times, it was only a matter of looking at the problem from a different angle."

Boss man Silas pushes the tech aside. "Brutus was at times our personal counselor." He winks at a redhead lady seated in the second row and the slightly younger man holding her hand. "He taught me the difference between love and jealously, passion verses possession. If it were not for Brutus, my wife and I would not be happily married today."

Another man appears, sounding choked up and struggling to speak. "It was back on Earth during the Freedom Day uprising. I was severely wounded and had taken multiple shots on my back. I could no longer walk up the starship ramp. Brutus ran down and scooped me up like a potato sack, all while taking hits. Safely inside the starship, I watched him run back down the long ramp to rescue countless others. I saw him tear at the sight of the militia beating those unlucky souls who never made it aboard the *Atlantis*."

After a brief lull, Admiral Turk takes his time stepping onto the stage. Scanning the sea of puzzled faces, he takes the mic. "As many know, Brutus and I were not what anyone would call the best of friends."

A woman wearing nursing attire emerges from the crowd. She leaps onto the stage, grabs the mic from the admiral's hand, and introduces herself only as Nurse Jasmine.

"I recall the Titan Incident like yesterday. Seventeen-hundred and thirty-five aboard the *Inca* and the *Calypso* lost their lives, my own husband being one of them. Magnetic crusher drones had attacked our starships. The *Atlantis'* shuttle #2 was flattened with captain Murray and Brutus still inside. Turk brought them aboard his ship and personally oversaw treatments using the armada's most advanced medical devices. I know for a fact as I was a nurse in training aboard the *Aegean* and was there when Brutus was wheeled into surgery." Pointing a finger at Turk, she winks at the crowd. "So don't let this man fool you. The admiral has a terribly huge heart."

To a round of deafening applause, Jasmine leads Turk off stage. In a flash of inspiration, Turk turns about. He runs back and grabs the mic off its stand. "Now, if any gypsies feel inclined to divulge the fabulous Booger Stew recipe, it would be greatly appreciated."

As the solemn moment breaks into laughter, Turk finds a seat next to his scorning wife. Jasmine, on the other hand, takes praise as she sits amongst *Inca* and *Calypso* survivors and families of the not so fortunate. The crowd stirs, awaiting the final eulogy.

On one side, Mila pokes Andorf in the ribs. Ayla likewise jabs him from the other side. "Now, be nice, Father," Ayla says, as he rises.

"And don't run everyone off this time," Mila whispers.

Andorf activates a lapel-mounted clip-on microphone. Walking the stage, he winces at his kids' soured expressions before scanning the apprehensive faces of those seated and the many spilling out the exits. He smiles tentatively at the cameras supplying video feeds to the quarter million refugees scattered throughout the armada's forty-four starships.

"Such touching tributes. How dare I attempt to top them?" Andorf removes a tart pino drink from his pocket. With so many sarcastic thoughts filling his head, he sips slowly at the drink. Heeding unspoken warnings from both daughters, he clears his throat.

"Thank you everyone for granting me the honor of the closing eulogy. As many recall, Brutus, Serin, and I were a triad back on mother Earth. But my dealings with Brutus dates further back ... back to our childhood days, when he was a ..."

Andorf pauses at the sight of the apprehensive faces scattered about the packed auditorium. He feels their nervous anticipation of his impending words. Scanning the front row, he spots his daughters' warning lips.

"Don't say it," Mila whispers.

"I'll disown you," Ayla mumbles.

"Dear friend," Andorf says.

With many sighing aloud, Andorf runs through condensed scenarios. Converting Brutus' shortcomings into triumphs, he portrays his old friend as the hero in each tale. "Brutus and I tag-teamed around the Canine Empire while our wife, Serin, covertly gathered loyal teams of renegades. We three overpowered Evil Max and his elite guards. In the heat of the cavalry's arrival, we packed the *Atlantis* and her sister ships with those desperately wanting to escape the evil Canine Empire. Amongst the chaos, Brutus kept his cool. Like always, he barely broke a sweat."

Pol, the *S.S. Atlantis'* navigator, suddenly leaps onto the stage. He crowds Andorf and shouts into the Goshi's clip-on mic in his native middle-eastern accent. "During takeoff, Peter, Murray, and I were overwhelmed by massive gravitational forces. Even our beloved captain Thom was struggling to maintain consciousness. It was Brutus who pushed the captain aside, climbed into his seat, and then piloted our overloaded starship during the harrowing escape. Brutus is truly the one to whom we owe our freedom. Every last one of us on the *Atlantis* should honor this man."

"And there you have it, folks," Andorf says, stepping away from Pol. He raises both hands high in the air. "Without Brutus at the helm, none of our forty-four starships would be heading for planet Nero. I expect each and every one of you to keep the *Atlantis'* chief engineer in your thoughts." He pauses for a moment to facetiously wipe his dry eyes. "And my condolences also go out to the families and the surviving members of the *Inca* and *Calypso*. Those who perished are deeply missed."

Andorf steps off the stage to join his son and daughters in the receiving line. Forty-four starship captains and crew are the first to voice final farewells to Brutus' empty casket. Tuning it all out, Andorf hobbles on his bum knee out a back door heading for Brutus' private elevator.

*

Exiting the auditorium, Andorf senses someone following behind. He turns about.

"You did this!" Sarak yells out. "You put papa in the replicator and it killed him."

"What?"

Andorf leads his son into a storage room behind the auditorium's stage. Soon as the door shuts behind, Sarak shouts at his father. "I heard about how you threatening that #6 would be the death of him … how it would spew out dozens of replicas of him."

The door opens. Mila steps inside and closes the door. She shakes her head. "That was years ago. I never told anyone about that incident."

"The techs heard what you said," Sarak yells. "And now papa's gone."

"No, Sarak! You're wrong!" Andorf yells. "Your papa was cheating on your mother with that damn replicator. I bet you never heard about that."

"Eww, Father. That's sick."

"No, not physically. He was emotionally involved with the machine."

While Mila nods, Sarak shakes his head.

"Go ahead, son. Ask any of his techs. They will all back up what I am saying."

"S—so what you're implying is …"

Andorf nods. "#6 feared sharing Brutus so she consumed him." He turns to exit the closet but pauses, hand on the door handle. "I admit, your papa accomplished a great many things but like the rest of us, he had his shortcomings. I shall no longer mention them. I suggest you and Mila do likewise. Now, you both must excuse me. There is a personal matter which I can no longer ignore."

C H A P T E R   1 9
A Sore Knee
ANDORF

The door to his 'once-best-friend's' private walk-in storage closet opens to Andorf's outstretched hand. With the exception of Serin's hanging clothes and her personal items, the room with the open toolbox appears hauntingly similar to Gregory's walk-in closet back on Earth. Standing on his toes to reach Gregory's most-prized shoebox on the upper shelf, he cannot help but inhale the trace scent of his late wife's wild mountain perfume lightly scenting her collection of peasant blouses. His thoughts immediately flash back to the fateful day he met Serin. Back in Gregory's living room, he was holding a kitchen chair high over his head, so ready to take out at one of the intruders. But discovering Serin on the floor sobbing, he began to panic, looking for a quick exit.

"Don't go," Serin said, in a voice so sweet he still shivers.

Feeling weak-kneed, Andorf grabs hold of the overhead shelf. The teetering shoebox falls and returns him to the present. He drops to his knees and inventories the box's spilled contents on the floor before him.

- Three squeeze tubes of reformulated analgesic rubbing cream
- Seven hundred and forty-one dollars and sixty-nine cents
- Two stick flags from the infamous rugby game
- One folded-up index card

Unfolding the index card and seeing all but the last item scratched through, he chuckles. *Introduce Andorf to Serin.*

"Some things are destined to be, my old friend," he mumbles, refolding the card. He pockets one of the cream tubes and returns everything else to the shoebox. Careful not to inhale any more of Serin's intoxicating perfume, he places the shoebox back on the overhead shelf. His eyes are then drawn to the story-telling chair stuffed in the corner. Again, his mind drifts, this time visualizing his then five-year-old Ayla sitting on her Uncle Gregory's lap with his best friend spinning one of his wild tales. He trembles, reliving the event of her discovering Uncle Greg had passed and the horror of her running across the linoleum floor while screaming for help.

Looking about the closet, he spots six tic-tocs which once hung in Gregory's entryway. Unlike their time displays, the once-animated eyes were kept in perfect unison. He turns to leave but pauses at sight of the weather-worn 'Andorf for Mayor' yard sign. Thinking about how Gregory had so proudly planted it in his front lawn, he cannot help but examine the Earth dirt still clinging to its metal leg.

Andorf hobbles out of the storage closet. With a wave of the Goshi's hand, the door closes and locks. He labors down the twisted hallway, up one flight of floating steps, and then down the long, winding A-deck hallway. Sitting atop the bed, he rolls his pants leg up. A good squirt of the analgesic cream should ease his throbbing knee pain. Unaware of the reformulated cream's psychoactive effects having intensified over the years, he messages in a second squirt for good measure. Suddenly, his thoughts drift back to that terrible evening back on Earth when Binky escaped.

Serin had rubbed this same analgesic cream on my sore shoulders. But why was she wearing gloves? She could have just as easily used her bare—?

Andorf's fingers begin to tingle. At first, he attributes the sensation to the twenty-four hour fast imposed upon every man, woman, and child over the age of three to honor the late Brutus Bittner. Again, he recalls that fateful evening, lying motionless on his bed, straining to comprehend Serin and Brutus' fading voices.

They were speaking of me in third person, as though I were not in the same room. And the next morning, I awoke hearing everyone's thoughts. Everywhere I went, I was hearing unspoken words.

With the knee pain fading, he visualizes images scrolling along a jumbled timeline. "Oh, no! Not this crap again," he says, eyes narrowing upon the analgesic cream tube. Squinting at the fine-print wrapping around the time-dulled squeeze tube, he struggles to rotate it between his numbed fingers. Through blurred vision, he sees tiny hallucinogenic warnings divide into dots and subdivide again into unreadably specs. With everything about him dancing in squiggles, the tube slips from his hand and falls beneath the bed. His eyes roll uncontrollably to one side. Andorf tries to stand but collapses face first onto the bed. As before, he is down for the count.

CHAPTER 20

The Kaanta
ANDORF

The Goshi awakens, barely able to raise his head. Through foggy eyes he scans the room from the limited perspective. With much effort, he rolls onto his back. The throbbing knee pain works its way down to his calf. He manages to scoot his head against the headboard, only to grab at his pounding skull to prevent it from twisting off his neck.

Segments of wild adventure games crammed together in random sequences play out in his head. He not only covers his ears at the men screaming devious schemes but shuts his eyes at the graphic imagery of women clinging to loved ones' legs while begging for them not to carry out their schemes.

When Andorf blinks, he appears in a damp, dark cave with water dripping from everywhere. Surrounded by scantily-dressed Neanderthals, standing barefoot in shallow pools of water, he squints through dim, dust-filled light at what he suspects may be the last vestiges of humanity. Starry-eyed in wonder, many of the cave dwellers pick at his clothing.

After sneezing, he finds himself kneeling defensively in front of an angry mob, all with bloodied nose. Threating him with huge clubs, they appear the same except for the red or blue shades of their clothing and the lean of their tilted stances.

The floor suddenly separates, allowing him to peer into a deep chasm where thick, gooey tar-like substance bubbles up from beneath heavy excavators. Mining equipment marked in Tenulian words are working the unstable ground, perhaps digging for the long promised Ghengis stones.

"Planet Nero," Andorf mumbles as a slimy creature scampers over his leg. With shadows overtaking him, he peers up to see screeching pterodactyls with gigantic wingspans and rows of teeth swooping down on him and the miners. He takes refuge behind a large stone to reflect on a primitive time such as this back on Earth. He flinches at a three-legged creature poking at him with a crooked stick. "Grimple," it growls. Out a corner of his eye, he sees similar creatures disappearing and then reappearing, taunting Tenulian miners.

Another sneeze returns Andorf to his cabin on the *Atlantis*. Feeling along the floor, he staggers to his feet. He grabs a wet hand towel to futilely wipe at white chalky mess staining his pants. Lifting his shirt, he examines fresh skin wounds aligning with new holes in the material. He then bends down to pick lichen off his pants and his shoes.

With horrific images fresh in his mind, Andorf stumbles toward the desk where Serin once worked. In the years since her passing, his late wife's works space has been left virtually untouched. When he reaches for the chair to stabilize himself, a bundled set of molecular markers flies into his outstretched hand. By instinct, he stuffs them in a pants pocket and hobbles out of the cabin.

Andorf's fast-sweeping hands draw highly-graphic scenes onto a straight section of hallway. The drawings progress from crude scribblings to three-dimensional abstracts, depicting multiple images if one was to turn their head just so.

He works tirelessly for hours until grinding to a sudden halt. Like the molecular markers, his energy has run dry. He leans against the opposing wall to admire the indelible artwork spanning a fifty-foot section of the starship's A-deck hallway.

Onlookers soon gather to gaze in awe at the strokes of chartreuse, vermillion, puce, and blends of other colors portraying his wild visions in full public view. Many cover their mouths, gasping at the large birds swooping down on the miners of planet Nero. Others wince at strange words, yet to be incorporated into the official Tenulian language.

After the eleven-hour ordeal, Andorf is too drained to explain much to anyone. Titling the fifty-foot mural as the 'The Kaanta–Life's Guideposts', he hobbles toward his cabin for a well-deserved rest.

CHAPTER 21

Sisters
MILA

The girls gather at Andorf's bedside, each taking turns checking breath and pulse. Mila smiles at Andorf's the first sign of their father's awakening. Propping him upright, she fluffs the pillow beneath his head. She feels good about having the only male in her life back home safe in the cozy cabin they've shared for the past twenty-seven years. Mila tasks herself with hand-feeding him.

Andorf accepts a sporkful of dim-sum dumplings. "How long was I out?" he asks, smacking his lips at taste of the exquisite concoction.

Ayla shrugs her shoulders. "Two days, maybe longer. All I can say is your next-door neighbor wasn't at all pleased to find you curled up in his closet. If he didn't know who you were, I'm sure you would have been severely beaten and dumped in the hallway. Honestly, I wouldn't have blamed him."

Mila inspects Andorf's marker-stained hands. "I hope this little marathon of yours has ended, Daddy. Everyone aboard the *Atlantis* including the captain thinks you've gone mad. Ayla and I are beginning to agree."

Eyes bouncing between her sister and father, Ayla nods.

Andorf snarls at the girls. The back of his hand pushes the next sporkful of dumplings aside. "Captain Jobi, ha. Crazy in *this* life perhaps but mark my words. I shall become a prophet not long after I'm gone."

Ayla cringes. "Quit speaking of your demise, Father. I've read your medical records. Sickbay gives your old bones another thirty years."

"And I suspect your little men in their starched lab-coats were less than helpful." Andorf smiles mischievously at Ayla. "Oh, I know about those medical records and the endless barrage of stick figure flash cards. Their blunt questions will put anyone to sleep." He stretches while yawning long and hard. "Don't act so surprised, girls. Little transpires aboard the *Atlantis* of which I am unaware."

Mila rolls her eyes and mumbles. "How many times must we hear this?"

"It—it's all your talk about mother," Ayla says. "She's been gone nearly thirty years."

"Twenty-seven," Mila says.

Andorf scans his daughters' long faces for a long moment. "So, tell me, my sweet ones, besides my longing to be reunited with my late wife, what troubles you so deeply? What may I ask lies beneath those pouty faces? Hmm?"

The girls exchange awkward glances. Ayla takes hold of her father's hand. "We counted over forty drawings out there in the hallway, each one quite unique."

Andorf smiles. "The mural portrays forty-two events to be exact."

"Promise me you won't do that again, Daddy." Mila raises her voice. "They're scaring everyone on the *Atlantis*."

"They're too abstract. No one knows what they mean," Ayla adds. "And what are those strange words? They're not from any known root language and certainly not Tenulian."

Andorf smiles wider. "Give it time. Everyone will understand my Kaanta in good time."

"Kaanta? Is that what you call those murals?"

Andorf nods.

Mila winces. "What about the drawing of miners? Can we assume our descendants eventually land on planet Nero?"

"What happens afterwards?" Ayla says. "Do they make it back to Earth in one piece?"

Andorf's mouth twists as if souring. He turns away, taking deep breaths before facing his daughters. "Nero is not the hospitable place everyone expects. Our miners will enter an unsavory world, face horrors on a scale you girls cannot begin to imagine. From the moment our descendants set foot on planet Nero their critical mission will be in jeopardy. Did you not see the pterodactyls I drew? The birds are only one of such horrors."

Ayla chuckles. "Birds? Those were birds? Are you telling us the miners will be frightened by birds?"

Andorf's face pales. He grabs hold of Ayla's arm and squeezes. "These are big birds—really big birds … not like the ones you find in starship terrariums. These raptors can eat a full-grown man and return for dessert. Did I not get that point across in my drawings? Did you miss the three-legged creatures who poke at you with sticks and then disappear and reappear at will? I thought everything was clearly portrayed."

Ayla sits beside her father on the bed. She and Mila stare bewildered. "What about the mobs of what looked like people wearing red and blue? Everyone was at each other's throats."

"As my mural depicts, many terrible things happen even before our descendants reach Nero." Andorf squinches his face. "The universe is a frightening place. Words … drawings … they simply cannot warn everyone of what lies ahead. What occurs in short time will forever change mankind's perception of space."

Mila runs off. She returns with a cool, wet compress and applies it to Andorf's sweaty forehead.

Wide-eyed, Andorf lifts his head. "When our descendants arrive back on Earth, the place will be a much different world than the one my generation left behind. Cities will be gone. In fact, there will be no trace of former civilizations. Humanity, if that is what you call it, will resort to living in caves."

Ayla winces. "Cities? Caves? Tell us about the last drawing. It depicts a starship being blown to pieces."

"Oh, that one." Andorf takes a moment. "There is a twelve-percent chance such an event will never occur. It all boils down to a matter of misappropriated lead ... two-tons of shielding missing from the *Atlantis'* secondary engines," he mumbles.

"What?" Ayla yells. "How would anyone be so fool-hardy?"

Mila's jaw drops. "If the secondary engines ever engage, there'd be wide-spread radiation poisoning. Everyone on the *Atlantis* would die."

Andorf nods. "Within minutes."

"Without anyone to maintain the starship, critical systems will fail," Ayla adds.

Mila's jaw drops. "The *Atlantis* would blow itself to pieces."

Andorf tells them about the duopoly planet where violence frequently erupts between people who lean to one side or the other. He details the last vestiges of humanity, eating lichen off walls in dark, dripping caves. Pausing in mid-thought, he casually mentions what becomes of the armada like a mere afterthought.

Mila flashes a puzzled look. "I don't understand. Why would the muskrat polarize the armada? How could he send half the starships off in different directions?"

"We lost several starships to his fanaticism before the S.O.B. and his followers were overthrown," Andorf retorts. "But the damage had been done. The armada was splintered, left a fraction of its original size."

"Stop!" Ayla yells, grabbing at her ears. "You're both making my head spin, describing future events as if they've already occurred."

Mila's eyes widen. "Tell Sis the tale of the woman offering a man forbidden fruit, Daddy. That's my favorite."

Andorf freezes in the memory of Serin offering him a dehydrated-apple slice after narrowly surviving *Atlantis'* rough takeoff. He rubs the graying hair on his chin for a moment. "How could you possibly know such things, Mila? I have never spoken of this to you or anyone else."

Before Mila turns to face her father, she grits her teeth at Ayla.

"Living with you nearly my entire life, is there no doubt I've acquired a few of your telepathic abilities?"

Andorf turns to his biological daughter. "There is a matter of heredity, Ayla. Your mother also had telepathy. I expect you have this ability as well."

Ayla shudders. "I—I've been having nightmares about many things in your drawings. Only mine were not such detail and vibrant color as those in your Kaanta."

"I suspect Sarak will have similar visions if ever he discovers himself."

"You've been spreading your DNA all over the *Atlantis*, Daddy. Think how many children have you fathered with your donations?"

Ayla smiles. "Generations of Tenulians will become visionaries as well."

"I'm banking on it," Andorf likewise smiles. "How else will Tenulians be able to survive the many epic events depicted in my Kaanta?"

The girls stare deep into their father's eyes. His face hardens as they try to lick away at his inner thoughts. They feel him resisting, clearing his mind of every event which has yet to occur.

"No!" Andorf yells. "There are too many things you girls need not know. No one can handle them … certainly not the both of you. One day the mystery will unravel, right before everyone's eyes. They will then understand the true meaning of my Kaanta … hopefully in time to heed its warnings." Andorf casts a dry, solemn look. "But until then, no one needs not know … not until the first visitors arrive."

"Visitors?" Mila says, raising her voice. "You mean aliens?"

Ayla covers her mouth with both hands. "How will we ever …?"

"We shall appear as aliens to the visitors as well," Andorf's eyes narrow. His face then saddens. "I regret to say our beloved *Atlantis* may not survive long after. Did I mention there is a good chance of the radiation-related catastrophe never occurring? But no worries. Everyone goes mad and turn on themselves long before the starship actually explodes." Andorf half-grins. "Of course, nothing is certain. Circumstances may skew us away from our present timeline."

The sisters exchange dazed glances. "But what about us? What becomes of Mila and I?"

With weighted eyes, Andorf yawns. He settles his head into his cushy pillow. "All I can say is, you both outlive two husbands. Beyond that ..." Andorf's broken words fade as he cozies beneath his covers.

"A second husband?" Ayla yells. "Wait! Father! What happens to Emin?"

Mila rolls her eyes. "Me? A husband? Like I can believe that."

Barely awake, Andorf mumbles. "Jules. Mila's husband will be named Jules."

C H A P T E R 2 2
While Daddy Rests
MILA

Examining details of their father's colorful artwork, the sisters walk the full length of the fifty-foot mural along the Atlantis' A-deck. "How could the *Atlantis* be destroyed?" Mila says. "Thousands would lose their lives."

"And father's masterpiece will be destroyed."

Mila raises her brow. "Perhaps his Kaanta needn't be lost after all."

"What are you implying, sis?"

"What if daddy's drawings were somehow copied onto our sister starships."

"But it'd take days ... weeks to duplicate the drawings."

"Not if we use daddy's rubbing cream," Mila mumbles.

"Wait! What about father's rubbing cream?"

"Well ..."

Ayla cringes. "And what if we were caught? Being the admiral's daughter-in-law, things could get really dicey."

"Isn't Turk planning to turn the reigns over to his son? Last I recall, you were married to Emin. Besides, everyone already believes we Johnsons are nuts. Even your husband thinks so. I've read it in his thoughts."

"Well, I don't know." Ayla appears to ponder the dastardly deed. Clenching her teeth, she sucks air between them. "We'd need to pull an all-nighter … do it between work shifts."

"That'll give us six … seven hours at best."

The girls return to Andorf's cabin and peer at their father sleeping soundly in the back bedroom. Hovering above, Mila raises a brow and whispers. "Did you know, daddy's inner thoughts are readily accessible while he sleeps. You should see some of the batty stuff he dreams. How do you think I know so much about what transpires throughout the starship?"

"Stop it, Mila. You shouldn't be doing that. Father's entitled to his private thoughts." Ayla raises a brow. "Damn! Listen to me. I'm beginning to sound like Emin."

Andorf snores loudly as if in agreement. The girls lean closer, checking to see whether he is truly asleep. A much louder snore sends the girls backing up.

Ayla stares at her sister. "What kind of batty stuff are you talking about?"

"Well … uh …"

Before Mila answers, Ayla's spots something on the floor at her feet. She bends down to pick up the spent rubbing cream tube. After taking a sniff, she shoves the flattened tube in her big sister's face. "What do you know about this stuff, Mila?"

Mumbling, Mila turns away. "It's what intensifies daddy's visions."

Ayla reaches out to turn Mila's guilt-stricken face. "Ah ha! I knew it! You've been using the rubbing cream. That's how you've been reading father's thoughts. How much of this crap have you been using?"

Baring incisors, Mila pinches a thumb and index finger together. "Just a wee bit. And if you rat on me, I swear I'll—"

"Don't think about using those scissor-finger chops on me, Mila. I'm not as easily persuaded as Sarak." Ayla lifts her head, as if proudly. "I'm married to the admiral's son."

Mila shrugs her shoulders. "Daddy mustn't know. Else, he would've said something … acted differently."

"He's been toying with you, Mila. Father toys with everyone."

"Not so. You're jealous of me spending so much time with him."

Ayla grins. "Please. I've got my own family … a demanding husband and a baby to contend with, lest you forget. And tell me, Mila, why is it you have no significant other? Living with father and doting on him like a lost puppy all these years, it's no wonder you have no mate."

The girls ball up their fingers, ready to strike. Eyes narrowing, Mila feels it is only a matter of seconds before she or Ayla takes swings. She lowers her fist and slowly backs away grumbling. "If only I could find someone who looks at me the way daddy did when he found me. I wouldn't waste another breath being single if there was anyone out there like him."

"Now fess up about your visions. You bear none of father's blood."

"Well, after your mother passed, I discovered her remains before they were added to the soil. I snuck a cupful out of the terrarium. Over several months, I added a sporkful of the granules to my meals. Within a few weeks, I was hearing other's thoughts as clear as my own."

Ayla squinches her nose. "Mila! What a horrible thing to do."

"What do you expect? I was only five. After spending months on my own, I so desperately wanted to be a part of Daddy's world … be a part of him like Serin."

Ayla's brow narrows. "You mean like his wife?"

"No. No. No." Mila winces. "I wanted to be entrenched in his soul. But hard as I tried, I could not read daddy's thoughts. Years later, I discovered your mother's special rubbing cream. Everything changed."

Ayla's jaw drops.

"I know where Daddy hides the cream. I'll bet there's another tube in there." Mila leans over Andorf's nightstand. Pulling the top drawer open, she finds nothing but notes.

The sisters scuttle about the room, opening drawers and lifting folders. They approach their father, hover above him. After a long moment, the sisters jostle. Ayla raises a brow. "Did you see those people in caves?"

"What I saw was three-legged creatures threatening me with sticks." Mila peers back at her father. She suddenly grins mischievously. "Ah, ha! There's rubbing cream in Uncle Greg's storage closet … in a fiber shoebox."

"What's a shoebox?"

"Oh, yeah," Mila says. "You wouldn't know. You were born on the starship."

Ayla nods.

"I saw it on an overhead shelf."

"I've tried to get inside Uncle Greg's closet but it's locked tight. I bet our brother has a key."

"Nah. Sarak would never go for it." After a moment, Mila's eyes widen. "Daddy merely waves his hand and doors magically open. I've seen him do so on many occasions."

"A lot of good that'll do us. We can't very well cut off Father's hand and we certainly can't drag him down there while he sleeps."

Mila hovers above her father, reads his more-accessible outer thoughts. She then runs across the room to his work desk. The middle drawer inches open to greet her reaching hand. An unlabeled key flies into her hand.

Ayla's jaw drops. "How much of the cream have you been using, Sis?"

"Never mind that," Mila dashes out the cabin door. "Hurry, Ayla. We've got work to do."

To avoid being seen, the sisters enter Brutus' vacant cabin. No one has dared taken up residence in the enormous master suite next door since the chief engineer's passing. They take the private elevator down one level and march along the B-deck hallway.

Unlocking Gregory's walk-in storage closet, Mila leads Ayla inside. The girls look about the closet. They find a metal box on the floor containing a variety of unfamiliar tools. Random clicking sounds draw their attention a few feet to the left. They turn their heads to focus on a collection of kitty clocks with animated eyes intermittently moving back and forth.

"Uncle Greg's tic-tocs," Ayla bursts out. "Remember how they used to line his entryway?"

Mila peers up. "See that? That's what a shoebox looks like." Her foot clumps against the open toolbox as she stands on her tiptoes and reaches for the upper shelf. The teetering shoebox falls onto the floor. Mila drops to her knees and reviews the spilled contents.

- Two reformulated analgesic cream squeeze tubes
- A handful of various coins and decorated paper with numbers and faces thereupon
- Two stick flags
- One folded-up index card

After pocketing one of the cream tubes, Mila stares bewildered at the remaining items, pondering their significance. She runs her fingers over the paper money, savoring the feel of the foreign material. The coins also feel odd as she manipulates them between her fingers. Ignoring the stick flags, she unfolds the index card on. Every item but the last is scratched through. *Introduce Andorf to Serin.*

"A bit late for that last one, Uncle Greg." Mila refolds the card and returns it and the other items to the shoebox. Lifting it over her head to organize things on the shelf, she spots her sister rifling through Serin's collection of peasant blouses.

Ayla peels off her shirt to slip a lavender blouse over her head. After her foot clunks against a metal twenty-five-gallon drum, she selects a pair of pliers from the toolbox. With much twisting of the plier handles, the four-inch cap spins off. Her brown eyes widen as does her devious smile. Before Mila can stop her, younger sister has not only dipped her fingers inside but wiped them across the neckline of the lavender blouse. "Look, Mila," she says, dabbing a bit of the sweet perfume behind each ear and then holds a finger out for Mila to sniff. "I've found mother's fabled perfume. Ah, it's very much the enticing fragrance I've always imagined. Come here. You've got to—"

Mila slaps Ayla's face. "What the hell are you thinking? You want daddy to go totally insane? The moment we get back, you'll remove this blouse and wash off that damn perfume. Do you hear me? I forbid you from wearing either of them."

Ayla's face reddens. Watching her sister uses the pliers to seal the metal drum, her fingers curl into a fist.

"First, an old man instructs daddy to find Serin," Mila yells. "Then Sarak encourages him with time-travel stunts. Now it's you wearing your mother's lavender blouse and her enticing perfume. Can't you see? Daddy's teetering dangerously over sanity's ledge. This could trip his loose footing and send him tumbling over the edge. Do you want that? Huh? Do you?"

While Mila tosses the pliers into the open tool box, Ayla backs out of the closet, keeping well beyond an arm's length of her older sister.

Mila pauses, staring at the 'Andorf for Mayor' yard sign with its dirt encrusted metal post propped up in the corner of the closet. "Hmm. I've seen that sign in daddy's visions."

"Never mind the damn sign," Ayla yells, directing Mila outside. Keeping their distance, they take Brutus' private elevator up to the A-deck. Back in Mila's cabin, they climb atop her bed. Both keep watchful eyes on each other from opposite sides of the single bed.

Mila reaches deep into her pocket and tosses the cream tube on the bed between them. At the backdrop of acapella snores emanating from the next room, the girls take turns glancing at the analgesic rubbing cream as if daring the other to be the first.

Ayla finally grabs the tube. She squeezes thick cream lines across the length of both arms and rubs them in. Rotating the partially spent tube, she reads the fine-printed warnings spiraling around the tube. "Did you know this stuff causes severe hallucinations? I don't think we should—"

"Like duh," Mila says, grabbing the partially spent tube and rubbing thick layers of the creamy contents from the tube onto both arms. "I've only used small dabs. Never globs like this. You know, this batch smells much stronger than—" Mila's speech slurs. Her eyesight becomes unfocused. She spots Ayla lying face down across the bed, still wearing her mother's lavender blouse and still reeking of Serin's enticing mountain-flower perfume. Losing coordination, her head wobbles. She leans to one side and collapses onto the bed beside her sister. Everything goes blank.

CHAPTER 23

Dangling Over Sanity's Ledge
ANDORF

Andorf dreams he is once again walking hand in hand with Serin, strolling past rows of tall sunflowers back at City Park. The large seed heads pivot to face the pair as they stroll past. There is a rumble at their feet. He looks back to see the ground behind rising over their heads. With everything nipping at their heels, he and Serin—

A THUMP THUMP THUMP on the cabin door jostles Andorf awake. He jumps out of bed to peer through the tiny peephole. He sees a woman dressed in a white smock, fiftyish, pacing the hallway outside. By time he throws on clothes and cracks open the door the hallway outside his cabin is vacant. Turning about, he senses something amiss—another's presence—someone who belongs elsewhere.

Under dim light of the second bedroom, he spots a blonde woman, lying face down beside Mila. Both appear fully dressed and sound asleep. For a brief moment, he wonders if Mila has finally found a mate. Stepping closer, he notices the blonde wearing a lavender peasant blouse.

Inhaling a fragrance nearly forgotten draws him closer. Breathing deep, he hovers above the girls, gazing first at Mila and then at the woman with platinum-blonde hair running halfway down the back of her blouse. Depressing the mattress in the dimly lit bedroom reveals a bit more of the blonde's face.

Andorf's eyes widen. Right in front of him, barely a foot away, he sees a woman with a larger than average nose … a nose which could only belong to one of two girls. But only one wore this intoxicating perfume and a peasant blouse, lavender at that.

Memories slosh about his brain like suds during a heavy wash cycle, overwhelming all reason. He grabs his spinning head with both hands and stumbles backwards until he is flush against the cabin door. Eyes rolling about, he runs through the A-deck hallway screaming out Serin's name uncontrollably at the top of his lungs.

CHAPTER 24

Passing The Torch
MILA

Lying on her bed, Mila is first to awaken. Eyes half-open, she elbows Ayla more than once, trying to get her sister to stir.

Fingers curling into fists, Ayla mumbles in her sleep. "Strike me again and I'll …" A stiff finger-jab in the ribs finally awakens Ayla. She sits up ready to spar with her sister in another staring match. During long moments of awkward silence, neither girl moves.

Mila uses both hands to hold her droopy head upright. Her wiggling feet feel for the floor. Sliding off the bed, she staggers about the cabin, bumping into furniture like an errant pinball. "Oh, my pounding head," she says, squeaking out the words. "This never happened with the other cream. I must have rubbed on too much this time."

Chuckling at the sight of her older sister stumbling about, Ayla struggles to prop herself against the headboard. Taking her time, she rubs feeling back into her arms. Laboriously slipping one foot and then the other off Mila's bed, Ayla also grabs her own head. She likewise teeters back and forth across the room.

Mila sits on Andorf's unmade bed, wiping her face with a damp washcloth. She grins at the sound of her sister stumbling about in the next room. "I dreamt I heard Daddy screaming," she calls out. "I wonder where he's run off to now."

Ayla appears in her father's bedroom, holding a damp washcloth to her head. "You're not going to try to hit me again, are you?" she says, sitting apprehensively on the bed beside Mila. She looks about the bedroom, waving her hand as if to touch things not there.

Mila's eyes glaze over. She grabs hold of Ayla's shoulders to stabilize her sister's wobbliness and herself as well.

Ayla peers back through partially-opened eyes. "I had the most-real dream of wandering through a damp, dark cave. Water was dripping everywhere. I was surrounded by barefoot, half-dressed people. One of them grabbed at my …" Ayla sneezes. "Clothes."

"At least you weren't chased by three-legged creatures who kept calling you Grimple. That's right. One dared call me a Grimple." Mila twists her face. "I know I've gained a few pounds recently but really … do I look like a Grimple?"

Ayla shrugs her shoulders.

"I mean, the creatures appeared right out of thin air and then disappeared just as quickly. One of them even poked me with a stick. Here, look at this hole in my blouse." Mila lifts her shirt to examine a flesh wound beneath.

"Where the hell did *this* come from?" Ayla asks, picking lichen out of her damp, long blonde hair. she then cringes at the sight of Mila's wound. "I warned you about tapping into father's visions, didn't I?" She again sneezes.

"These weren't just visions. I believe we were actually living inside daddy's dreams." Mila lifts her blouse again to reexamine the fresh wound.

"More like reliving his nightmares." Ayla staggers to her feet. "Hurry, Mila. We need to draw these visions before they escape us."

Standing on wobbly feet, Mila hobbles towards Andorf's desk. As she grabs for the chair to move it aside, a bundled set of molecular markers flies into her outstretched hand. Ayla reaches out as well and a bundled set flies into her hands. The girls freeze, staring at the markers and then at one another.

"Why not all the markers?" Mila says, gazing at a third bundle remaining on the desk.

Ayla is already a few steps out the door. "Hurry, Mila. Evening work shifts are about to change."

With markers in hand and little time to spare, the sisters run along opposite sides of the seemingly endless A-deck hallway. Mila is first to reach the teleportal. "I'm heading for *Starship Phoenix*."

Catching up, Ayla nods. "I've always favored the *Mayflower*."

CHAPTER 25

In Your Dreams
SARAK

F ather. Father. I got here as soon as I could."

Lying flat on his back, Andorf awakens. He flinches at first sight of Sarak's face hovering inches above his own. Struggling to move his arms, he finds them bound to the bed. "Where am I, Son? Why am I not in my own bed? Why am I restrained like this?"

Sarak towel-wipes his father's sweaty face. "I've been told you are being held for observation. They say you're secured for your own safety."

"By those men in the white coats I presume," the Goshi grumbles.

"What do you expect? This time they found you wandering the *Atlantis'* hallways in terrible mind and screaming out mother's name."

"I know it may sound crazy, Sarak, but you must believe me. I saw her. She was so close I tasted her sweet scent on my lips. Serin was …" Andorf raises his head, periscopes the room as much as the restraints would allow. "Wait. Where are your sisters? I would have expected the girls to be here at my bedside."

"Mila? Ayla?" Sarak chuckles. "No one's seen them for a better part of the day. Whatever those two are up to. It's none of my business. I don't want to know. I want no part of it."

Sarak watches his father look around the bland white room as if taking note of the framed pictures of Vincent Van Gogh and Pablo Picasso. Andorf points out the framed picture entitled 'The Goshi', which depicts men in lab-coats carting off the starship's most famed person in a strait jacket.

Andorf smirks. "It appears I have joined the ranks of the famed."

"I must admit," Sarak says, rubbing the fine hairs on his chin. "You'll be hard-pressed to top this one."

"Definitely not my best pose." Andorf squinches his nose and the picture of the restrained Goshi morphs into himself smiling.

"Hey! Wait! How'd you do that?"

The Goshi cracks a similar smile.

"You cannot be rewinding everything you don't like. That's not how time works. It has hard-fast rules."

Andorf smirks. "Some hard-fast rules are meant to be bent. Like you said before, what good are a few fractions of a second?"

Sarak stares oddly at the picture and then back at his father. "Huh? What? Are you implying this event has occurred before … that you've somehow changed it?"

Examining the bindings securing him to the bed, Andorf's eyes narrow. The chain links creak and stretch. Within seconds, the metal links have untwisted enough to allow the Goshi to stretch free. He reaches up and taps Sarak's shoulder.

"Mila … Ayla … I felt them peeling away at my thoughts while I slept. I suspect they found the key to your uncle's walk-in storage closet and have been in there snooping around."

"Indeed. Uncle Greg's closet has been picked clean. My thieving sisters made off with mother's clothes … jewelry … even her industrial-size drum of I.Y.D. perfume."

Beginning to chuckle, Andorf suddenly quiets. His jaw drops. "Wait! That twenty-five-gallon drum of cleaning solution was actually Serin's perfume stash?"

Sarak nods. "According to my research, only one batch was ever manufactured. Laced with pheromones, the wild-mountain flower solution was formulated in celebration of a certain girl's twenty-first birthday. And do you know by whom?"

Andorf shrugs his shoulders.

"The customer was my maternal grandpa. He supplied mother with a lifetime supply of the enticing … in your case, intoxicating, perfume."

Andorf slides off the bed to pace about the sterile-looking room "Why yes. I.Y.D. makes perfect sense. In Your Dreams is what Serin told Brutus and I whenever we asked." Andorf chuckles. "And all this time we believed she was blowing us off."

Sarak rolls his eyes.

Red-faced, Andorf slaps his forehead. He turns to face Sarak. "That was Ayla I found lying face down across Mila's bed. She was wearing Serin's lavender peasant blouse and the I.Y.D. perfume. In the dim light, I mistook her for your mother. It is no wonder I went insane. You cannot blame me, Sarak. What else was I to think?"

"I'm not blaming you. Any man would have gone crazy thinking his wife dead for the past thirty years had returned."

Andorf closes his eyes for a long moment. He begins to wobble.

"Father? Are you okay?" Sarak rushes to Andorf's side.

"Mila and Ayla … I see where they have been. I know what they have been up to." Andorf grins at Sarak. "The girls transcribed my visions onto walls of our sister starships, the *Phoenix* and the *Mayflower*. And they have added a few drawings of their own." Andorf grins. "It appears the Kaanta has become a family affair." He gazes back at Sarak "How long did you say I have been here?"

Sarak shakes his head. "Eight or nine hours, I suppose … maybe longer."

"Yes, The girls had plenty of time. Hmm, their additions shall prove quite interesting."

Sarak takes Andorf's arm to steady him. "Rest, Father. You've been through a lot these past few days. First your eleven-hour artist session and now this." Sarak tugs on Andorf's arm. "Come, I'll escort you back to your cabin."

"By the tone of your voice earlier, I suspect you are still fearful of your sisters."

"We've had our differences concerning a certain Goshi. Let's just leave it at that."

"I cannot allow them to bully you any longer."

At Andorf's nod, Sarak leads him out of the room and up the starship's floating steps to the A-deck landing. They walk the long, twisting hallway in silence. At the wave of his hand, Andorf's cabin door opens. Sarak helps his father into a finely-upholstered easy-chair.

"Thank you, Son, but you must leave now. I must prepare for a run-in with a contemptuous visitor. Yes, I see her now dressed in a white smock and heading this way. On your way out, would you mind dimming the lights?"

CHAPTER 26

A Hard Sell
JASMINE

A woman in her mid-fifties appears to the Goshi's cabin door for a second time in as many days. This time the door eases open to her firm knock. The woman peers beyond the cracked door before stepping cautiously inside. Her soft-spoken voice peppered with hints of sweet Sudanese accent precedes her entry.

"Andorf? Andorf Johnson? My name is Jasmine Townsend. Mr. Johnson. Are you in there? Hello?"

Movement within dark shadows of the dimly lit room startles her. Back-stepping, she finds herself in the hallway with the cabin door slamming shut behind.

Letting herself back inside, Jasmine looks about, squinting at the tidiness of half of the room and the disorder of the other. It is as if a demarcation line had been drawn across the middle. On the sloppy half, she spots tack-it notes stuck to furniture, walls, and chairs. Walking about, she feels deep emotion in the many hand-drawn sketches of the great Serin Gray lining the walls. Each sketch oozes with Andorf's longing to be with her again. A sudden creaking draws her focus to a finely-upholstered easy-chair at the far end of the room and the veined hands within beckoning her closer. The middle-aged man in the chair appears tranquil enough, friendly but undoubtedly hungering for things all straight-men crave.

Stepping cautiously, she senses her every move being scrutinized. Jasmine gathers her wit. She reaches to shake the man's unwelcoming hand. "Am I correct in assuming you are Andorf Johnson … the one many call a Goshi?"

The man's twitching eyes pierce the room's shadows as though he were reliving painful events. "You think you can help me?" he says, snickering between words. "Many have come before you, promising a cure for one ailment or another. From the old-crow chanting 'what's it matter?' to the narcissistic carnival barker who staged a bogus assignation on himself to raise his ratings. I have seen it all, lady."

Jasmine raises a brow at the sorrow-filled voice she has not heard in three decades. She was then in her late-twenties. A much younger Andorf was curled up on the floor of sickbay, bawling his eyes out like a baby. Though Jasmine has much to say, she finds the words difficult. This time she is the one asking favors.

"So, what makes you special, lady? Why should I listen to someone who barges into my home uninvited?"

Though the man's bluntness joggles painful memories, Jasmine reaches out and manages to shake his hand. "Let's start over, shall we? My name is Jasmine Townsend. You may not remember back thirty years ago, but I was the attending nurse at your late wife's childbirth."

Andorf's free hand prompts her to continue.

Jasmine's mouth tightens to form her best salesperson smile. "What would you say, Mr. Johnson, if I told you your wife needn't to have died that day? That if we had acted on your insistent claims of performing a blood transfusion, she may have survived childbirth—would you be interested?"

Andorf is instantly on his feet, yelling. "It is much too late for all this now. You and your buffoon medical staff should have believed me while my beloved still had breath in her lungs." He grabs Jasmine's arm to escort her out of the room.

Standing her ground, Jasmine yanks her arm free. "Don't you understand? I'm here to rectify a bad decision in the distant past. If there's any truth in what I've heard about you reliving your life over and over, I just may be able to help." Jasmine raises a brow. "In ways you cannot begin to imagine."

"Oh, I can imagine a lot … much more than what people consider healthy, as I am frequently reminded." Andorf scans a few tack-it notes before turning an ear toward Jasmine. "Have you ever lost a loved one, Jasmine? Can you even imagine the lingering pain which bites every nerve of your soul at every breath?"

Feeling Andorf picking at her thoughts, Jasmine gazes at the floor tongue-tied. After a long moment, she gazes back at the Goshi. "It was during the Titan incident. My husband—"

"Dougie," Andorf blurts out. "Your husband's name was Dougie. He was aboard the *S.S. Inca*, handling refueling operations when those dreadful magnetic-crusher droids attacked the armada."

Jasmine's jaw drops. Again, she is speechless. *Only a Goshi could read thoughts like that.* She peers up to see Andorf's probing eyes. "As you must know, my Dougie was among the thousands who lost their lives that terrible day. I believe Captain Murray was lost as well."

Andorf suddenly recalls Binky's premonition. "Ah, the grieving widow," he mumbles before lowering the tone of her voice. "The late Brutus Bittner, was in the shuttle that day with Murray. Unlike your captain, he somehow survived being severely crushed."

"I myself still have nightmares about The Incident," Jasmine says. "You see, I was stationed aboard the *S.S. Aegean* when Brutus was wheeled into sickbay. Your friend was flattened like a pancake and suffering from multiple lacerations, crushed ribs and cracked vertebrae. It took weeks of progressively inflating the three-hundred man. If the chief engineer was not healthy, he would never have survived the stretching procedures, not to mention those months of intense physical therapy."

Andorf snarls. "Who believed Turk of all people would have had the most medically advanced ship in the entire armada? Or he would take such good care of someone he once considered him a mortal enemy?"

"Rumor has it the admiral was desperate to discover some secret ingredient."

Andorf smirks. "Booger Stew. A secret the gypsies refuse to divulge to this day."

"But you know what it is, don't you? You know about the secret ingredient."

The Goshi raises a brow in silence.

While he looks away as if trying not to laugh. Jasmine covertly slips a syringe into her hand. "Nowadays I find myself believing in the possibility of many things."

Andorf whips his head around. He stares down the nurse. "Show me see what you are hiding there."

"Whatever do you mean?"

The Goshi sweeps a hand over Jasmine's clenched fist. Her unfolding fingers reveal a 10ml syringe.

"Please," Jasmine begs. "Allow me to draw a small blood sample to determine your blood type … see if it's possible a—"

"Match?" Andorf's eyes widen at the large collector tube hanging off the syringe. "Stop right there. Even I know blood-typing requires but a few drops. What are you really up to?"

Jasmine hesitates, then speaks. "In truth, I'll be checking for complex compounds. See, I've got a theory why everyone around here believes you're—"

Andorf's eyes narrow. "Crazy?"

"Now, I didn't say that. Must you complete my sentences?"

"Look, Jasmine, if you're here to sell me another scam, I'm not buying." Andorf reaches for her arm.

Jasmine again pulls away. "No! Wait! If you humor me with a blood sample, it may prove my theory."

At the Goshi's reluctant nod, she swabs his arm and then covers the area with the vacu-syringe. Andorf's blood is sucked up just as quickly. The nurse injects the sample into a portable scanalyzer. Moments later, she smiles at the initial findings.

"Ah ha! It's what I suspected all along. You are O negative, a universal donor. But you already know this. You are also recovering from severe salt depletion. Of course, I'll have to do a full analysis back in the lab to finalize the results."

Discarding the syringe wrappings in the recycle bin, Jasmine discovers a spent rubbing cream tube. She rolls her fingers along the length of the flattened tube and analgesic cream spurts out in a blob. Using a second vacu-syringe, she injects the cream into the scanalyzer's secondary port. She then waits, studying the Goshi.

Seconds later, the scanalyzer display reports its results. "I believe I've found the source of your delusions, Mr. Johnson. This rubbing cream terribly depletes vital body salts. It causes severe convulsions and wild hallucinations not to mention irritability and paranoia. The ingredients are immortal."

"Huh? What do you mean by 'immortal?'"

"The chemicals never leave your bloodstream. In most cases, they get passed onto your offspring."

Andorf gulps. "Serin used the cream in the past. She delivered twins that day … Ayla and Sarak."

Jasmine's eyes widen. "The twins will have these symptoms as well as their own offspring."

Without warning, the floor vibrates. Andorf leans closer. After scanning Jasmine's timepiece, he takes her arm and hurries her out of the cabin. In the hallway, Jasmine grabs a rumble rail as directed.

When the tremors lessen, she and Andorf dash toward the view portal in time to catch sight of Andorf's finely-upholstered easy-chair drifting in space away from the *Atlantis*. Staring up at Andorf in total disbelief, Jasmine drops to her knees. Her voice quivers.

"Good gosh! Goshis even know when things are about to occur."

Andorf helps Jasmine to her feet. Feeling faint, she holds his arm until her wobbly legs stabilize. He leads her back inside the cabin while grumbling about the missing chair and looking around for additional missing items. "Murray Disturbances have a history of relocating items. Perhaps I shall move my easy-chair to a safer location next time."

"Ah ha. Just as I suspected. You *are* able to change things."

Andorf clears his throat. "Now, as you were saying, Jasmine. How could you possibly help me? Everyone tells me it is impossible to bring back my beloved Serin no matter what I do. Even my own daughters tell me to give it up."

"What about your scientific son? How does he feel?"

"The jury is still out."

Jasmine walks around the living area, examining the many hand-drawn sketches of Serin. She smiles, awkwardly back at Andorf. "You must deeply believe your late wife can be saved. Why else would you be entertaining my presence?"

Andorf's eyes narrow upon the nurse. "Okay. You have five minutes to explain yourself before trouble arrives. Go ahead. You had better make it quick."

"But … but it'll take much longer to …"

"Trust me, Jasmine. You will want to be elsewhere when my eldest bursts through the cabin door. I feel her on her way and in a foul mood, wanting only to sleep."

Jasmine gulps. "Then I'll make this brief. Let's begin with you trusting me. The last thing I want is to inflict more pain." She takes a deep breath.

Folding arms tightly against his chest, Andorf appears to be waiting patiently.

"The morning of the Titan incident. Dougie and I had a terrible fight and I was running late. I had fed my pet squirrel, Aquino, but fled without fixing my own breakfast. I know it sounds crazy, but there's a good chance I may have taken you more seriously if you had mentioned me feeding Aquino … or skipping breakfast … or the fight."

"With your late husband?"

Jasmine nods, woefully. "Now, what if there was a way of passing this information onto your younger-self ... sometime before your wife's death?"

Rubbing rough whiskers on his chin, Andorf begins to pace about his half of the living area. "There were a few times in the past when I could possibly have done such a thing. I could have relayed something about your fight or skipping breakfast or your pet squirrel to old man Chester. He could have in turn warned Serin when he saw her at the Cos.

"The Cos," Jasmine says, taking in a deep breath."

She would then inform my younger, quite naïve self during her confession right after *Atlantis'* launch. My younger-self would then mention it to you at the operating table and Serin would have been saved."

Jasmine nods. "Go on."

"Or perhaps I could bring it up directly with my younger-self," Andorf says. "I recall my last evening back on Earth. It was in the Last Stab Diner where I stirred creamer stick after creamer stick into my coffee, trying to make the face in the cup reappear." Andorf pushes his octagon-framed glasses further up the bridge of his nose. "Yes, it was me ... my future self, trying to warn the younger me." Andorf's eyes wide. "Wait! This has yet to occur. I can still warn my younger-self."

"Oh my gosh. That's it."

Andorf freezes. "No. Wait. This could not possibly work. It was brief and only an image. There would be no way my younger-self could possibly understand the warning."

"But you've got to try, Andorf. Perhaps your younger-self learns how to lip read. Now, tell me about this Chester fellow. Maybe he holds the answer."

"Yes, but I recall, Chester had memory issues. It is no wonder. He was well into his nineties. The old timer could never be entrusted to remember any details." Andorf pauses, staring at the squirrel tattoo occupying five-square inches of real estate on Jasmine's wrist.

Jasmine's eyes widen. "Aquino," she says, quickly pulling down her sleeve to cover additional tattoos. "I know Tenulians frown on skin markings but you must understand ... Aquino was the last of my babies. There'll be no other squirrels aboard starships. I doubt anyone born on starships has the slightest knowledge of squirrels."

"One of many things we have sacrificed over the years. How long have you had that crisp tattoo of Aquino on your wrist?"

"It was my first, inked a few days before Serin Gray's passing."

Reviewing the Aquino tattoo, Andorf shakes his head. "Impossible. That was thirty years ago. These colors are as crisp as though it was inked yesterday."

Jasmine looks around. She leans close and whispers. "I have a friend, a touch-up artist, right here aboard the *Atlantis*. The guy repairs things but also does inking." Jasmine's eyes twinkle. "My young friend has ways of making everything old glisten."

Andorf winces. "What if I could go back in time? My son, Sarak, has proven such a thing is possible. But it was for barely a fraction of a second. He mentioned the cause was lead contamination in his original teleportal design. If only he could reintroduce the lead in much greater quantity …"

Jasmine's eyes widen. "You could go back in time to advise Chester on what to tell Serin."

"Or I could do it when—"

The cabin door slams shut. "What the hell is *she* doing here?" Mila yells, hands on hips and looking over Jasmine's white nursing smock and the belt-mounted scanalyzer. "We've been through this before. You can't be opening your door to every crackpot who …"

Jasmine's face reddens. Temper swelling, she uses choice words to swear in her native Sudanese tongue before reverting back to Tenulian. "Why you little bitch! I've been practicing medicine longer than you've been alive. In fact, I was the one who bundled you up in a blanket and handed you off to your father when you were born."

Mila stares at Jasmine as if quite confused. Andorf clears his throat. "Mila is my adopted daughter, Jasmine. She was already five when the twins were born."

"What the hell's going on, Daddy?" Mila yells. "Who's this woman? What's she doing in our cabin?"

Andorf examines Mila's marker-stained hands and then points toward her bedroom. "Get some rest, young lady. We shall discuss yours and Ayla's expansion of my Kaanta tomorrow."

"Whatever," Mila says, in a whiny voice. Rolling her eyes, she heads for the bathroom, yelling without turning about. "Why can't we get beyond this? Serin's never ever coming back. Never!"

At the sound of the bathroom door slamming, Jasmine turns for the door. As Andorf escorts her out, she slips a fiber strip in his hand. "Here's my cabin number. Don't hesitate to contact me. You'll need help planning this out."

CHAPTER 27

Then There Were Three
ANDORF

A ndorf Johnson, please pick up," the comm-box blasts from its undersized speaker. "This is Captain Albie of the *Starship Phoenix*."

Expecting the overdue call, Andorf winces at the terribly distorted but seemingly urgent message. Without delay, he presses REPLY. "What can I do for you, Captain Albie?"

"We've got a situation here aboard the *Phoenix*, one I believe you'll find quite interesting." The captain clears his throat. "Please teleport over at your earliest convenience."

"I shall meet you in front of your new mural in say ..." Andorf glances at the time reflection above his work area. "An hour?" He reaches to disconnect.

"Very well, Mr. Johnson. But how'd you know about the—?"
CLICK!

*

Andorf takes note of how identical the *S.S. Phoenix* is to the *Atlantis*

134

as he exits the shuttle. Stepping onto the landing, he rides the floating steps up to the A-deck hallway where he examines the fifty-foot mural of individual drawings staining the wall. Though the drawings appear radically different from those of his own Kaanta back on the *Atlantis*, they carry similar themes. The longer he examines the mural, the more complex the artwork appears.

"And an hour it is." Captain Albie releases the timepiece dangling on a well-polished silver chain around his neck and drops it inside his collared shirt. "I saw you taking a shuttle, Mr. Johnson? Are we having problems with the teleportal again? I'll put a halt to them if they're endangering anyone's life."

"If you must know, Captain, I am uneasy with new technology … especially one which exceeds my mental grasp."

Albie looks at him as if baffled. "But wasn't it your son who first invented the teleportal?"

Andorf nods. "If you must know, I find traveling difficult without surrounding walls."

The captain wipes his brow. "I'm relieved. In spite of their occasional glitches, our teleportals are much more reliable. Besides, you never know when those finicky pilots will pull another strike." Albie chuckles. "I heard rumors of an old geezer once running up twenty-years of transit tolls. Who would believe anything so outlandish?"

Knowing Albie's reputation for bluntness and getting right to the point, Andorf is concerned at the captain's subtle pleasantries. "I am surprised to see you on your A-deck. Starship captains rarely venture this far off their bridge while on duty."

Albie's joviality thins. His brow rises as does the tone of his voice. He uses his arms to point out the fresh artwork. "Have you no eyes, Mr. Johnson? Can't you see the graffiti staining my starship's otherwise pristine wall? Why, we've got vandals in our midst … plagiarists at that. You may get away with this on the *Atlantis* but things are quite different here aboard the *Phoenix*. Just take a look at this crap. It's covering a fifty-foot section of my A-deck from here all the way down to there. My techs scrubbed for hours using our strongest cleaning solvents. Nothing seems to touch it. It's like the vandals used some kind of ..."

Eyeing the flaring pen strokes, Andorf runs a hand over the multi-colored sketches. He turns an eye toward the captain. "Molecular bonding pens. I've been told nothing short of a sandblaster will remove it."

Captain Albie growls. "Out of the question. Botanists would scream bloody murder at anyone merely suggesting use of their precious terrarium soil. That's sacred stuff, you know. Remains of everyone who's died on the *Phoenix* over the past three decades have been recycled into that soil."

"Is that so?" Andorf mumbles, continuing to run his hands across the elaborate drawings.

"You may not be concerned, Mr. Johnson, but I consider this a security breach. This section of the A-deck must have been locked down for hours during the whole third shift. And would you believe, no one saw a damn thing. Not one person left their cabin while the bastards performed this dastardly deed. It's as though everyone on the A-deck section had been brain-washed."

Andorf steps to the other side of the hallway to examine the wider pen strokes with greater interest. "Hmm. I seem to recognize this handwriting. I may even know the artist."

"Aren't you even the least bit concerned? Vandals have undermined your Kaanta. Why, they've made a mockery of it. Whoever did this, we must find them." The captain takes a series of breaths just shorter than his patience. "Wait! Did you say artist ... as in a single person?"

"Yes, and definitely single," Andorf mumbles.

"Impossible! Look at all this graffiti. It'd take days ... weeks."

"If my suspicions are correct, this can only be the work of a certain talented individual."

"We must apprehend this bastard ... lock him up right away."

"Careful using such words, Captain. I believe you are speaking of my eldest daughter, Mila." Rubbing his chin, he smiles at Albie. "I believe you will find similar drawings covering the *Mayflower's* A-deck as well ... my other daughter's handiwork."

"Daughters or no daughters, there must be consequences for their actions." Albie reaches for the nearest wall-mounted comm-box. He manages to press a few buttons before Andorf rubs his thumb and two of his fingers together.

The comm-box's CANCEL button engages.

Eyes narrowing upon Albie, the Goshi takes a firm grip of the captain's shoulder. He stares deep into the captain's emerald eyes. "You will do nothing of the sort, Captain. Instead, you shall bless these drawings as an extension of my original Kaanta."

Albie growls as he steps away from the comm-box. "But this blasphemy … it's an eyesore … an insult to your Kaanta."

Again, Andorf homes in on Albie's thoughts. His hand squeezes the captain's shoulder much firmer. "You shall conduct a series of tours. Everyone aboard the *Phoenix* must become intimately acquainted with these drawings. No one may yet comprehend their meaning but it is absolutely critical these become deeply ingrained in the people's collective mind." Andorf drops his hand and heads for the floating steps.

Captain Albie nods. "Wait," he calls out. "Aren't you going to explain the meaning of any of these drawings?"

Andorf takes his time, turning back to Albie. "No offense, Captain, but I am afraid they are currently beyond yours and most everyone else's comprehension."

"B—but where are you going?" the captain stutters.

"I must deal with another starship captain about a similar matter."

"If it's captain Waters of the *Mayflower*, my friend, you'll need to be more persuasive. The man's got a keen eye for the fine arts. He won't be nearly as receptive to this public nuisance."

*

Andorf discovers captain Waters stooped down on his knees, micromanaging a cleaning crew. He chuckles at the sight of techs holding their noses with one hand while scrubbing relentlessly on the *Mayflower's* latest art display with the other.

"You can certainly pick out the work of a southpaw can you not, Captain?"

Captain Waters staggers to his feet. Inside a split second, his crooked nose is jammed in Andorf's face. "Did you know the *Phoenix's* captain Albie found similar graffiti staining *his* A-deck? They are not as complex pieces such as these but it is graffiti just the same. Whomever did this will spend years in my brig."

Andorf rubs an open hand over the nearest colorful drawing on the fifty-foot mural. "I see."

Waters folds both arms tightly into his chest. Appearing put out by Andorf's serenity, he winces at the Goshi. "Just look at the rough, non-uniform lines of this piece. It's definitely the work of beginners. I suspect it is the work of those Q-nots ... you know, the cancel culture. Or perhaps those Michael Stipe revolutionaries. Oh, they'll be losing far more than religion after I'm through with them."

Hand on chin, Andorf walks the full length of the painted wall, noting particular segments of radically different style than his own. He smirks back at Waters.

"Must I remind you, Captain, every last one of the first-generation passengers was a revolutionary, including you and I? We not only stole the pride and joy of the Canine Empire by hijacking their fastest starships, but snatched up their most talented citizens as well."

"Jean-Claude."

"Who?" Andorf says, surprised by the captain's sudden warm up.

"Call me Jean-Claude ... Jean-Claude Waters. I take it you are Andorf Johnson of the *Atlantis* ... the armada's infamous Goshi?"

Andorf reluctantly nods.

Jean-Claude squints at the mural. "I've seen the crude sketches of the original Kaanta. You are a minimalist, using the fewest brush strokes to express points. But these drawings ... they are definitely drawn by someone of ..." The captain clears his throat. "Not to belittle you, Mr. Johnson, a more refined taste. I see many new scenes, a few much more frightening."

Andorf raises a brow. "Are you telling me you actually understand the meaning of any of these drawings? I never expected—"

"Quite the contrary. One need not understand what something means in order to appreciate its beauty." Waters laughs. "If such were the case, not a one of us guys would be married."

"True," Andorf admits, stepping closer to the captain.

Waters casts his hands outward. "Stay right there! Don't come any closer. I've witnessed first-hand how Goshi mind tricks work. Once your eyes narrow and you grab hold of—"

Andorf clamps one hand onto the captain's shoulder. Waters grovels. Then the captain's anguish-ridden face relaxes, as if recognizing Andorf as less of a threat. "I once heard my great grandparents were aghast by the Beatles' White Album on their first listen. After hearing the music a second time, they could not stop singing the songs."

Jean-Claude cracks a smile. "It is the same with fine art, Andorf. May I call you Andorf?"

Andorf nods.

"Like a fine wine, some things require time to digest." The captain steps to his right and points out one of the sectional drawings. "Take this more advanced piece for example. See how each color flows into the next? It's as they say, handwriting on the wall. As a fellow artist, I read deep meanings … well beyond what untrained eye sees on the surface of such refined artwork."

Andorf smirks. "I suspect this to be the handwriting of my youngest daughter, Ayla."

"Sacre bleu! A thirty-year-old did this?"

"She will actually be thirty-two soon."

Waters scans a second piece from top to bottom. His eyes narrow on the scene where Tenulians are backed into a corner by a gathering of thorny, three-legged creatures. He carefully inspects the tapering pen drabs. "This piece reveals traces of Picasso but with more subtle strokes. Has this younger daughter of yours had formal education in fine art appreciation?"

Andorf shrugs his shoulders.

"With your approval, I would love to take her under my wing as they say … teach her everything. I shall explain in great detail the many pictures of the Guggenheim … the Sistine Chapel … the Louvre."

Relieved, Andorf smiles. "Yes. I believe Ayla would make a great student."

"Now I question this drawing … the one of a blonde woman delivering twin babies."

Andorf's eyes begin to tear. He stares at the abstract piece for the longest time before abruptly dashing away in silence.

CHAPTER 28

Sarak's Lab
ANDORF

Andorf appears in the bowels of the *Atlantis*. He barges into Sarak's lab, clearing his throat loud enough to gain his son's attention. "About your mother …"

Sarak's head appears from behind a rack stuffed with interconnected equipment. "As you can see, I'm nearing completion on the original teleportal rebuild. This version contains none of the lead impurities which caused the time displacement."

"I wish you had not fixed that," Andorf mumbles. "If memory serves me, I recall you accidentally sent your papa Brutus back in time when you teleported him. Thus, we know time travel is possible."

Sarak nods. "Yes, indeed but it's no longer an issue. The teleportals are much safer since engineers removed that side effect when they miniaturized the circuitry."

Andorf peers around the lab at all the elaborate equipment but more importantly, noting that they are alone. "What if you were to reintroduce the lead, this time on a much grander scale to send me back thirty-two years?"

"Thirty-two years? What occurred then was for the slightest fraction of a second. It would take an awful lot of lead to do what you are asking."

"Well, how much lead are we talking about, Son?"

"Hmm. Thirty-two years would require …" Sarak's eyes roll about for a second. "It would require nearly seven and a half tons of lead. There's simply not enough available lead in the entire armada."

"What if we were to merely …" Andorf draws quote signs in the air with his fingers. "borrow that much of the stuff? Would it be possible then?"

Sarak paces about the lab, rubbing his chin as if deep in thought. "I suppose. Lead is used as engine radiation shielding making it an extremely rare commodity. But it would take years to accumulate so much lead." Sarak laughs. "You'd have much better luck gathering as much gold."

"Radiation shielding … hmm," Andorf mumbles.

Tipping his head, Sarak's mood sobers. "Isn't living in the now just reward for surviving our past deeds?" He stares at his father. "No! Wait! Don't even think about it. Mother has been gone far too many years."

"Remember when I mistook Ayla for your mother?"

"How could I forget? It's only been a few weeks."

"It was a sign. Not a day has gone by these past years where I have not longed to be with my Serin. If there is even the tiniest sliver of a chance …" Andorf places an arm on his son's shoulder. "I'm begging you to reconsider, Son."

Sarak throws both hands up. "Time-leaping isn't instantaneous, you know. It's not like what's portrayed in movies. You're what … sixty now?"

"Sixty-one."

"You'd age another thirty-two years … be in your mid-nineties. No! I refuse to entertain this madness any further."

Andorf winces. "Early nineties. I will take my chances."

"You could never survive the time-leap," Sarak yells. "And even if you could, you'd arrive as an old man lacking rational thought. Odds are you'd end up crippled." Sarak winces. "Did you know, each time I sent test fruits into the past they returned brown and all shriveled up?"

Andorf winces. "Those were fruits, not a human beings and … and this shall be a one-way trip."

"I'm telling you, Father, a time-leap so far back in time would literally kill you. There'd be no way in hell you could possibly survive. Besides, long ago I'd promised papa Brutus not to pursue this time travel matter any further. If I assisted you with this, he'll surely gather his soilenated pieces together and haunt me for the rest of my life."

Andorf shrugs his shoulders. "Then we will not tell him, will we?" He again slides an arm over Sarak's shoulder, leans into the experimenter. "Oh yes … you will also need to send me back to Earth."

"Earth? Why would anyone in their right mind want to go back to that wretched place?"

Andorf nods.

"Sending anyone such a distance would require more power than the *Atlantis* can muster up. And even if such a thing were possible, Turk's engineers would notice the power drain and shut us down before the equipment could complete its task. You'd be forever stuck in limbo."

"What about the Galactic Drives? Will they not be coming online shortly? Surely, they could supply enough power to send me back to Earth."

"I guess. But when the drives fully engage, we'll be traveling at too fast a clip to send anyone beyond the realm of the armada's starships."

"I suspect it takes time for the drives to power up. What if we tapped their power before they are fully engaged?"

"I don't know." Sarak grabs his chin to pace about the lab. "Theoretically it could be possible … our timing would have to be impeccable. The window for tapping drive power would be measured in seconds."

"A matter of seconds … hmm," Andorf mumbles. "My plan seems to be coming together. But there are a few minor details I seem to be forgetting … three of them in fact."

"Those minor details of which you speak," Sarak says. "You know what they are?"

Andorf stares.

"Number one … changing anything radically would irreversibly corrupt the current timeline. Number two … the odds of sending you back exactly thirty-two years are infinitesimally small. A sixty-one-year-old could never survive such an arduous time-leap. Number three … the precision required to land you at a specific place on Earth is beyond astronomical. With the Galactic Drives coming online in a matter of weeks, there is little time to gather the required lead. So, no! I won't help you. I refuse even to entertain this far-fetched notion any further."

Andorf scratches his head. "Nope. None of those are the details I cannot seem to remember." Andorf turns away, mumbling as he heads for the door. "Perhaps the nurse lady will clue me in on what I seem to have forgotten."

"A nurse lady?" Sarak races to stop Andorf's exit. "Father!"

"You must delay the Galactic Drives from coming online for however long it takes to complete your modified teleportal. Surely you can devise a reason … like … like some sort of safety flaw. We cannot engage the drives with dangerous safety flaws."

Sarak takes a firm grip of his father's arm. "Even if everything else was possible, there are too many obstacles. Mila for instance … s—she hears everything. She's even got people listening. I believe she's got the whole damn starship bugged."

Andorf brushes off Sarak's hand. "Calm down. Mila is a prominent member of the Third Council. It is her job to keep tabs on everything transpiring aboard the *Atlantis*."

"You saw how she hates kids. Remember what she's threatened to do if she caught wind of me assisting with your hair-brained, time-travel scheme? I have no doubt she'll slip inside my cabin one evening, come to my bedside when I'm sound asleep, and—" He forms cutting scissors with two fingers. "Snip. Snip."

"Damn, Sarak! Quit being so paranoid."

Perspire drips off the experimenter's forehead. He stares back at his father in disbelief. "I may want a second child someday … perhaps a daughter."

Andorf scratches his chin. "I shall bring it up with the Third Council. Perhaps they could send Mila away for a few months. Hmm. That is one but what the hell are those two other minor details?"

"Then there's the matter of Ayla. Have you seen the way she bosses her husband around? Emin is Turk's son for gosh sakes, in line to become our next admiral. She's just as adamant against this time-leaping business."

"I would be alarmed otherwise. Your sisters are merely exercising their newly-found telepathic skills."

"The girls are evil I tell you … pure evil."

Andorf's eyes widen. "I just remembered another minor detail. I am terribly sorry, Son, but I have got to do this." He grabs Sarak's arm and twists it behind his back until it snaps.

"Hey! Oww! What the hell are you doing? Are you—?"

"Crazy? Considering I have just advanced *your* personal timeline you may say so." Andorf 's eyes widen. "You will thank me in a few days when you are back to your old self. In the meantime, you will find the last tube of analgesic rubbing cream in your uncle's walk-in storage closet … in a shoebox … upper shelf. I believe you already have a key."

"But—ow—Father. You broke my arm."

"Nonsense. It is merely dislocated." Andorf grabs his son's arm again and twists. Again, it snaps. "Trust me, Son, your arm will heal soon."

"Trust you? Why should I trust you?" Sarak screams. "You ripped my arm out of its socket."

Andorf half-grins. "But I put it back, didn't I? I advise you to double up on your salt intake for the next few days." Andorf mumbles as he exits the lab. "Yes indeed. The plan is coming together. Now if I could only remember that last minor detail."

CHAPTER 29

Refining The Plan
JASMINE

A series of knocks draws Jasmine to her cabin door. She peers through the peephole before allowing Andorf inside. Her door shuts and locks at the whisk of the Goshi's hand.

"We have a big problem, Jasmine. My son tells me traveling back over thirty-two years would age me by as many years … that I would arrive back on Earth as a feeble and disoriented old man with possible health issues. I have rehashed the plan over and over in my head. Every way I look at it I cannot make things work."

Jasmine gazes at the crisp tattoo on her wrist, the one of her pet Aquino. Eyes widening, she smiles at Andorf. "What if you wore a series of tattoos bearing instructions? Each tattoo would step you through what you need to do. My inker friend has sweet magic in those hands of his." Jasmine's face deepens in color. "Like how he bows and says 'at your service, ma'am."

"That's nice, but I fail to see how this pertains to me relaying messages to my younger self?"

"Two weeks ago, the young man operated out of a repair shop hidden behind the G-deck's sickbay. But with skin markings frowned upon, he may no longer be there."

Andorf gazes at his unblemished hands and arms. "It—it will never work. My journey would span thirty-two years. Short of having your tattoo guy in tow, imprinted instructions would become unreadable in far less time."

"Back in the day, Sudanese plastic surgeons experimented with skin grafts. During early trials of covering skin lesions, they discovered light exposure was the cause of skin-overlays peeling. Nowadays, skin grafts can last well beyond ninety days, but still, there's peeling issue. You'd need to protect them from light exposure. Perhaps use some form of sheathing."

Andorf's eyes widen. "Is this real?"

Jasmine extracts a small pad from her belt-pack. After a bit of finger-scribbling, she tears off the top sheet and hands it to the Goshi. "Check this guy out. He's the best skin grafter in the entire armada. I've sent him countless patients over the years."

Andorf grins. "Let us begin with your young man … the tattoo artist. I am certain he will not be advertising. How will I ever find the guy with the magic hands?"

A wide grin stretches Jasmine's cheeks. Her face again reddens. "Magic hands indeed. Oh, if only I were half my age I would—"

"Jasmine?" Andorf snaps his fingers to bring the nurse back to reality.

"Oh, right, the techno-whiz. Have you got anything in need of repair?"

Andorf looks about Jasmine's uncluttered cabin. After a long moment, he smiles at the ticking of a wind-up clock. His eyes widen. "My old friend, Gregory, had a shoebox full of animated tic-tocs. I suspect after all these years they all must require repair."

Jasmine walks Andorf out of her cabin and into the hallway. She pauses at the doorway. "The techno-whiz frequently works a table at the weekend swap-fest." She begins to whisper. "You may get lucky and find him there. He's identified by a gold star tattooed on the back of his left hand."

Andorf nods. He again apologizes for Mila's rude behavior. "She was coming off of intense visualizations and badly needed rest. I expect her to be more tolerable in a few days' time."

Jasmine laughs. "Of course. Now don't forget about my Dougie. As much me and that S.O.B. fought, I'd do anything to be back in his husky arms."

"If I am successful, Jasmine, your husband will be stationed elsewhere during the Titan Incident. Tattoos and skin grafts, hmm. Yes indeed, the plan is coming together. Now if I can only remember that last minor detail."

Listening to Andorf's departing words and footsteps, Jasmine ponders the ramifications of the Goshi actually saving his late wife and warning Dougie.

Perhaps the four of us will have dinner … hang out. Wait. If he succeeds, there'll be no getting together as friends. This meeting we just had will have never occurred. Life with Dougie will continue as it had before the Titan incident interrupted our routines. No one will be the wiser.

CHAPTER 30

The Weekend Swap-Fest
ANDORF

Gregory's walk-in closet door on the B-deck creaks open at the wave of the Goshi's hand. As Sarak had mentioned, the sisters have ransacked the closet. Every last one of his late wife's peasant blouses and her collection of personal items have been picked clean. Even the twenty-five-gallon drum of I.Y.D. perfume is gone. He finds Gregory's most-treasured shoebox tossed carelessly onto the floor. Except for a wadded-up index card and loose currency, the shoebox is empty.

"It appears Sarak found the last rubbing cream," he mumbles, stooping down to stuff the index card, coins and hundred-dollar bills into a pants pocket. Andorf gathers up Gregory's once-animated tic-tocs and gently places them gently in the shoebox. Sighting the 'Andorf for Mayor' yard sign in the corner of the closet, he freezes deep in thought. *It was Gregory who so proudly made those signs. How he bragged as he pounded them into the courtyard lawn.*

A commotion in the hallway jars Andorf back to the present. He peeks out the door and finds the B-deck hallway filled with energized people toting boxes brimming with whatnots rushing past. He extends an arm outward and the yard sign flies into his expectant hand. He then pulls his hoodie further over his enlarged ears. With the shoebox of tic-tocs in one hand and sign in the other, he starts to head back to the A-deck cabin. Instead, the building euphoria convinces him to follow the rowdy crowd down the floating steps.

Nearing the transportation deck, the ambient noise is absolutely deafening. Chaotic bantering of swappers bartering their wares spills out of the repurposed shuttle-bay. Entering the packed room, everywhere he looks, Andorf sees tables and chairs, people giving massages, trimming beards, and painting toe nails. At the tap on his arm, he turns about.

"How much for the sign, mister? Will you trade it for a Benghazi berdoli?"

"Benghazi berdoli?"

The youngster nods. "Yeah. They come in a variety of colors, from bright balloon yellow to a serin grey so dark it can disappear within the night."

"Like my wife, so dark she easily evaded the authorities," Andorf mumbles. "Not for sale," he growls but the kid has already moved on to haggle with another trader. He works his way around the bunching crowd before finally pulling one man aside. "What is all this? What is going on here?"

Appearing confused, the man gasps. "Where ya' been, pal? It's the weekend swap-fest. Say, do any of those antique tic-tocs work?"

Andorf shakes his head. "Not for many years. Besides, they are not—"

"What about your yard sign?"

Andorf grins. "I turned down an offer for a Benghazi berdoli."

Looking the weather-worn sign over, the man runs a light finger over the rusty post. Examining the dirt onto his finger, the man grins. "And I suspect you're passing this off as Earth dirt?"

Andorf nods.

The man bursts out laughing. "Are you kidding me? If this was real, uncontaminated Earth dirt, the guy would have offered you a whole warehouse full of berdolis. This sign is worthless but this much Earth dirt would draw a small fortune." The guy pauses to read the sign. "Who the hell is Andorf Johnson?"

Andorf shrugs his shoulders. "Someone I used to know."

"Well, what about the tic-tocs?"

"It is questionable if they can still tic or even toc, but they are definitely *not* for sale."

"Come on, buddy. Everything's for sale or trade if the deal is right … even you and me."

"The clocks are only here for repair." Tucking the shoebox tightly under his arm, Andorf feels another tap on his arm.

"There's a guy way over there who fixes old things … even old relics like those ancient tickers. He's the best there is … a techno-whiz if ever there was one."

Andorf's eyes widen. "Techno-whiz? Did you say a techno-whiz?"

"Yep. Over that a-way," the man says, nodding and pointing off into the distance.

Andorf works a path through the packed crowd, waving off anyone displaying the least interest in the yard sign or tic-tocs. He stops frequently beneath signs mounted on tall poles to check out one item or another, each time asking 'Have you seen the techno-whiz?' He is repetitively met with conflicting finger points and traders interested in his sign and tic-tocs. "Not for sale," Andorf repeats, as he weaves a crooked path toward the back of the room.

One trader jumps in front of him, blocking his path. "What about a photograph of the Singapore Freedom Rally of '45," he says in a sharp, jabbing Asian/Hotot accent. "It's even autographed by the great Rama Santosh himself."

Not that anyone in the crowd would recognize him, Andorf pulls his hoodie further over his enlarged ears. He zigzags around the trader and others who show him the slightest interest. He soon finds himself at the tail-end of a line extending up one row and down the next. The Goshi waves one hand and those ahead graciously step aside. Avoiding eye contact, he advances to second in line. The man ahead thumbs a comm device on the table then collects an unidentifiable gizmo under his arm.

Advancing to the table, Andorf peers apprehensively at tattoos spanning the young man's arms. Spotting a gold star on the young man's left hand, he places the shoebox filled with tic-tocs on the table. The goateed man, young enough to be one of his kids, reaches for the bright orange tic-toc with cat whiskers painted on its face.

"May I?"

At Andorf's nod, the guy fingers both of the clock's once animated eyes before reaching around the back side to wind a small, recessed knob. Listening to the tic-toc sound, his eyes follow the clock's mechanical eyes sweeping back and forth. Gazing up at Andorf, the young man offers a wide smile. "When I was a child, my grandfather had an orange tic-toc like this one hanging in his entryway. I haven't seen another since. And here you bring me a box full of them. Are they for trade or repair?"

For a long moment, Andorf stares hypnotized at the orange tic-toc's eyes sweeping back and forth. Before he can reply, the techno-wiz has wound every last one of the tic-toc's knobs. None of the other animated clock eyes comes alive. People crowd around to watch the hypnotic ticker's eyes sweep back and forth.

"Uh—repair," Andorf blurts out. "All six are here for repair."

The techno-wiz reaches into a small pouch and plops a handful of gum nuggets in his mouth. A strawberry aroma saturates the air as he chews open-mouthed. "If you change your mind, I will give you three-hundred credits for the collection as is. You won't find a better deal, mister, not here nor anywhere else in the entire armada."

Andorf winces at the thought of selling Gregory's treasured collection. "I could never part with them. They belonged to an old friend who is no longer with us. Lining my friend's entryway, all twelve eyes moved together as one. They are a matched set and all must be working. Can you repair them?"

"What? Are you implying all eyes moved together as one?"

Andorf nods.

"To keep them in perfect sync like that, your friend must have been an eccentric perfectionist."

"That he was."

The young man snickers. "You know, these tickers kept terrible time. At best, they were accurate twice a day."

Andorf likewise snickers. "Accuracy is not important. They must have their eyes working again."

Returning the orange tic-toc back to the fiber shoebox, the young man stares into Andorf's eyes. "Well then, I could open them here but gears and springs would certainly fly out and be forever lost. Each tic-toc requires time to repair. I suspect those in line behind you wouldn't want that, would they?"

Peering at those gathered behind who are shaking their heads, Andorf catches the techno-whiz taking interest in his elongated ears. He draws the strings of his hoodie tight.

The techno-whiz peers around before beckoning Andorf closer with an inching finger. As Andorf leans in, the young man whispers. "I run a repair shop hidden behind the rear service access of G-deck's sickbay. No promises but if you bring the tic-tocs by after 5pm, I'll have a closer look. The orange one works fine. It only needed winding. I suspect the others may be repairable."

Andorf nods.

The goateed man continues to lean close and whisper. "You'll find a narrow, unmarked door with recessed finger holes in place of a knob. A short twisting hallway leads to a second door. Knock quickly three times." The techno-wiz spits the strawberry gum wad into his hand and then reaches beneath the table. His hand returns empty. "If I repair the lot, I get to keep the ticker of my choosing … perhaps this dark blue one."

Andorf places the blue tic-toc on the table. He gathers the shoebox in one hand and yard sign in the other before turning to leave. At the techno-wiz clearing his throat loudly and pointing to his tip jar, Andorf reaches deep into his pocket. He extracts a coin from his pocket along with the wadded-up index card and places them beneath the comm device on the table. He grins slyly at the techno-wiz before walking off.

CHAPTER 31
A Hidden Workshop
ANDORF

5 pm drags its feet arriving as Andorf lingers in the dark, nearly-forgotten recesses at the far end of the *Atlantis'* G-deck. He looks for finger holes of the hidden door, frequently pausing as people come and go through sickbay's patient door. He feels his way along the darkened walls. He soon discovers a hole the size of his index finger. Opening and then quickly closing the narrow door behind leaves him in total darkness. Toting the shoebox full of tic-tocs in one hand, the Goshi bumps his way along the eighteen-inch-wide corridor with the other. He takes multiple 90-degree turns before appearing at a faded sign mounted above the narrow door. 'Retro Bob's Cleaning Service' he reads, staring up at the faint illumination of a miniature bulb dangling by frayed wires above.

As advised, Andorf knocks three quick times on the door. After his knocks goes unanswered, he waves a hand. The entry door creaks open to reveal a collection of whatnots stacked from floor to ceiling everywhere he turns. Red string tags and wires dangle from things the Goshi cannot begin to describe. Unfamiliar chemical smells tingle his nostrils. He begins to sneeze but instead pinches his nose.

He steps cautiously between stacked whatnots to discover the goateed techno-whiz at an overcrowded workbench tapping his feet to whatever is being pumped into his head through temporal taps stuck to his head. Diligent fingers of one hand are working at a feverish pace on the piece held in his other hand. After clearing his throat loudly goes unnoticed, the Goshi twiddling index finger has the temporal probes sliding down the young man's face. The techno-whiz lifts his head.

Andorf looks about the cramped quarters. Recalling how his father was once a tinker of sorts, he feels right at home. "Retro Bob, I assume?"

The techno-wiz raises a brow at the visitor's sudden appearance. After recognizing the worn box of tic-tocs in Andorf's hand, the young man relaxes. "The name's a ruse, intended to discourage those wanting to shut me down. Nowadays, nearly everyone needs an alias, you know, to protect their guilt." The young man puts his work down and then extends one of his ink-stained hands. "You may call me Artemis. Welcome to my humble abode."

Andorf stares at the gold star tattooed on the back of the Artemis' left hand as he warily shakes the young man's ink-stained hand. "My name is Andorf … Andorf Johnson."

"The mattress over there in the corner is where I catch a few z's whenever I find time. I eat what little scraps I can dig up and work at this bench. The rest of my time, I'm out peddling repairs. Now, let's see. I believe you had a few antique tic-tocs needing repair."

Andorf half-way smiles. "My father once had a yard full of scrap. He collected and worked on all sorts of electronic gadgetry, many of which became prototypes for starship control systems."

Artemis returns the smile. "Ah, the son of a scrapyard dog."

"I would have expected a repair shop to smell more like burned resistors and heat sink grease. This place reeks of …"

"Busted," Artemis mumbles. "I dabble in inks as you've undoubtedly noticed. While I consider myself an amateur tattoo artist, I'm more adept than ninety-nine percent of the inkers out there. Have you seen their shoddy work? The colors fade after only a couple of …" The techno-wiz pauses at the sight his visitor's dazed look.

Andorf does his best not to feel out of place. Still, he smiles awkwardly.

"That's right. There's quite of few of us practicing the craft. But we're all driven into hiding in back rooms such as this one. Every last one of us must be poised and ready to flee at a moment's notice. Despite Tenulian restrictions, someone must fill the high demand for quality tattoos. It's only a sideline right now but I'm steadily building a group of loyal clients." After locking eyes with Andorf, his eyes narrow. "You are not here for repairs, are you? How'd you find out about me?"

Careful not to bump against anything which would cause an avalanche, Andorf worms a hazardous path closer. He places his shoebox of tic-tocs on the only vacant real estate on the techno-wiz's workbench. "You may recall a nurse named Jasmine. A few weeks ago, you touched up a tattoo of a pet squirrel on her wrist. Aquino … Aquino was its name."

"You must understand. I cannot divulge, let alone acknowledge, anything about my clients." Artemis returns his attention to the piece sitting half on the bench and half on his lap. The ceiling above their heads begins to pound in a repetitive rhythm. The overhead ventilator fan squeals. As if by habit, Artemis picks up a stick and taps a small overhead box. After a few taps, the fan housed within quietly churns.

"I've repaired that blasted ventilator motor countless times." Artemis winces. "Still, it freezes up whenever the tenants begin doing whatever they're doing up there. I don't know what it is but it won't stop. I've pounded on the ceiling to no avail."

Andorf peers at the artwork scattered about the room. Noticing a tattoo on the artist's arm similar to Aquino, he approaches the inker. Face inches away, Andorf catches himself gagging at the stale breath of someone who has skipped far too many meals. Binky's last words return to his thoughts. The Goshi's eyes widen.

"You are the starving artist … the one Binky had mentioned."

"Binky? Who's Binky?"

Andorf steps away for a brief moment before returning. "I have a job requiring ten precise tattoos, four of which are to be applied atop artificial skin."

The ceiling over their heads begins to pound in a repetitive rhythm. Gazing suspiciously at Andorf, Artemis grabs the tapping stick. This time he points it at Andorf. "I don't know who you are or why you've chosen me but best you leave now."

Andorf's voice sharpens. "I am dead serious, Artemis. This is a time-critical task, requiring detailed work to be completed in phases."

Artemis takes a wadded-up index card and presents it to Andorf. "Look, mister. Do us both a favor and forget about me. Forget who I am and forget where you found me."

Andorf grins wide. "Open the card. Read it."

The inker opens the wadded-up card. His hand begins to tremble. "Y—you were to meet the great Serin Gray ... conspirator of the uprising against the Canine Empire?"

Using both hands, Andorf slowly lowers his hoodie. "My late wife."

Artemis' eyes widen at sight of Andorf's elongated ears. "The Goshi!"

Andorf whisks one of his hands aside. A path clears all the way back to the entry door. The narrow exit door opens. Beginning to exit, he turns back to face the starving artist. "I shall return in three days' time bearing stencils. I advise you to clear your calendar."

PART 4
The Flimsy Plan

CHAPTER 32

Change In Wind Direction
ANDORF

Andorf is surrounded by odd machinery everywhere he turns. Each time he reaches to touch anything in the lab, a voice from somewhere within warns him not to touch it. He then walks about the lab, looking for his son.

"So, tell me, Sarak, what the hell is all this stuff?"

Sarak appears from behind racks stuffed with equipment briefly before disappearing. "We can't have you zooming through space without the comforts of an environmental chamber, can we?"

Andorf smiles. "Whatever changed your mind? A few days ago, you were so adamant against helping."

"It began the day after you dislocated my shoulder. I began to have crazy visions." Sarak's head again surfaces. "There I was leaving sick bay with a sore shoulder when I remembered the analgesic cream in Uncle Greg's walk-in storage closet. After rubbing a good bit of the goop on my shoulder, I barely recall returning to my cabin."

Andorf places a hand on Sarak's shoulder. "Look, Son, about your dislocated your shoulder. I hope you realize it was for your own good … a necessary evil of sorts. Besides, it is due time you came into your own. We cannot have your sisters bullying you any longer, can we?"

"The next morning, I awoke having wild hallucinations dancing around my head and with my wife's worried face hovering above. In a semi-conscious state, I somehow stumbled out of bed only to arrive back at your cabin. As I reached your cabin door it opened on its own. You and Mila weren't there. I went to your work area to leave you a note and a bundled set of markers flew into my outstretched hand. Then things got *really* crazy. As if inviting me inside, papa Brutus' cabin door opened before me."

Andorf raises a brow.

"I took papa's private elevator down to the B-deck … dashed toward my cabin expecting to tell my wife just what happened. A few steps outside the elevator my feet directed me toward the nearest wall. My hands began working overtime and before I knew it, my hallucinogenic visions were on full public display along a section of the starship wall."

"A fourth Kaanta," Andorf mumbles, rubbing his chin. "The murals are growing faster than my family tree. I see your inherited skills are emerging. You shall no longer fear your sisters."

"Unlike *your* Kaanta, *my* drawings depict a more immediate future. The first scene portrays me sending you back to Earth."

Andorf raises a brow. "I never had that vision."

"Another drawing depicts you as an old geezer on a walker, greeting mother at the Cos. She was ever so beautiful, as I've been told. There's even one scene of me and the girls going at each other's throats. A stranger wearing a white smock was intervening."

"Jasmine." Andorf sighs long and hard. "Say, with all this fancy machinery of yours, would it be possible to send a message to my younger-self?"

Sarak chuckles. "Well, I guess. Why not? Where and how far in the past do we need to send your message?"

"Earth—thirty-two years ago."

"To go that distance, I'll need something from Earth … a trinket of sorts."

Andorf leaves and returns to the lab twenty minutes later wearing a pair of worn-out pants. Reaching within deep recesses of the pants pocket, he hands Sarak a crinkled slip of paper.

Sarak holds the paper up to the light as if trying to read the faded words. "What's this?"

Andorf grins. "The words have long faded but it is a receipt from my last meal on Earth … back at the Last Stab Diner."

While Sarak reviews the faded paper scrap, Andorf digs deep inside his pants pocket and eventually extracts a second treasure.

"Aha, I knew it was in there." Unfolding the flattened paper tube, grains of coffee creamer spill onto the floor.

Sarak inserts both papers into a sleeve in one of the machines. "I must warn you, Father. This can be done only once … a few seconds at most. It can be nothing more than an image. Go stand over there."

Andorf slides the octagon glasses further up the bridge of his nose. Sarak lowers a mind probe over his father's head. He presses a few buttons and then says "now." When the transmission begins, Andorf does his best to tell his younger-self about nurse Jasmine. The transmission ends much too soon.

"Your message has been sent. All seven seconds of video."

"But there was not enough time," Andorf yells. "My younger-self was not able to hear anything I said. I need audio to tell him about nurse Jasmine and her pet squirrel, Aquino."

Sarak shrugs his shoulders and steps away. "Take what you get, Father."

Andorf grumbles. "So, show me how your time-leaping gadgetry works."

Sarak leads Andorf to a command console in the center of one floor-to-ceiling equipment rack. Every inch of the cabinet is filled with busy-looking gadgets connected by plastic tubes and wires of various lengths and colors. "First, we tap in the destination ... Earth in your case. Then we pinpoint an exact location … preferably a wide-open space. You wouldn't want to get stuck inside a solid object, like a wall, or drown face down in some lake."

"A park! What about City Park?" Andorf reaches around Sarak and finger-swipes across the screen. The image zooms into Earth's northern hemisphere. Another swipe brings up what were once the Eastern states of the Canine Empire.

"Keep in mind, Father, this data was imported from thirty-five-year-old Canine Empire maps."

Andorf raises a brow. "Back when there were seventy-two states."

"What the hell's a state?" Sarak asks, watching his father's finger-tweezes. The display zooms past the tallest mountain of Mid-Virginia and then hones in on a large ball field.

"Right there … City Park. This is where I want to go. Send me right there."

"As you wouldn't want to be falling upon arrival or worse … be buried six feet under. I assume you know the destination's altitude?"

"Exactly fourteen-hundred and five feet, plus eight point five inches."

Sarak taps in Andorf's numbers and the screen displays 428.45 meters with many preceding zeros.

"Is that it?" Andorf asks, eyeing the empty environmental chamber within the partially wrapped lead-lined vault.

"Not quite yet. We must set one thing, the all-important parameter … your arrival date."

"September 2nd," Andorf says, much too quickly. "I will need time to prepare."

Sarak chuckles as he enters the date. "If I am not mistaken, that was three months prior to the infamous soccer game … the one which triggered events leading up to the starship hijackings."

"You are absolutely correct except it was a local rugby match. Oh, I remember the match like it was yesterday."

"First-gen teachers gave their students first hand details of the game. It was as though they attended the match."

"Indeed. Many were watching from bleachers. You see, I went there to meet your Uncle Gregory." Andorf splits attention between Sarak and the pair of frozen numeric displays. He then cringes. "Say, why is that large square button flashing?"

"Nothing happens until I enter a password and press the sync button. The instruments will then sync up with the power source, determine the position forty seconds in the future, and then set the proper displacement vectors which …" Sarak pauses at the sight of Andorf's glazed over eyes.

"Speak plain Tenulian, Son. You know very well I am not technically astute."

"Argh," Sarak says, rolling his eyes. "If only papa Brutus, rest his soul, was still alive. He'd appreciate the technical details of what spatial time travel entails." Sarak sighs, taking a moment to refine his verbiage. He stares, displaying disappointment at his low-tech father. "Let's just say, if all goes according to plan, forty seconds after I press the flashing button, everything inside what I hope will be a completed lead-lined vault goes on its merry way through time and space, back to the days of Yestermore. Theoretically, the environmental chamber and everything within vanishes, leaving the lead-lined vault in a shroud of dense fog. Of course, it's never actually been tested on a real live person."

Andorf scratches his head. "Lead shell? I only see a shell around what appears to be one of those heated roll-around cabinets like they use in food services. Where is the lead vault?"

Sarak's face saddens. "Well, that's just it, Father. I'm lacking enough lead to complete the vault. Without the required quantity, the chamber goes nowhere in time."

"Rats," Andorf mumbles. "We are so close and yet so far."

"Then there's the matter of needing a target reference. A few ounces of dirt would be preferred."

Andorf laughs. "Dirt? Why would dirt be a problem? Every starship terrarium is filled with Earth dirt. I am sure the arborists would not miss a few ounces of the stuff."

"No. No. No. The dirt must have originated from within a few miles of the target destination."

"I believe most of *Atlantis'* terrarium soil was excavated from sites near City Park."

Sarak winces. "You don't understand. Terrarium soil has been contaminated with remains of those who have perished over the past three decades."

Andorf rubs his head.

"And to make matters even worse, Galaxy Drives are due to come online in a few days. Though it'll slice travel time to Planet Nero by a factor of ten, the *Atlantis* will be speeding too rapidly to safely send anyone beyond the realm of the armada."

"Again, please humor your low-tech father."

Sarak sighs. "Give me strength, Papa," he says looking away. He turns back to face his father. "If we don't send you back to Earth in the next few days, all bets will be off."

Andorf gasps. "A few days, you say? I have only begun to sketch the tattoo outlines."

"Tattoo outlines?"

"Conjure up with excuses, Son. Tell the engineers you have discovered serious design flaws in their Galactic Drives. Get arbiters involved if you must. The drives absolutely cannot go online until we are ready."

CHAPTER 33

Last-minute Plans
MILA

And don't you be hanging around with loose women while I'm gone," Mila barks while prancing around the cabin and gathering personal items to place in a roll-around cart. "I don't want to come home to find you've married some floozy."

Working at his desk, Andorf slides his rough outline aside. He throws both hands up as if insulted by the accusations.

"What was the Council thinking? How could I possibly leave you alone for ten weeks? Who'll be here watching over you?"

"Now now, Mila. I am sure the Council has their reasons. And against common belief, I am quite capable of taking care of my sixty-one-year-old self."

"It's a fact-finding tour for gosh sakes. They could've picked anyone to perform such a mundane task."

"Are you not the one who goes about telling everyone how you will get to the bottom of things?"

"Yes, but ..."

Andorf laughs. "Apparently, you have become the victim of your own ambition."

Mila smirks as she realigns items within the imaginary halfway line demarcating their shared living area. "It's not right, Daddy. Cleaning up after you alone has become a full-time job."

"You are months shy of another birthday and quite deserving of your own life. It is time you ventured off on your own … socialize with others your age."

"Whatever," Mila yells. "There you sit at that desk all day scripting. Your friends no longer speak to me. Now I'm off to who knows where on some bogus fact-finding tour. Something's not right."

"As I said, the Council has its reasons."

Mila grabs hold of her father's shoulder, stares directly into his eyes. "You know, I'll have people checking up on you."

"I would expect no less," Andorf mumbles, looking around as if trying to locate Mila's latest hidden cameras.

Tossing more items onto her cart, Mila grumbles.

"You know, there will be surcharges on those extra items, young lady."

Mila ignores her father as she overloads the cart.

"Galactic Drives!" he mumbles. "Not only are Galactic Drives coming online but I am fighting both of my two grown daughters."

"Don't start again with that jumping back in time to save Serin nonsense. Even you know it's impossible. Sarak better not be helping you."

"I know you have both been threatening him. Oh, the things I have heard … things too indignant to have come from either of my daughters."

"They were promises," Mila mumbles. She turns back to straightening up a few of the hand-drawn sketches of Serin lining the cabin walls. "You must forget about her, Daddy. It's driving you—"

Andorf interrupts. "Crazy?"

Growling beneath her breath, Mila kisses her father's forehead before putting her weight behind the heavy, over-loaded cart and storming out the door.

Sweeten The Deal
ARTEMIS

Lying on the bare mattress stuffed in a corner of the workshop, Artemis is awakened by the bundled stack of sketches landing on his chest. His foggy eyes strain to focus on the visitor hovering above.

"As promised, I have completed the ten drawings," Andorf says, proudly. "I know they are rough sketches but it is the best I could muster up in three days."

Artemis's legs stretch into a wobbly stance. He unbinds and then fans quickly through the pages of shoddy drawings before tossing them in a waste bin. "You expect me to use such trash?"

At the wiggle of the Goshi's fingers, the outlines fly out of the waste bin one by one and reassemble in a neat stack on the inker's workbench. Artemis peers at them bewildered. He attempts to again toss them away until his hand freezes.

"I suggest you take a closer look, my friend." Andorf lowers his hand to release control of the inker. "I am afraid my hands are not as precise as those of someone your age. I have little time and much less skill. You will note, the work requires accurate orientation and placement as noted thereupon."

Taking a deep breath, Artemis holds the sketches up to the overhead light. "How do you expect me to work with these scribblings? Why, it'd take me weeks to transcribe them onto workable outlines."

Andorf paces about the tight quarters, stopping here and there to examine the artwork on the surrounding walls. "That will not do. The first four tattoos must be ready in three days."

"Three days?" By habit, Artemis peers nervously over his shoulder. He scans the hallway monitors before locking eyes with Andorf. "Are the Q-nots after you?"

"Q-nots?"

"You know ... the radical cancel-culture aiming to eliminate most everything, including us inkers. I'm surprised you haven't heard of the extremist group. They knock on doors in a certain pattern ... two hard knocks followed by a soft knock and then a loud one."

Andorf winces. "A 'Q' in ancient Morse code?"

Artemis nods. "But sometimes they barge right in without knocking and take to trashing everything. I've devised a secret escape just in case."

"I assure you, none of those maggots are after me. Now about the scenes in my rough drafts ... they are no ordinary events. What transpired there were events leading up to the first of the starship hijackings."

"So, they're of historical nature," Artemis says, flipping quickly through the eight rough sketches and two instructional pages. He then tosses them atop his over-crowded workbench.

Being on a tight schedule, Andorf hands the stack back to the inker. "The first set of four are to be inked on my arms and legs. The next four will be applied atop artificial skin. Lastly, the all-important instructions are to be applied to the back of my bare hands."

"Artificial skin?" Artemis trembles. "There's no way in hell I could do this. Inking artificial skin is way too complex. There's way too many things to go wrong." Eyes blinking nervously, he peers back at Andorf. "I'm sorry, Mr. Goshi, but I'm not the right guy for this job. The precision required far-exceeds my skills."

Taking deep breaths, Andorf glares at Artemis. "I have no time to find another inker … one who can let us say …" The Goshi looks around the crowded workshop. "Be discreet."

"In all your wizardry, Mr. Goshi, I've no doubt you'll find my work disappointing. But I can name a handful of others who …" Artemis freezes at the weight of the Goshi's eyes bearing down upon him.

"The last of my friends have turned against me," Andorf mumbles. "Even my daughters are standing in my way. Fortunately, Sarak, has had a recent change of heart."

Artemis' eyes widen. "Sarak? Sarak? Did you say Sarak … as in Sarak Johnson, the guy who single-handedly invented the teleportal?"

Andorf nods. "My son."

"Why of course. I never put the last names together. I've heard he's been dabbling in time travel, sending objects off into the past. When can I meet him?"

"Well, I …"

"Wait a minute," Artemis says, scratching his head. "If Sarak is really your son, why are you using antiquated shuttlecraft?"

Andorf slaps his forehead. "Is there anyone in the armada who does not know?"

Artemis shrugs his shoulders.

"I shall make you a deal, young man. In exchange for the tattoo work, I shall trade you dead even my box of tic-tocs … all six of them. You told me they are quite rare."

"Well …"

"In addition to the tic-tocs, I will introduce you to my inventor son. If you are lucky, he may grant you a tour of his lab." Andorf extends an open palm. "So, what do you say? Have we got a deal?"

Artemis rubs his chin while taking his time to shake the Goshi's hand. "I guess so, but why the rush?" The inker's eyes grow large. "Ah. That's the point, isn't it? You don't have much time."

"My eldest, overbearing daughter for one thing was hampering my ability to turn out those outlines." Andorf winces. "I had the Council send her off on a ten-week fact-finding tour. Needless to say, my life will be a living hell if/when …" The Goshi clears his throat. "The girl catches wind of all this. Then there is the matter of the Galactic Drives coming online any day now. That alone nullifies any chance of my traveling back to Earth. My son is doing his best to postpone the drive integration but he cannot hold them off indefinitely."

"I admire your underhandedness. Perhaps we'll work on an air-tight alibi for your daughter."

"If I get the timing right, no alibi will be required."

Artemis's eyes widen. "First, tell me what it takes to become a Goshi. Barring obvious paranoia, can anyone become a Goshi? Does it require special training? Will I need years of intense wizardry training?"

Andorf cringles his nose. "Paranoia, ha! You have no idea. I would not wish this curse on anyone. It is much more than the average person can handle."

"Please, Mr. Goshi. I'm begging you. Get me out of this hell-hole. Working with old, dilapidated tools is tearing up my hands. A—and I inhale ink all day in this tiny, poorly ventilated joint. Fumes are doing terrible things to my brain. I feel them eating my insides." He holds both hands out. "Just look at these shaky—"

Roof joists moan in agreement. The small ceiling ventilator fan whining and then coming to a stop has Artemis and Andorf gazing upward.

"Whatever is going on up there is overloading the beams … one day—FWAP!" Artemis slaps his hands together. "The F-deck will come crashing down. It's even more reason to get me out of here. Don't Goshis ever need apprentices?"

Artemis again feels the Goshi's eyes narrowing upon him. He begins to tremble from his shoulders down to his ankles. Doing his best to cover his head with one hand, he swats at imaginary things flying around with the other. And just as suddenly, the imaginary things are gone.

"Hey! How'd you do that?" Artemis screams. "What'd you just put in my head?"

Andorf smiles mysteriously. "Whatever do you mean?"

"I was just in an earie place, sitting on a rock beneath a blackening, orange sky watching men work excavators. Then being twisting on the ground, being picked apart by giant winged-things before being eaten. One winged-thing even swooped down bearing massive teeth as if I were destined to become its next meal. And—and I saw three-legged creatures who were there one minute and gone the next. Where in the world did you send me, Mr. Goshi?"

"What you witnessed, my friend, was a future work detail. Those were Tenulian miners battling the elements of a hostile world known as planet Nero. These are but a few of the many horrors facing our descendants when they attempt to excavate Genghis stones on alien soil. Citizens will soon discover warnings of many such horrors buried within the Kaantas."

Still swatting the air, Artemis' eyes widen at the sight of white chalky mess on his shirt. His hands wipe futilely at the stains. "What the hell's this pasty crap? Did you smear something on me while you had me tranced?"

Andorf snarls. "Think of your recent vision as having lived the dream. Although the bird droppings will eventually wash out with soapy water and much scrubbing, the horrors you experienced will forever stain your soul."

"You mean …" Artemis gulps. "I was actually on planet Nero?"

"You were momentarily astro-projected there." Andorf clears his throat. "Now about these tattoos. Rumor has it you have inked surgically-applied skin on many occasions. If this is true, you should have no problem inking the second set of tattoos."

Artemis wipes sweat beads from his brow. Face reddening, he turns away. "You know how guys exaggerate from time to time. We're always bragging about things we've never done." He gazes back at Andorf, pinching a thumb and index finger. "Is it so dishonest to warp the truth a wee bit every once in a while?"

Filled with anger, Andorf's voice revs up. Drawings around him peel off the walls. In a whirlwind, they sail around the room. "Dammit, Artemis! We had a deal. You are to ink ten tattoos in exchange for my antique tic-tocs and me introducing you to Sarak."

"I—I don't know, Mr. Goshi. Artificial skin is—"

Andorf's eyes narrow. "You say you would like to revisit the Tenulian work detail on planet Nero?"

Artemis takes another swat at the air above. "No! Certainly not. I—I never want to see that dastardly place ever again." He runs over to scoop up the errant artwork scattered about the floor. "I—I just want you to know there are dozens of other inkers with much more experience at this sort of thing. I'd hate to mess up anything of such great historical importance."

Andorf approaches. He places a firm hand on the inker's shoulder. "You will do just fine, Artemis."

Pausing to review the Goshi's rough sketches, Artemis tips his head to one side, again pinching fingers. "How about if you were to sweeten the deal a bit?"

"Such as?"

The inker raises a brow. "Upon completion of this project, you shall …" He looks slyly at the Goshi. "Grant me a couple nights with three ladies … gifted professionals who will satisfy my every desire for hours on end."

Andorf rolls his eyes. "I will arrange a single night … but only after I am totally satisfied with your work. All ten tattoos must be crisp, right down to the very last detail of shadowing and color. Only then will you have your pleasures met by these three …" Andorf clears his throat, loudly. "Ladies."

Wiping his slobbering mouth on an ink-stained rag, Artemis smears a rainbow of colors across an already-filthy face. "And your son, Sarak, when can I meet him?"

Andorf's fingers touch Artemis' shoulder. Within seconds, Artemis calms. "First, explain the tattooing process. What am I to expect? Is it painful?"

Sighting Andorf's scowl, Artemis's glee completely shatters. "Shit, yeah it hurts. Actually, it's more of a painful discomfort. But hey, anything's tolerable if you want it bad enough. You've got to want it more than fear it."

"And what about ink depth? I need an absolute guarantee your colors will not bleed through the skin sheathes into the layers beneath."

Artemis gulps. "You're not kidding me, are you? Y—you really want stacked tattoos?"

Andorf nods. "As I said, my plan requires two layers … the first set on real skin and the second set atop surgically applied skin grafts. Limited to my arms and legs, two layers are required for the eight mappings. The final, most-important tattoos providing instructions about the other time-released maps are to be applied on the backs of my hands."

The inker's mouth drops. "So, these tattoos … I take it they're kinda like hidden treasure maps."

"Only these maps lead to a beautiful young woman." Andorf raises a brow. "A special someone I so long ago."

"Ah ha! I knew it. There's a woman in every sad story." Artemis snorts. "Passion always leads to mankind's downfall."

"Little do you know, Artemis," Andorf mumbles. "Little do you know."

Artemis' eyes widen. His voice again ramps with excitement. "I'll use my latest high-tech inks … ones artists back on your Earth have only dreamt about. Reduced gravity is the key to unlocking the finest particles. Working them is tricky, but the results are literary out of this world."

"As skin grafts begin to degrade in normal light, the second set of tattoos must be inked under dimmed lighting."

"I have no light dimmers."

The Goshi snaps his fingers and the overhead light dims.

Artemis sighs. "I must warn you, Mr. Goshi. Working under reduced lighting requires more time."

Andorf raises a brow.

"And your chicken scratches will need to be redrawn on transferable outline sheets. We're talking a good ten days, maybe fifteen."

"No," Andorf yells, taking a moment as if to step through the timeline in his head. "We are on an extremely tight schedule. I give you three days. No longer than three days."

"What you are asking of me is impossible. Even if I work twenty-four hours a day it'd take me a week."

"What if I introduce you to Sarak after the first four tattoos have been completed?"

Artemis grins. "I shall work day and night, starting tomorrow."

At the wave of the Goshi's hand, the narrow exit door creaks open. Artemis becomes startled by all the drawings on the walls seemingly staring at him. He again swats the air above his head. "Okay. Okay, Mr. Goshi. You'll have your proofs in three days. I'll begin work right away."

CHAPTER 35
Credentials
JASMINE

Jasmine peers out her peep hole and spots her new friend pacing about the hallway as if disorientated. She invites him inside.

"I found your tattoo artist, Jasmine." Shaking his head, Andorf takes a seat at the kitchen table. "But I have reservations about the kid. Are you sure he is really the best inker out there?"

Jasmine takes a seat beside him. "Believe me, there's no one like him. While Artemis may appear amateurish, his work excels all others."

"I am concerned whether his tattoos will withstand the test of time. He seemed awfully paranoid and totally unreliable. Why should I risk everything betting on this guy?"

"You must understand. There are many people trying to shut him down. Beginning with that weird counter culture, the Q-nots." Jasmine's eyes narrow. "Those S.O.B.s are not the only ones. I'm frequently reminded marking one's body is not the Tenulian way. Those of us bearing tattoos are looked down upon."

Raising a brow, Andorf peers at his unblemished, pale white limbs. "I shall keep that in mind."

"Now, what about your son? Will his updated teleportal be ready in time?"

Andorf's eyes widen. "You should see what Sarak has accomplished over the past few weeks. He built a complete environmental chamber for my traveling comfort. The only obstacle I can see is him acquiring enough lead to encase the chamber in a vault."

"A vault? How much lead are we talking about?"

"Seven and a half tons."

Jasmine gasp. "There's also a matter of nourishment during your hibernation. I must visit your son."

CHAPTER 36

Our Little Secret
ANDORF

ndorf returns to the little-known service area hidden behind *Atlantis'* G-deck sick bay. He feels his way through the dark, narrow, twisting passage leading to the inner door. Squinting up at the overhead sign illuminated from a dim light dangling above by frayed wires, he knocks three quick times before entering.

His eyes are drawn immediately to Artemis and the hands moving at a rapid pace. The young man appears to have been working on the rough sketches non-stop since their last meetup.

Artemis pauses to glance up at his visitor through bloodshot eyes. "I'll be with you shortly, Mr. Goshi. I'm just now finishing up the last of the instructions."

After peeling off his shirt and pants, Andorf stretches out on a fold-up table. "Remember, the tattoos must be crisp enough to be read by an impatient old man … one possibly struggling with failing eyesight. An occasional nudge in the right direction will undoubtedly be required to assist a forgetful man in his nineties."

"Okay. I've cleaned up your scribblings to create incredible drawings."

Artemis puts the outlines aside to wash and shave Andorf's left thigh. He disinfects the area with alcohol and then pad-dries it before centering an outline on the thigh. Artemis begins to trim the edges. "Remind me of the significance of these instructions."

Andorf peers down at the inker. "No," he yells, ripping the sheet away. "Instructions are last to be inked. They must be the first thing I see when the skin on the back of my hands peels off." He shuffles the outlines in reverse order and then hands Artemis the top sheet. "Begin with #10 … the one with a woman's rump and a fat syringe sticking out of it."

The inker smirks as he warms up the inks. Andorf stares nervously at his pasty white thighs. "This is for your, Serin."

He then grins up at the inker. "Serin and her brother were about to escape a political prison known as the Cos. An orderly awoke prematurely and was about to activate a panic button. In a final burst of energy, Chester tripped the orderly and injected her with a dose of her own sedative."

Artemis runs a roller over the stencil. After lifting corner, he blows lightly on the crisp black outline left behind on the Goshi's thigh.

Andorf watches the image begins to take shape at 500 pricks per minute. Sensing the ink penetrating his skin cells, he redirects his thoughts to the memory of last week's visit with Sarak before drifting back to the night of the starship hijackings.

"There I was, enjoying my last Earth meal when the vision of my current sixty-one-year-old-self appeared in the coffee cup. The image appeared to be a warning. There was no sound. After a few seconds, it was gone. I remember stirring in creamer stick after creamer stick trying to make the image reappear. Perhaps these tattoos would be unnecessary if only that seven-second clip had had sound. You know, I recently sent that message." Focusing on the inker's busy hands, Andorf wipes at his drooling lips. "Damn! I miss coffee, nearly as much as—"

"Coffee? What's coffee?"

Andorf winces. "Of course you have never tasted coffee. You were born on this starship, were you not?"

The inker nods.

"Coffee was a wonderfully warm, caffeinated drink … like chocolate but lacking the aphrodisiac side-effects. It was more of a stimulant, usually accompanied by a sweet treat … such as a donut or a tasty little French pastry. If I do make it back to Earth, enjoying coffee and a plateful of beignets will be the first items on my agenda."

Artemis' eyes widen. "If this choc-a-lot is as you say an aphrodisiac, I'm definitely visiting Earth."

"You would be shocked by the many strange customs, ones we first-gen Tenulians painfully left behind."

"I don't understand. Why would anyone give up such incredible things like coffee and choc-a-lot?"

"We never gave such things much thought. Everything was so plentiful back then. But I guess those items competed with vital food sources on star-ships." Andorf casts an open hand upwards. "Or perhaps the processes were too complex to replicate." He takes a deep breath. "Now getting back to the plan, certain event corrections must be injected into the timeline."

"Huh?"

"I must somehow inform my younger counterpart about Jasmine … like the fight she had with her husband … about her skipping breakfast … perhaps mention her pet squirrel, Aquino."

Artemis refocuses on his work. "All this sounds moxie but I fail to see how any of this possibly ties back to me."

"You see, my younger-self needs to point out one of those things to nurse Jasmine. Only then will she take him serious enough to perform the vital blood transfusion which hopefully saves Serin's life."

Artemis' eyes glaze over. His jaw drops as he lifts the machine and pauses. "You can't be doing this. It'll seriously skew the timeline. I've seen such things in movies. Things get really complicated. Nothing good comes of it."

Andorf grins. "And who is to say the current timeline has not already been skewed? Perhaps we are presently living in the guise of altered timelines. What if I messed it up the first time? I will need to correct it on a second … or a third attempt."

Artemis winces. "Well, yes. I suppose that could have happened. B—but you're implying we've done this at least once before."

Andorf scratches his chin. "It has been a while but I do not recall Chester having tattoos."

"I see what you're trying to do, but timeline warping is scarily dangerous stuff. What if you don't get it right and things get even more screwed up?"

"Then I shall go back and do it again until I get it right."

Artemis gazes at Andorf as if confused. "When do you know to stop? When will the madness ever end?"

"When I never lose my Serin."

"Perhaps what I've heard is true." Artemis' nose squinches. "That a Goshi accumulates all-knowing powers from reliving his life over and over."

"Things are different each time. New iterations occur so they are never the same twice." Andorf scratches his head. "And who is to say this is the first time … where it all begins?"

"I—I want you to know … I don't feel good about any of this, Mr. Goshi."

"So noted."

Artemis goes back to work. Using a second machine with a larger needle, he moves onto shadowing. He then switches to the much finer needle of a third machine for coloring in the outline. Afterwards, he preps Andorf's right thigh and moves onto outline #9.

"I suppose this yellow-haired woman was your wife?"

"Indeed. The late great Serin Gray."

Artemis cracks a smile. "You were really Serin's husband?"

Andorf half-smiles. "One of them."

"I didn't know she married twice."

"Only once."

"Ah," Artemis says, rolling his eyes.

"This event is where Serin meets Chester inside the Cos." Andorf fans out both hands. "Imagine guards and staff scattered about the floor, sleeping off their tainted meals. Searching for her brother, Serin rounds a corner only to discover the old man from her thoughts. His feeble hand takes hold of her arm. Grasping it as firm as he is able, he warns her of never seeing the births of her children. Perhaps this is where he should tell her about Jasmine and Aquino."

"He can't," Artemis says. "Serin will be too traumatized about not seeing her kids. She'll never remember anything about the nurse." The inker shakes his head as he moves onto outline #8 on Andorf's left arm. "What about this next scene where Serin appears to be sitting inside a large metal box?"

"Now, back up a good twenty minutes, Artemis. Serin was inside one of the apprehended cargo vans waiting for the Cos' entry gate to open. As old man Chester imposes thoughts upon hers, he instills an urgent need for her to speak with him inside the Cos. This may be the better time."

"Too much information may scare her. Informing Serin about nurse Jasmine at this point may not be my best option." After a while, the inker moves onto outline #7. "And what about this last outline? I see a long vehicle and a car chasing after it with flashing lights. There's Chester speaking with someone much younger, apparently your younger-self."

Andorf smiles. "This event occurred across the road from my apartment complex. Believing I had killed a recently-reacquainted childhood friend, I was on the run, scared. I got spooked when old man Chester appeared out of nowhere. He was peering over his shoulder repeatedly and acting irritated. He mentioned an impending date with a certain girl … how his ride would be arriving at any moment."

Artemis' eyes widen. "Perhaps *this* is where Chester should tell the younger you about the nurse and her pet squirrel. What's the squirrel's name again?"

"Aquino," Andorf says, shaking his head. "Think about it, there will not be enough time. With flashing blue lights quickly approaching, I ran across the street. I looked back in time to see Chester was being apprehended instead of myself."

Artemis colorizes the tattoo. He terminates the session by dabbing Andorf's arms and thighs with moist rags before setting off to clean his tools. "I hope my work exceeds your expectations."

Andorf examines the tattoos. He smiles at the accomplished artist. "These will do just fine, Artemis. I trust the tattoos covering my skin grafts will appear equally as crisp?"

The inker peers over Andorf's shoulder at his work. "I warned you before … tattooing artificial skin is tricky business. They're never of such pristine condition as those on real skin. But if you insist, I'll do my best. Now don't forget, these tattoos need time to breathe. You must allow at least two weeks before covering them."

"Ten days you say?"

"Quit doing that! If you expect sharp ink quality, you must allow the full two weeks. And when you get those skin grafts, you must allow the new skin another two weeks to stretch. You wouldn't want the next set of tattoos to end up looking like my great grandma's wrinkled hands."

Andorf shivers at the thought. Gazing up at the creaking joists overhead, he adjusts the critical timeline in his head. He stares at the inker waiting for a reply … any debatable reply.

Artemis remains silent as he puts putting away his inks and tools.

"We are cutting this awfully close. Mila's return is fast approaching." Andorf breathes deep. "Mark your calendar. I shall return in twenty-eight days for the second set of tattoos."

Artemis sighs. "I must warn you of one particularly shady skin doctor aboard the *Atlantis*. Whatever you do, stay clear of a wacko named Ivan Sardonicus. I've heard horror stories about the mad stitcher and his nut job assistant, Jillian." After looking about, he leans into the Goshi and whispers. "I hear they have some sort of business romance going on."

"Sardonicus, right." Andorf rises to examining fresh inks lining a counter in the rear corner of the room.

Artemis reaches around the Goshi to gather up his special inks. "The satin-flows I'm experimenting with fade around the edges over time, revealing more vivid tattoos beneath. They kind of take on a 3-D effect."

Andorf winces. "Are you telling me I won't need to bother with all the artificial skin?"

"Those inks are in trial stages. But if I can work with your son and his time-travel device, I could ramp up testing. Imagine me jumping back say a month … tweaking my processes … returning to immediately evaluate the results. After a dozen or so leaps, I could perfect these inks." Artemis' eyes widen. "Hey, I could even layer them on you."

"According to Sarak, each day you travel back and return, ages you two days." Andorf grumbles. "And every day I waste adds another two days to my journey. Look at me, Artemis. I am a sixty-one years old man. I am already taking enough risk arriving on Earth as a ninety-three-year-old. I will need to work quick to inform my younger self as odds are I won't live much beyond ninety-three."

The inker's eyes brighten. His voice rises. "I'll go with you. You'll need help remembering long-forgotten details. Adding another thirty-two years to my life will put me in my sixties, I'll still have most of my wits. I won't be a hindrance. I swear. I can guide you every step of the way."

Andorf raises a brow. "Hmm. That makes you the same age as my son and his twin sister, Ayla. I would not, could not, expect this of anyone. You would be sacrificing too many critical years. No. I absolutely cannot bring you along."

"But think how I could advance the art. With everything I know, I could advance the inking process far beyond my lifetime. I'd be performing tricks my counterparts have only dreamt about." Artemis begins to salivate. "I'd set my own prices … turn customers away by the droves."

"Definitely not, Artemis. You would have no friends upon arrival. Hell, chances of my own survival are not guaranteed."

"And what about you, Mr. Goshi? You'll have no friends … certainly not any at the ripe old age of ninety-three."

Andorf's mouth sours. "Most everyone I ever cared about … Serin, Gregory, and Brutus are now gone. Even my pet bunny, Binky, has long passed."

Artemis reluctantly smiles. "It appears you won."

"Where is the winning in surviving all your friends?" Wiping a tear, Andorf takes a deep breath. "One more thing, Artemis …"

The inker holds his breath for a moment, as if hoping Andorf has reconsidered a travel companion. "Anything, Mr. Goshi. Just name it."

"All this time leaping business is strictly confidential. Far too many people are trying to put an end to it. Why, if my daughters … or captain Jobi … or even Turk caught wind of this—"

"As an artist and friend, you have my word." Artemis projects a curved digit as if trying to pinky-swear. "It'll be our little secret."

CHAPTER 37

Whittling Time
ANDORF

With Mila gone, Andorf for once in his sixty-one years feels lonely. He visits Sarak's lab deep within the lower bowels of the *Atlantis* only to find his son performing experiments using various test fruits to send who them knows where. "Can I rest assured you have delayed the Galactic Drives from coming online?"

Sarak pokes his head out of an equipment rack. "Against Turk's liking." Sarak clears his throat loudly. "I've uncovered erratic fluctuations within the vibrawave modulators. The project has been pushed back three weeks."

"Three weeks?" Andorf yells. "Not good enough, Son. You have got to uncover more complications for the engineers to resolve."

"Don't worry. I'll get your full six-week delay as promised."

"Still not enough time," Andorf says, pacing about the lab. "We need another eight weeks." He peers at an incomplete segments of the lead encasing Sarak's environmental chamber and the door covered with the dull metal. He steps closer to examine the shell's fortified door hinges.

"I see you have been working on my travel chamber." Andorf eases around the door and peers inside. "There appears to be little room inside."

"The chamber started out much larger. Then I added thick super-insulation and redundant sets of gyroscopes to keep it vertically and horizontally aligned. We can't have you landing on Earth upside-down."

"No. Definitely cannot have that."

Grinning wide, Sarak approaches the partially enclosed 6-1/2-foot cube designed around two roll-around pastry cabinets. "The chamber has also been equipped with an air cleanser, heat exchanger, and humidity controls." Sarak lowers his voice to a whisper. "It's all powered by a radium 226 power source."

Andorf falls back a step. "What? Are you telling me this thing is nuclear?"

"Shh!" Sarak places a palm over Andorf's mouth while looking around the lab. "Watch your words, Father. Saying the wrong thing too loud will have more than one group of people shutting us down. Not only will Turk and his crew be breathing down our throats, but the Q-Nots are sure to visit."

Andorf gulps. "You know of the Q-Nots?"

"Do I ever. There is nothing good to say about those lying bastards. Their slimy hands are in most everything. They've already recruited a great many of the armada's ruling Council. And their cult is spreading like cancer."

"Is that so? Perhaps the Council is in need of cleansing."

CHAPTER 38
Turk's Rant
TURK

Turk pounds insistently on the cabin door. Spotting someone peering through the tiny peephole he pounds harder. At the door opening, he barges inside. The admiral's eyes are immediately drawn to the imaginary line drawn across the living area. One half of the room appears congested with stacks of documents while every knickknack on the other half has been placed in its proper spot. He turns about to stare down the encroacher.

"There's an urgent matter we need to discuss, Andorf. It's about your other daughter ... my daughter-in-law. I'm doing my best to groom Emin as my successor but Ayla's insidious sarcasm keeps undermining my efforts. How will the young man ever take command of the armada when he lacks self-confidence?"

Andorf winces. "Sarcasm? No, not my sweet Ayla."

"And another thing ... a couple roll-around pastry cabinets have gone missing. You wouldn't know anything about them, would you?"

Andorf shrugs his shoulders.

Turk scans the divided living area for a second time, noting Andorf's clutter taking up more than his allotted half. "I take it your eldest daughter is still away on the fact-finding tour?"

Andorf nods.

"I know Mila. If you don't fix this, she'll be steaming mad when she returns."

Andorf grumbles.

"Oh yes, another thing," Turk says. "One of those high-security foot-lockers plastered with bio-hazard labels has also gone missing. According to the armada manifest, it was supposed to be located in the *Atlantis'* L-deck cargo hold. What worries me greatly is it was filled to the brim with dangerous Carnga nuts. You know, the ones exported from Earth's Madagascar Islands."

"Carnga nuts?"

"The rare nuts are supposedly tasty as pistachios. I am told Carnga nuts permanently stain your skin a pale olive-green color."

Andorf squinches his face, while staring at his pasty-white hands.

Turk leans into Andorf and whispers. "I hear the delicacies are known to have extreme aphrodisiac effects. Why, ingesting merely a handful causes one to lose all sexual inhibition. Could you imagine having all that pent-up, unfulfilled desire? It's no wonder those partaking in the delight eventually go mad."

CHAPTER 39

Mr. Skin
ANDORF

Steering clear of anyone exiting sickbay's main entrance, Andorf covertly slips through a door marked 'Medical Staff Only'. In the backroom, he strips down to his briefs. By previously instruction, he scrubs both arms and thighs with antiseptic foam before rinsing them at a small sink. Waves of ultrasonic air ensure his limbs are absolutely dry within seconds. He slips on a gown, takes a seat, and then waits.

The back door suddenly swings open. A distinguished gentleman dressed in a teal green surgical smock steps inside with a woman half his age wrapped around his arm. They proceed to slip personalized skin-tight gloves over their well-manicured hands, his embroidered with 'IS' and hers 'NJ'.

"The enchanting Ms. Jillian will be assisting me today. Am I correct in saying we are to perform skin grafts on all four of your limbs?"

Andorf nods.

The doctor pulls back Andorf's gown to examine his tattooed arms and legs. "Jasmine prepped me on this rare quadraplex procedure but one thing troubles me. Why'd you request thirty-day skin when we offer a much higher quality ninety-day skin. Both require the same surgery and recovery time."

Andorf explains the scheme of alternating layers of skin and tattoos, emphasizing how this round requires the less-durable thirty-day skin. "On the next session, my limbs are to be covered by ninety-day skin. The back of my hands will require sixty-day skin."

Jillian smiles facetiously at her patient as she fills a 15ml syringe with a milky solution. As she offers it to the doctor, Andorf hears her unspoken words.

I would die to have long blonde hair like the girl tattooed on his right thigh. Why would anyone in their right mind cover up such vivid graphics?

Andorf sneers at the assistant. "No one would be foolish enough to accuse a Goshi of being in his right mind."

Jillian raises a brow. Her widened eyes bounce between the doctor and Andorf. "But I never …"

The doctor swabs the area, takes the syringe, and then injects the solution below Andorf's right shoulder. He turns to the assistant. "Mr. Johnson has been reading your thoughts, Jillian. The Goshi is known for such things."

Andorf winces at the sharp jab. Seconds later, his arm falls limp. Jillian reaches across him to place a fresh syringe on the surgical tool tray.

The doctor takes a moment to review Andorf's medical history hologram. Displaying perfect teeth, he offers a wide smile. "Without complications, the quadruple procedure should take roughly three-and-a-half hours."

Jillian grins at her patient. "Records indicate you are good with nitrous gas. Is that correct, Mr. Johnson?"

Andorf nods.

The doctor again studies the holographic medical record projected before him. "Now, before we proceed, I must warn you. You will be marginally awake during this procedure. While under the influence of nitric, you may experience wild fantasies … distorted visions of what will be taking place. For everyone's safety, I insist you remain calm and be secured in your seat."

"This should prove interesting," Andorf mumbles beneath his breath as the seat reclines.

The assistant snickers while dimming the lights. "You wouldn't want to jerk a limb in the middle of the good doctor's delicate procedure, now would you, Mr. Johnson?"

Jillian tightly straps on at Andorf's shoulders, wrists, hips, and ankles. He feels her slipping a mask over his face and then securing it around the back of his head while advising him to breathe normal.

Andorf smacks his lips at the sweet taste of nitrous gas infiltrating his airways. Catching Jillian peering into his dilating eyes, he begins to hallucinate. In his mind, Jillian and the doctor are laughing like crazed-hyenas. Jillian duplicates the doctor's wide, painful, cactus-eating smile.

"The gas appears to be working, Doctor Ivan."

Shivers run the length of Andorf's spine at the mere mention of the doctor's first name. His head lurches forward the little bit his shoulder straps allow. "Ivan … as in Ivan Sardonicus?" he mumbles, through the rubber mask. "The mad stitcher?"

The good doctor smiles wide, this time flashing a set of pointed teeth. "Indeed. You may call me Mr. Skin," he says, before bursting into insidiously wicked laughter.

Jillian presses her palms firmly against Andorf's shoulders, driving him back into the reclining seat. She secures the seat's binding straps ever tighter. Treating his chest as work space, she unrolls a med-pack.

A light mounted atop the doctor's forehead illuminates Andorf's arm as he begins to whistle an off-key rendition of the classic 'Hi Ho! Hi Ho! It's Off to Work We Go'.

Much to Andorf's dismay, the assistant hums along with the doctor in her own off-key harmony.

From his obstructed view, Andorf watches Mr. Skin methodically measure, cut, and lap new skin over the first tattoo. He focuses on the doctor's bulging eyes as the first overlay is methodically sewn in place. Mr.

Skin's face distorts into the very face of Doctor Frankenstein from Andorf's recently viewed late-night movie. While weaving the needle rhythmically back and forth down one side of Andorf's right arm and up the other side, the doctor then appears to morph into the legendary mad stitcher.

Meanwhile, Jillian's gloved hands rub the good doctor's shoulder, as she oversees the rapid motion of his busy fingers working the nearly invisible thread along the edges of the artificial skin. Andorf can only imagine what seductive words she is whispering in the doctor's ear.

Andorf feels a sudden, sharp jab to his left shoulder. Seconds later, his other arm falls limp. Before he knows it, the doctor has completed his left arm and has repeated the process on each of his thighs.

With both legs tingling, Andorf begins to lose patience. Shifting in the seat, he feels Jillian applying weight against his flailing legs. "Another few minutes, Mr. Johnson. You must be still. The good doctor is nearing completion."

Mr. Skin finally tosses his needle and thread onto the work tray atop Andorf's chest. Flashing a perfect set of pearly whites like a smile of success, the doctor steps back to proudly examine his work.

"The procedures went as planned, Mr. Johnson. You can expect slight discomfort over the next week along with moderate itchiness along the overlay's perimeter. I strongly advise you to resist scratching. And must I remind you to wear the protective sheathes at all times? The thirty-day skin begins to deteriorate the moment it is exposed to bright light. I take it you understood these preconditions when you accepted the unreadable fine print?"

Strapped tight against the reclining seat, Andorf does his best to nod.

After removing Andorf's mask and straps, Jillian slips protective breathable sheaths over each of her patient's limbs. Then she maliciously applies pressure on one of the shoulder injection sites. When Andorf flinches, she breaks into a wicked laugh. "I thought Goshis were impervious to pain."

With Andorf's eyes narrowing, the assistant's eyes go cross-eyed. She hastily exits the room, holding her crotch.

The doctor grimaces at his assistant's speedy departure and the pee trail left behind. "Of course, it'll take time to get used to the overlay's weight, texture, and—"

Andorf again nods. "Must I wait the full two weeks before having the new skin tattooed?"

The doctor smiles at Andorf. "Nurse Jasmine advised me of your plans. I have reservations of you inking my attractive skin overlays but of course it's your call." The doctor spots the Goshi's raised brow. "You *must* allow time for the skin to stretch. According to your layering schedule, I shall be ready to apply your second skin layer in four weeks."

Examining the sheaths. Andorf nods. "That'll be the ninety-day skin. Your mid-grade sixty-day skin must be applied to the backs of my hands," Andorf quickly adds.

Doctor Ivan smirks. "Curiosity prompts me to ask, Mr. Johnson. Why the layering? This all sounds as though you're planning some sort of treasure hunt. What in the world could possibly be worth so much trouble?"

Andorf takes a deep breath. "I am on a quest to recover something very dear to me… someone I lost so very long ago. Oh, to hear my beloved's voice … to get lost in her gorgeous brown eyes once again."

CHAPTER 40
Visitors
ANDORF

Back safely within the comforts of his cabin, Andorf stares at the clutter line running through more than half of the living area. He gazes at items packing his side of the room and the well-organized emptiness of Mila's side. Despite admiral Turk's warning, a flick of a few fingers causes items to shift a tad more onto Mila's side. Scratching at his chin, Andorf paces about the living space. A second flail of the fingers shifts items a bit farther across the imaginary boundary. "Better … much better."

A tap on the cabin door draws him to the peephole. At the door cracking open, nurse Jasmine pushes past and then quickly shuts the door. She freezes at sight of the imaginary line running down the middle of the room. "I take it your eldest daughter's not here, that we are alone?"

Andorf half-smiles. "For the moment. She is still off on the extended fact-finding tour."

"Great. Let me see your limbs."

Andorf clicks his tongue and the room lighting dims. He rolls up one of his shirt sleeves and removes the protective sheath.

Jasmine runs a finger along the fine stitchery encircling the artificial skin. "Very nice work. What'd you think of Mr. Skin and his crazy assistant?"

"I usually do well under nitrous gas but this time things got really weird. I was visualizing all sorts of crazy things. As your inker friend implied, Jillian appeared to have romantic interest in the doctor while he was sewing my legs."

Jasmine rolls her eyes. "Mm, yes. We all have our idiosyncrasies, don't we? Now, back to your time travels. Must I remind you of saving my husband?"

"As agreed, I shall see your Dougie is located on a starship other than the *Inca* well before the Titan Incident takes place."

"Nor the *Calypso*. That starship also took heavy casualties."

Andorf nods.

"Good. Now lift your shirt."

Andorf complies.

"You need an intravenous chest portal. Everyone over fifty is getting them. They've become quite trendy."

Andorf winces. "A portal? You mean to see my insides?"

"Nah. They no longer do that." Jasmine chuckles as she moves her palm below his collar bone, presses the center of his chest. "It goes right about here. The portal will make Sarak's work much easier. Say, when are your next skin grafts scheduled? I'll make the arrangements."

"Exactly twenty-eight days."

Jasmine turns to leave. "After the procedure, head next door. The medics will be expecting you."

A second tap on the door has Andorf peering through the peephole. He turns to whisper but finds himself alone. Hearing the bedroom door shut, he replaces the sheath, slips on his shirt, and then opens the cabin door. "What can I do for you, Captain Jobi?"

"Just checking up on my friend," the captain says, sporting a jolly face while doing his best to peer around the Goshi.

Andorf folds both arms. "You were here yesterday checking up on me. What is going on? Are you spying on me for Mila?"

"Your daughter sends urgent messages. Four alone this week. I don't know why that girl expects *me* to keep tabs on you while she's …"

Andorf shifts back and forth, attempting to block Jobi's probing eyes. "Oh, Mila did, did she? I suspect you are not the only spy she has recruited."

"Are you alone?" the captain asks, sniffing at fading traces of Jasmine's perfume.

"A most popular question recently. Does it look like anyone else is here, Jobi?"

The captain's eyes do a fast sweep of the living area as he edges inside past Andorf.

"You can tell my prying daughter that her half of the room has gone untouched."

"It appears Mila's things have recently been moved," Jobi says. "I can tell by the dust. Oh, I wouldn't be messing with her things if I were you. You know her temper. She'll be raging mad when she discovers what you've—" Jobi's eyes widen at the sight of the breathable sheath covering on of Andorf's arm.

Andorf pulls the shirt sleeve further down over his arm. "It is not what you think, Jobi. Everything around here is perfectly fine."

"My gosh, Andorf! You've been in an accident. Captains are required to know such things about his passengers. Have you filed the report?"

"It is not what you think," Andorf snaps. "Nothing funny is going on. In my spare time I have taken a few liberties. That is all."

The captain again looks about the living area. "Oh, Mila's not going to be happy about any of …" Jobi pauses at Andorf's glaring stare. His face twitches as the Goshi intrudes his thoughts.

Andorf places a hand on Jobi's shoulder. He stares deep into the captain's eyes. "You will say nothing of this to Mila or anyone else. You will not mention anything about my intrusion into Mila's precious space. Not a single word. Hear me, Jobi?"

Beads of sweat drip off the captain's forehead. Beginning to twitch, he pulls away from the Goshi, ducking and swatting at imaginary things flying about his head. "What the hell are those flying things you just planted in my head? You want me to have nightmares? I'm really impressionable, you know."

"Be glad you do not have the itches," Andorf mumbles. "What I gave you was a taste of planet Nero, the armada's destination."

Jobi futilely wipes at the chalky, white streaks staining his shirt. He begins to exit but pauses at the cabin door held open by Andorf. Staring at the Goshi, he shivers. "I never want to see anything like that dastardly place ever again. Not for the rest of my life. Promise me, Andorf, you'll never do that to me again."

Andorf grins, mischievously. "So, we have an agreement, Captain?"

"You needn't worry. I won't mention any of what I've seen to Mila nor anyone else." Jobi runs off before the Goshi has another chance of planting anything else in his head.

The moment the cabin door shuts, Jasmine reappears. Making a beeline for the exit, she pauses at the door. "Good luck with your second skin overlays. And don't forget the chest portal. The medics shall expect you in twenty-eight days."

Fur Traders
ANDORF

Not only does their bulk weigh heavily on his limbs but man are the skin overlays are itchy. Instead of scratching at the breathable, flesh-colored sheathes, Andorf focuses focusing on a certain unfulfilled promise.

He pauses at the informational display outside his cabin door. A lone finger-swipe retrieves a redacted passenger roster. His flattened palm causes the bright red letters flashing 'RESTRICTED' to melt off the screen. He then sequences through stacks of floor plans, noting detailed passenger names and locations aboard each of the armada's forty-four starships. Sorting by job tasks fails to reveal anything remotely reasonable. Recalling what Artemis called the women, he speaks soft and clear.

"Locate professional ladies."

No response.

Andorf paces the hallway scratching at his fuzzy chin before meandering back to his cabin. Feeling a tad lonely, he scans the empty cupboard shelves, searches through drawers. He enters his bedroom's walk-in closet only to gaze at stacks of neatly folded clothes at his feet.

Sorting through a short stack of 'no longer worn' pants he discovers many covered in his late bunny's white fur.

Staring at the fur-laden clothing, he becomes entranced in thought. Eyes suddenly widening, Andorf dashes into the hallway. "Fur traders! Locate fur traders!"

Floor plans of the forty-six starships are again displayed on the panel. When he taps the outline labeled '*Atlantis*' the window narrows to a dozen cabins. All but one cabin portrays a single-colored dot.

"Not good," Andorf mumbles, maintaining focus on the highlighted cabins. One particular cabin at the far end of the F-deck with three flashing dots suddenly grabs his attention. When he presses a thumb on the cabin, an index appears. Blonde 'Candy' is linked to a yellow dot and brunette 'Devine' to a brown one. The name 'Camarilla' is associated with a bright red dot. Tapping on each color, a woman's visual profile is displayed.

Startled at sight of Camarilla's rusty steel-wool hair fanning out far beyond her head, Andorf jumps back. He grabs the low-gravity hold to prevent a fall. He returns to the display and reviews the vixen's profile before dashing off. Despite of the crowds, he makes good time traversing the A-deck's twisting hallway. Arriving at the floating steps, he waits in line to descend.

Scanning ascending door numbers on the F-deck, an overpowering scent permeating down the hallway draws him closer. Only one person could possibly have the audacity to wear sassafras patchouli and he is about to discover who it is. Pausing at the opened door of the last cabin, Andorf peers inside. His nasal passages itch as he gazes at the castanets dangling from the bedpost vibrating in sync with a jazzy tune emanating from somewhere within. Andorf steps cautiously inside but freezes at sight of the rusty-red-head's electrified hair, glowing brighter than the phosphorus-red tri-hazard labels plastered about a footlocker at the base of a super-king-size bed.

He eases back out into the hallway. *What the hell was I thinking? This lacks any sign of decency.*

Between curiosity and his commitment to fulfil the promise, he dares himself to take another peek. The speckling of spent nut shells scattered across the floor reminds him of Turk's warning about tasty, cashew-like Carnga nuts and their aphrodisiac effect ... how merely touching them will permanently stain one's skin a dull olive-green color.

Stomach churning with regret, he steps further inside the maiden's chamber. Carnga shells crunching beneath announce his reluctant entry. Olive-green hands flash across his peripheral vision as he is pulled him further inside. Within seconds, his shirt has been removed and tossed atop a heap of clothing in the middle of the room.

Andorf's eyes are immediately drawn to the head vixen's naked form. From her painted toes up to the shiny amulet wedged between her full-sized breasts, every bit of the rusty-redhead appears to be smiling. Though he knows better, his reaching hands have a will of their own. Camarilla palms the back of his head, pulls his face into her cleavage. In a fraction of a moment, he is staring close up and cross-eyed at the amulet held in his hand. He quickly uncovers the source of the sassafras patchouli.

"The grand prize for brightest hair ... third year in a row," Camarilla says, purring out the words.

Andorf releases a sweaty grip of the piece and pulls his head away from the pillowing delight. Hearing women's wicked laughter, he backs up, gazing suspiciously at Candy and Devine sitting naked with their backs against the huge bed's headboard and beaconing him closer with spread legs and olive-green hands.

Candy appears entranced by the Goshi's elongated ears. "Where'd ya' get such long horns?"

"Why ya' still dressed, Nanook?" Fanning legs like an accordion, the buxom Devine snickers at her latest conquest. "What about it, Nanook? Wanna' play dirty Eskimo?"

"Yeah, Nanook," Candy adds. "How about a four-way Eskimo sand-wich? Wah-kah. Wah-kah."

Thoughts of being in the middle of an Eskimo sandwich flash wildly through Andorf's head. Barely a straight man in his right mind could turn down the opportunity of having three voluptuous women at the same time. Even this Goshi is having difficulty as he scans the variety of sex toys scattered about room like a well-stocked adult gift shop. His eyes widen at the gallery of animal photos wallpapering the room, the footlocker plastered with phosphorus-red tri-hazard labels, and the bed with its dangling castanets dancing to fast-paced tunes. His heart rate surges to nearly the beat of the music. Sweat drips off his forehead as he fixates on Camarilla's hand, swinging her shiny amulet about as if impatiently waiting a decision.

Camarilla smirks. "You're wondering about the animal pix, aren't you?"

Andorf gulps, sheepishly.

"Now, don't get the wrong idea," Camarilla says. "We aren't into bestiality."

Devine nods.

Candy's face slightly reddens. "Well, not recently."

"In what was once a farm in Montana, Uncle Fred raised a whole lot of pigmy ponies." Camarilla grins. "The old codger made his actual fortune growing waxy strings and selling them in little flip-top boxes."

While Candy smiles invitingly at Andorf, Devine runs a moist tongue across her Botox-injected lips. "Now, how about that four-way, Nanook?"

The head vixen points at the 'no one rides for free' sign hanging diagonally from a crooked nail above the bedpost beside the dangling castanets. "It won't cost you much more than a double."

Feeling good and evil jousting for his soul, Andorf is overcome by conflict. Although only there to arrange a rendezvous for his inker friend, before him lies the promise of every straight man's dream. He peers at his shirt on the clothes pile while plotting a quick getaway. "Y—you must believe me … I am only here for a friend … someone other than me requiring your services."

The Devine beckons him closer with curling olive-green fingers. "That's what everyone says."

Candy raises a brow. "Why so shy, Nanook? Drop those pants and come to bed."

"B—but you do not understand," Andorf says, squeaking out the words. "I am here merely to set up a trade … in exchange for a friend's services rendered. Artemis is a young tattoo artist who—"

"Everyone trades," Camarilla smirks. Her eyes narrow. "If me and the girls take on this artist friend of yours, what can you do for the three of us right now?"

Pondering for a moment, Andorf stares into the women's eyes, probing each of their thoughts. "You," he says to the blonde. "You have lost something very dear to you … something which has eluded your search for quite some time." He points across the room. "You will find the item beneath the table leg over there."

Candy leaps off the bed. Crawling on hands and knees, she feels beneath each table leg. Rising to her feet, she holds a bent copper piece between her thumb and index finger. Tears stream down her cheeks as she smiles at Andorf and the others. "The heirloom from my mother's collection. It's been missing for years. Thank you, Nanook! I am forever indebted."

"And for you." Raising a brow, Andorf peers at Devine sitting, arms folded over her chest as if daring his discovery of *her* inner passion. "You have an unquenched thirst of making people laugh on command. I believe you wish to become a comedian."

The brunette's face reddens. "Why, this man's reading me like braille. Making people laugh is what I've always wanted but I've never known how to express it."

Andorf whispers in Devine's ear. Her eyes brighten at the Goshi revealing secrets of telling a good joke, from purposely misleading the audience to driving home the punch line.

Camarilla clears her throat, loudly. "Now what about me, Nanook? I'll bet both sides of an argument you cannot resolve my deepest desire."

Andorf probes the redhead's deep thoughts. Weaving slowly between layers of useless information, a horrid look suddenly consumes his face. "You long for that special someone … someone who feels your every emotion, every little twitch."

Camarilla smiles slyly at the Goshi.

"No!" Andorf yells. Keeping an eye on the redhead, he backs away slowly. "W—what you want from me is impossible. I can give you most anything but—but never that. My heart belongs to another."

Camarilla's friends chase after Andorf and grab his arms. Being pulled onto the oversized bed, Andorf finds himself too aroused to resist. He feels his pants removed, sees them tossed atop the clothing pile. Camarilla drags him closer. "I could tell you were Goshi material the moment you stumbled inside. How careful you entered but no one escapes Carnga nuts." She shoves a handful of Carga nuts in his gaping mouth.

Andorf immediately spits them out. In desperation, he reevaluates his escape. *I will grab clothes and high tail it out of—*"

Ripping off Andorf's briefs, Candy gasps. "It's true what they say about sizing a man up by the length of his ears."

Devine runs a tongue over her cinnamon-scented lips. "And I've heard a Goshi can feel your every desire."

"Like he is deep within your soul," Candy adds.

Camarilla joins the Andorf-grab. "If you won't give me your heart, I'll settle for a Goshi child."

Andorf musters up as much Goshi power as his soul allows. But with traces of the Carnga nuts lingering in his mouth and lust pumping through his veins, his desire becomes overwhelming. As he submits to lust, the voice of the late Flip Wilson flashes through his brain. 'The devil made me do it.'

The women chuckle at the Goshi's hands struggling to caress all their breasts at once. Arms and legs fly in every direction as the women wrestle each other to be the first to mount the Goshi. With so many olive-green appendages moving about, Andorf finds it difficult to determine which body part belongs to whom and which part goes where. To the sound of dangling castanets swinging back and forth with each bump and grind, everything appears to transpire in slow-motioned choreographic movements, to a twisted version of the catchy Overnight Sensation tune:

He edged inside the maiden's chamber,
stomach churning with regret.
Staring at three naked women,
and the dangling castanets.

The gals were masters of deception,
making any man believe.
That he was truly an exception,
when they only wanted to conceive.

The foursome carried on without a comma,
beneath the swinging castanets.
Though there was so very little drama,
the gals were known to hedge their bets.

This night all chirped like little monkeys,
spouting every kind of name.
The Goshi did his best to keep them happy,
tho he knows it was all in vain.

The women left him sore and out of breath,
Still a viable escape plan remained,
As the Goshi grabbed his clothes and hit the doorway,
The red-head shouts out his name.

November 23rd will be your last day,
with a girl a third your age.
You shall spend your last breath,
for the one who's up and left.

Camarilla lurches forward. She twists Andorf's head aside and stares deep into his tired eyes. "I see a young man's heart pining for lost love. He is willing to give it all up to be with her one last time. But his aching heart will lead to his doom as a dying, crippled old man."

Andorf pulls away to slip on his briefs but after inspecting the holes, he tosses them aside. Slipping into a pants leg, he hops about, sorting through the pile looking for the remains of his shirt. Daring not to look back, the Goshi dashes out into the hallway holding socks and shoes in hand. "Forgive me, Serin," he mumbles. "I did this for you."

Unabashed and stark naked, Candy runs out after the Goshi. Disturbed neighbors poke heads out of their cabin doors as she shamelessly calls out. "Come back, Nanook! What about desert?"

CHAPTER 42
Conditions
ANDORF

Returning to the A-deck cabin, Andorf finds his youngest daughter camped in the hallway with baby Misty asleep in her arms. Viewing the many bags, he summarizes what occurred. He does his best to smile at Ayla and his infant granddaughter.

"I can't take any more of Emin's belligerence," Ayla says, accentuating each whispered word. "It's like I've married the bastard's father."

Andorf breathes deep. He again smiles at Ayla and Misty. "Turk is merely grooming his son to one day assume control of the armada. You must grant Emin enough wiggle room to do whatever is involved in commandeering starships."

"But ... but!"

"There is no debating this, young lady. It is not your place to get involved in starship matters."

Ayla shifts the baby in her arms to wipe at her dripping nose.

Andorf peers at the many large bags, then back at his daughter and sleeping baby. "What about your brother?"

"Sarak? He has no room for me. He's got a wife and kid of his own. Please, Father. I have nowhere else to go."

"What about your sis …?" Andorf begins to ask. After an awkward moment, the cabin door opens at his outstretched hand. "This was not supposed to occur for another two months," he mumbles beneath his breath while struggling with the bags.

Ayla disappears into a back bedroom. In a minute, she returns without Misty. She begins to speak until Andorf hushes her.

"I am warning you right now, Mila is due back soon. There is simply not enough room for me, a baby, and two combative sisters."

Ayla kisses his cheek. "Thank you, Father. It'll only be a few …" Her eyes widen at sight of the breathable sheaths covering both of his arms. "Oh my! You've been in an accident. Are you okay? What happened? Have you filed a report?"

Andorf laughs as he pulls the shirt sleeve over the sheath. "Reports, ha. Like we need more damn reports. First, you shall forget what you just saw. Secondly, you are not to fuss about my living arrangements. Nor will you report anything I say or do to anyone … especially your sister. Lastly, you will either find peace with your husband or make other arrangements. I give you ten days. No more. Am I clear?"

Ayla again kisses her father's cheek. "You won't regret this," she says, running off to check on Misty.

"And there shall be no spying on me," Andorf calls out. "Mila already knows too much. She has been sending spies. And if I catch you trying to read my thoughts, you and lil-missy will be joining your bags out in the hallway."

Ayla returns, scanning the living area, she cringes at her father's what-nots occupying seventy-percent of the space. She reluctantly nods.

Offering a cautious smile, Andorf scrounges through snack containers in the pantry. "Now, with that settled, are you hungry?"

PART 5
A New Hope

CHAPTER 43
Layering
ANDORF

Andorf sneaks out of the cabin before Ayla and baby stir. He waits on patients exiting G-deck sickbay to pass before slipping through the inker's secret entrance. He spots Artemis amidst the congested workshop holding the final six overlays up to the overhead light. After dimming the lights, Andorf removes the protective sheathes from his arms and legs.

Artemis encircles the Goshi to marvel at the intricate stitching on the skin overlays. "Very nice work, Mr. Goshi. But as I previously warned, I've never applied ink to artificial skin."

"You will do just fine." Andorf places a hand on the inker's shoulder. "My youngest daughter moved in with me for a few days on condition she makes peace with her husband. Meanwhile, Mila has been recruiting countless others to watch me. Even Jobi is an accomplice."

"The *Atlantis'* captain Jobi?"

Andorf nods. "I suspect she even bugged our cabin before departing."

"With hidden microphones and cameras?"

"At this point. I would not put anything past her."

Artemis sighs as he overlays the first outline on the artificial skin of Andorf's left leg. "I see old man Chester is at it again. This time he appears to be in a courtyard, selling food out of some sort of flimsy contraption."

Andorf winces at the tickling sensation of the roller applying the outline. "Chester used a homemade portable vending stand strung together with bailing wire. He was selling sausages." Andorf's nose squinches. "Do not ask me what sausages were. No one really knew. We all had suspicions but ate them anyway."

The inker chuckles as he works his needle between sharp lines of the crisp black outline.

"He was always complaining about the government … warned how I was wasting my time. If only I had listened."

Artemis pauses. "Perhaps this would be a good time to plant thoughts of nurse Jasmine into your younger-self's head."

Andorf nods. Looking around, he spots new jars of custom ink scattered about the workshop. He notes deep lines spanning the young inker's forehead. "I see you have been working with Sarak." He reaches to touch the inker's aging face. "If I did not know better, I would say you have time-leapt many times during these past four weeks."

Artemis leans away, twitching at Andorf intrusion on his thoughts. "No! Don't do that. Don't put those frightful visions in my head. It's been twenty-eight days and I'm still plagued by terrible nightmares."

"Look at you, Artemis. You appear fifteen years older. Did I not warn of the irreversible aging consequences of time-leaping?"

"Well—I …"

"How many times, Artemis. How many times have you leapt?"

Artemis gulps. Sweat dripping down both temples, he begins to stutter. "A—at first it was to test a custom ink … another time to fix an overused additive. The one-month leap soon became two … then three. I soon became addicted to making changes … changing what I believed would improve my new line of inks."

"Artemis!"

"It wasn't easy setting up hideaways and avoiding my other selves who knew nearly as much as me. But I tested and retested, never knowing when to quit. I could refine my inks but leaping time changed nothing. I hate to say this, Mr. Goshi, but you'll be wasting your time going back to save your late wife. I've wasted years of my life … just as you'll be, trying to save Serin. Time leaps never change anything. My leaps prove this so."

The Goshi grabs Artemis' shoulder. For several minutes, he stares deep inside Artemis' quivering eyes. He then turns away, leaving the inker shaking. After a good while, Andorf grins mischievously at the inker. "As we had agreed, Artemis, you will get the box of tic-tocs. And you already have obviously met Sarak. Now about the—"

The creaking sound of bowing roof joists has Andorf and Artemis gazing upwards. While Artemis scrutinizes falling paint flakes gathering on the floor, Andorf rolls his eyes in thought of Camarilla, the girls, and what is certainly taking place directly above.

"I have not forgotten our arrangement with the three professional …" Andorf clears his throat. "Ladies. Details have already been worked out, my young friend. Upon completion of these six tattoos, you shall be justly rewarded. But I suggest you gather plenty of rest beforehand."

Wiping drool from his chin, Artemis returns to trim the next outline on the artificial skin of Andorf's other leg.

"This event occurred when I was standing outside Gregory's back door. I had been awakened by someone breaking into and ransacking my best friend's apartment directly below. So, I crept down the front steps. Peering past the kicked-in door, I spotted someone inside his apartment. I snuck around to the kitchen door. Of course, Gregory's back door was locked. But an inner voice kept telling me to check my pants pockets. There I found the spare key from the previous evening."

Artemis moves onto Andorf's left arm.

"If you recall, these tattoos are digressing in time. Event #2 occurred while Gregory and I broke into … I mean entered the Archives building."

"I take it this guy with the flashlight is a …"

Andorf raises a brow. "Night watchman."

Artemis completes the tattoo and begins to trim the last graphical outline.

Andorf describes the action taking place back at City Park's game field that night. "And some say what took place during the rugby match was the single event which triggered other events leading up to the original three starship hijackings."

The inker pauses. Taking a breath, he begins to chuckle. "Old man Chester is at it again, standing behind that flimsy contraption. This time he appears to be offering your younger-self a steaming-hot beverage."

"Chester was hawking coffee in over-priced mugs. He would yell out in a wheezy voice. 'I'm not selling coffee! I'm selling collectible souvenir mugs.' Between long-winded rants and coughing fits, he would bark about the ails of the authoritarian Canine Empire. At one time, the old guy actually caught himself speaking to me in an incomprehensible language." Andorf grins at Artemis. "Tenulian, he called it."

Artemis' eyes widen. "Tenulian? That proves he came from the future, spent time on an armada starship."

"And after Turk had assumed command."

Artemis hurriedly completes his colorizing of the last pair of tattoos. While trimming the most-important instructional outlines for the back of Andorf's hands, a series of knocks on the door interrupt. Two hard—one soft—another hard.

Andorf gulps.

"Q-nots," the inker whispers, fingers held to his lips. He hurriedly powers down his tools. "I don't know how but they've found me."

Andorf reviews the grainy image of two large men on the small view screen above the inker's workbench. He watches Artemis dart here and there, gathering inks and tools and shoving them inside a handbag.

"Take me back to Earth with you, Mr. Goshi," Artemis whispers. "I promise, I won't be much bother. My tools take up minimal …"

Andorf whispers back. "We've been through this before. There is barely room for a single grown man, let alone an inker with all his—"

The knocks become shouts and pounding. "We hear you in there, Retro Bob! Open the damn door before we bust it down."

While Artemis stuffs whatever he can into his pockets, the door bursts open. Two men dressed in militia gear force and bearing weapons force their way through the narrow opening. They hap-hazardously topple stacks of what-nots which were piled to the ceiling. Bottles of ink are smashed. Drawings are ripped off the walls and torched.

With everything crashing down around him, Andorf places himself between Artemis and the intruders. The Q-nots suddenly pause, eyes homing in on Andorf standing in the middle of the chaos. Both cringe at the Goshi standing before them in underwear and bearing brightly-colored tattoos spanning his limbs. The larger man shoves Andorf aside. The other goon grabs Andorf's arm and squeezes hard but releases at the sight of the Goshi's narrowing eyes.

The Goshi trances back to the evening he spent with Gregory in the dark, dusty Archives building where hordes of rats scurried over their shoes. He then opens his eyes and stares down the masked Q-nots.

One man suddenly jumps high in the air. The other begins to skip across the floor, knocking over more stacks of repair items while yelling at the top of his lungs. "Yeow! Something's bit my leg!"

Both run around the cramped space swatting with their hands and kicking at the floor. "Rats! We've been bitten by rats!"

"Look at them all," the larger man yells. "There's hundreds of 'em." Peering behind, he runs out the door leaving his companion nipping at his heels.

The Goshi laughs. "Well, Artemis, what do you think about that trick? Artemis?"

Scanning the trashed workshop, Andorf feels abandoned. He lifts the mattress stuffed in the corner and every box large enough to hide behind. "The intruders are gone, Artemis. You can come out now."

Andorf pulls the protective sheathes over his fresh tattoos, fastens them with ties, and then get dressed. Brightening overhead lights, he gives the workshop a second look, kicking boxes and peering here and there. He scours the workshop for the instructional outlines but finds only charred fragments. "This is not funny," Andorf yells, gazing at the tattoo-free backs of his hands. "Without instructions the tattoos are meaningless."

CHAPTER 44
Gone Without A Trace
ANDORF

Andorf dashes out of Artemis' hidden workshop and through the winding G-deck hallway. Locating a wall-mounted display, he flattens a palm against the screen until the restrictive overlay disappears. He speaks slow and clear.

"Locate a thirty-one-year-old man named Artemis, last known whereabout was aboard the *S.S. Atlantis'* G-deck."

After a long moment, a floor map of the *Atlantis'* transportation deck appears. Highlighting Artemis' personal data off to one side, it zooms into an area at the rear of the shuttle bay.

Andorf hops the descending floating steps. Nearing the transportation deck, he becomes immersed in the chaos of people bartering their wares. As before, there are tables and chairs, people cutting hair, doing body rubs, and giving pedicures. He sees sports memorabilia, collections of discolored event tickets, and many items he cannot begin to describe. With euphoria filling the room, he secures the hoodie over his enlarged ears and then heads towards the rear of the shuttle-bay.

He persistently pushes through the tightly-packed crowd to eventually arrive at the table where Artemis sat weeks prior. Shiny discs are scattered about the table where a bushy-haired man sits.

"Where is the repair guy? Why are you camped in his spot?"

The vendor gazes up in contempt. "Look mister, this spot's mine. The table was open and I claimed it fair and square. As for your repair guy, I have no idea in hell who you're talking about."

Grumbling, Andorf walks off to mill about the crowd of buyers and vendors. Frequently halting to inquire about the techno-wiz, he is met each time by shoulder shrugs or pointing fingers directing him elsewhere. Andorf feels down on his luck, in total despair. Then, a tap on his arm and a heard-once-before voice has him turning about.

"Say mister, aren't you the guy with those animated tic-tocs … the one looking for the techno-whiz?"

"Yes, the techno-wiz." Andorf winces at the young man. "Is he here? Have you seen him today?"

The lad nods. "He was here just ten minutes ago … at his usual table."

"Was he alone? What did he say?"

"The wiz was alone all right but he seemed troubled. He hurriedly took something from his mouth and stuck it beneath the table. I heard him mumbling something about retrieving inks. I blinked once and the wiz was gone."

Andorf returns to Artemis' old table. His eyes narrow upon the squatter camped out in the spot. At the whisk of the Goshi's hand, the man's chair squeals as it moves aside. The squatter scrambles to his feet.

"Hey! What're you doing? Why'd you kick my—?"

At the wave of two fingers, the squatter is silenced. Andorf gets down on his hands and knees, crawls under the table. His nostrils flare at the scent of fresh strawberry gum. The warm, moist wad stuck beneath the table easily peels loose. Scrutinizing the sticky find rolling between his fingers, Andorf runs for the nearest information display, squatter in tow. A palm press and finger swipe verifies what he suspects. Artemis is identified as standing at that very display console.

"I should have known," Andorf mumbles, staring at the fragrant gum wad between his fingers.

The squatter behind him gazes up as if dazed. "What'd 'ya mean, mister?"

"The guy who stuck this gum wad beneath your table … did you notice his hands? Were either of them bandaged?"

"Well, yes. Come to think of it, the guy's left hand was wrapped up. Blood was oozing out of the wrap but I didn't pay it much attention at the time."

"Damn! Artemis removed his chip!" Andorf says. "You see, ID chips are surgically implanted at birth. Only a few first-gen Tenulians like me are without them. It is why we wear ID lanyards around our necks. It appears the techno-wiz has joined our ranks. He can now roam about the starship undetected."

Andorf hops onto the floating steps and then speeds back through the dark passages of the G-deck. He finds both doors to the inker's workshop kicked in and dangling by single hinges. Everywhere he turns, he finds smashed inks and burned drawings scattered about the floor. For a second time, the room feels void of life.

Where the hell are you, Artemis? I know you are too clever to be apprehended by radical Q-nots. Have you setup shop elsewhere? Either way, you will certainly never return to this place, let alone the swap shop. With my instructions destroyed and no way of locating you, the critical instructions on the back of my hands will never be inked. The older version of me will be left confused when his skin overlays deteriorate and tattoos appear.

Closing his eyes, Andorf concentrates on a sea of abundant thoughts, beginning with the immediate vicinity and fanning outward. As if on a beach amongst thousands of strange voices, he sifts through sand for the inker's thoughts. Nada! Artemis' lone voice is not among them. His friend is forever gone.

Andorf walks about the workshop, gazing at empty clips hanging everywhere and the broken shelves which housed Artemis' custom inks. Everything points to a single conclusion but Andorf still refuses to accept the obvious. Lowering his head from exhaustion, his eyes widen at the faint ticking sound coming from across the room. He spots his fiber shoebox full of tic-tocs left for repair tucked in a corner of the workshop. Though the six clocks all display different times, their kitty-cat eyes sweep back and forth. A crumpled index card stuffed inside the shoebox wedges free and floats across the room to land in Andorf's outstretched hand. The inker's tale unfolds along with his scribbled onto the card.

My Goshi friend, you will find all windup clocks in perfect working order. I have no use for them where I am going. But have no worry. I shall catch up with you sometime in the past. For Serin's sake, don't be late.

Overhead lights momentarily flicker. Shuddering at the sudden power surge, Andorf runs through the winding G-deck hallway. *No! Artemis could not. He would not.*

CHAPTER 45

Another Power Surge
BURAK

There it goes again," the Aegean's second-in-command yells. "This one's much greater than blips I've witnessed over the past four weeks."

The navigator surfaces from behind his console. He joins the second-in-command at the helm. "What's going on, Burak?"

"Each starship has its own power signature, like this one here." Burak points out one particular area of his display. "See, this one's well within the normal range of a starship."

"Uh huh."

"Power usage sometimes spike but it rarely exceeding this maximum line. This last spike was totally off the charts."

As if confused, the navigator scratches his head. "The admiral's not going to like this."

Burak winces. "Especially when he learns of the source."

CHAPTER 46

Lost In A Fog
ANDORF

Deep within the dark bowels of the *Atlantis*, Andorf is greeted by Sarak's dead-bolted lab door. At the door opening to the wave of his hand, the Goshi wades inside through dense fog. An exhaust fan activates and after a good minute, he spots Sarak standing before him, holding a spent, cherry-smelling schooner and an empty syringe.

The young scientist shakes his head. "It's too late, Father. Your inker friend is gone."

The overhead fan nearly drowns out Andorf's swearing as he walks around Sarak in circles. He pauses, shocked by the many tattoos spanning the length of his son's arms. "How many times, Sarak? How many times have you sent Artemis time-leaping?"

Sarak takes his time as if counting the tattoos. "Dozens ... more I suppose. He kept coming back to adjust one thing or another as he perfected his ink brand."

"By the looks of your arms, it appears you were deeply involved in his research."

Progressively pointing out the tattoos, Sarak grins. "It started with this one, then this one, and then this one. You can really see his progress."

To contain his anger, Andorf takes several deep breaths. "Could you not see him aging? The last time I saw Artemis he appeared to be in his forties."

"What could I do? Unlike the crude pen-strokes of my Kaanta, the guy's an actual artist. I was only helping him develop his craft."

"Not only have you nearly doubled his physical age but you used *my* environmental chamber. How could you do that? How will I ever get back to Earth?"

Sarak directs his father's attention to the rear of his lab. "If you haven't noticed, I've retrofitted a second environmental chamber. Yours has advanced features such as—"

"We have a major problem. Artemis was about to ink instructions on the back of my hands when we were rudely interrupted. He disappeared before inking them. What am I going to do without my instructions?"

"What? How? Why?"

"Reality-denying Q-nots paid us a friendly visit. When they began to destroy everything, I stepped between them and Artemis. I soon sent them packing."

"Your ole rats in the head trick?"

Andorf nods. "When I turned around, Artemis had vanished. I went looking for him at the weekend swap-meet but he kept one step ahead of me. Then I found his ID implant in chewing gum stuck beneath a table. When I returned to his workshop, I discovered his remaining inks and tools were gone. All that was left were the repaired tic-tocs and this farewell note."

Sarak raises a brow as he reads the inker's note. "That explains Artemis' hand bag and bulging pockets."

"Damn, Sarak! If you sent him off to where I think you did, you have robbed him of three additional decades of life."

"I cannot tell you where he's gone, Father. Artemis had me swear on mother's grave. All I can say is it's not when and where you think and he was hell-bent on helping you with your quest."

"Or stopping me!" Andorf yells. "Artemis became adamant about me corrupting the current timeline." He begins to probe Sarak's mind as the young experimenter walks away. Every thought in Sarak's brain-path he finds blocked. "You are developing your new-found mind control, I see."

"Indeed." Sarak grins. "And I no longer fear my sisters' threats."

CHAPTER 47

Urgency

SARAK

Sarak appears outside Andorf's cabin. After the door opens to his outstretched hand, he steps inside and finds his father working intensely at his desk. "There's nothing else I could do to delay them. The Galactic Drives are—"

Andorf looks up as if surprise. Pressing fingers to his lips, he takes his son's hand and leads him into the hallway. "It's much safer out here."

"Safer?" Sarak peers at his father strangely as he is dragged into a nook, away from curious passerbys. "What do you mean by *much safer*? Wait! Did I smell baby powder?"

"Ayla and Misty have temporarily moved in with me. It is like she and half of the armada have been recruited to spy on me. In addition, I believe Mila bugged the cabin with listening devices before she departed on her fact-finding tour as there have been too many coincidental visits."

Sarak smirks. "Finally, you believe me about Mila. She's wicked I tell you."

Andorf smiles facetiously at the paused crowd in the hallway. He waves them off with both hands. "Now, as you were saying about the Galactic Drives?"

"Engineering teams have combed over the lop-eared couplers. They've tested and retested each triplexer injector during simulated startup phasing sequences. After removing the dozens of wobbulators I stashed inside, every drive component was disassembled, cleaned, inspected, and then reassembled. Now there is simply nothing left for them to possibly test. So, I'm sorry to tell you, Father, but the Galactic Drives are coming online at noon tomorrow. You'll need to be locked securely in the environmental chamber in my lab at least sixty seconds before the initialization sequence begins."

Andorf's face pales. His mouth curls as if wanting to spit. Taking hold of Sarak's timepiece, his eyes narrow. "Noon you say? As in twenty hours from now?"

Sarak nods.

"That is nineteen and a half minutes after the armada exits the current Murray Disturbance."

"Only you could track these disturbances so precisely."

Andorf grins. "I have to get the second set of skin overlays applied … also some sort of chest portal. Fortunately for us, Mila is not due back for another few days. I have strong feelings it may be much sooner."

"Like tomorrow?" Sarak yells.

Andorf nods.

"Why are we cutting something of such importance so close? Oh, by the way … I've installed dead bolts on my lab doors to keep Turk's goons from snooping around."

Andorf taps his son's shoulder. "You had better leave. I believe Turk has entered a teleportal and is currently on his way here."

Sweat gathers on Sarak's temples. "Turk? He'll be trying to shut us down. Aren't you afraid he's coming after you?"

The Goshi snarls. "I am little threat to the admiral, more like a cut that won't heal. Ayla being his daughter-in-law and our loose friendship nearly ensures my safety. Now you on the other hand are a totally different matter. He considers you as a splinter in his mind's eye."

Turk Returns
TURK

Turk pounds relentlessly on Andorf's cabin door. When the door opens, he barges inside. As usual, his eyes are initially drawn to the imaginary line drawn across the living area. He turns his gaze back to Andorf.

"A few more roll-around food cabinets have mysteriously vanished. You wouldn't know anything about them, would you?"

Andorf winces.

"There are too many odd things going on around here. Like the seven-and-a-half tons of lead shielding missing from the Atlantis' secondary engines. I am told. that's enough material to construct a six-and-a-half-foot cube one inch thick. You wouldn't happen to be hoarding any lead, would you?"

"Go ahead, Turk. Take a look for yourself."

The admiral quickly visits Andorf's back bedrooms and returns with a puzzled look and holding a baby bassinet.

"I am putting Ayla up for a few days while she and Emin settle their differences. And yes, I have already told her she must grant Emin more leeway.

Shaking his head in despair., Turk looks about the bathroom and living area to verify they are truly alone. "I believe Sarak is somehow involved in all these thefts. I don't care if he is your son, I'm getting to the bottom of this no matter what it takes."

To the admiral's chagrin, Andorf shrugs his shoulders.

"And each time I inquire about the Galactic Drives, engineers inform me of a new issue. After three decades of research, you'd think all these endless problems would have been resolved. I suspect your son has something to do with them as well."

Again, Andorf shrugs his shoulders.

CHAPTER 49

Wisdom In The
Midst Of Distress
ANDORF

Visiting Jasmine in her cabin, Andorf briefs the nurse on the latest details and his distress over the missing instructional tattoos.

"Damn Q-nots!" Jasmine yells.

Andorf begins to pace about her living area. "I'll be lost, not knowing what the tattoos mean whenever they appear. What the hell am I to do?"

"Get a grip, Andorf. You're a master Goshi. I assure you everything will work out. And don't forget your promise that my Dougie won't be aboard the doomed *S.S. Inca* nor the *Calypso*."

Andorf grins. "A Goshi's promise is good as already recorded in the armada's logs."

"So, how much time do we have?"

"That's just it, Jasmine. Sarak can no longer delay the Galactic Drives from coming online. They are scheduled to come online noon tomorrow."

Jasmine's eyes widen. "Then what are you doing here?" She grabs hold of Andorf's arm and escorts him out the door. "Hurray! We haven't much time. Go get your final skin overlays and then have the portal installed in your chest. I'll move up the appointments."

CHAPTER 50

Rush Job
ANDORF

Relieved that Ayla and the baby have departed, Andorf revisits the G-deck. After him waiting four hours for the second skin overlay it is doctor Sardonicus and assistant who appear put out. Having to reschedule other clients, both grill him with seemingly endlessly questions.

"And hasn't your inker friend made it clear?" the doctor barks. "Your skin needs a good two weeks to heal after the tattoos?"

As if recalling the results of their last encounter, Jillian's eyes narrow upon Andorf as she straps Andorf into the patient chair.

Andorf nods. "Extraneous circumstances have accelerated my timeline. This must get done right now." He watches the good doctor and his assistant lay out their devices across his chest. After having the anesthesia mask placed over his face, he feels a slight needle jab and then the deadening of his limb. He settles in to endure the off-key tunes from mid '60's cartoon movies.

*

Four hours later, Andorf heads next door to have the portal installed in his chest. "I don't know how you did it buy your procedure has been fast-tracked," the receptionist spouts, as she whisks him into a back room. Trying not to scratch at the new ninety-day skin, Andorf waits for what seems like hours listening to muzak pumped in from hidden speakers.

Suddenly, the Goshi is surrounded by a handful of medics speaking medical-talk amongst themselves. Each medic performs a series of discrete prep tasks. Andorf squints at the holographic vitals encircling him while being bombarded by a barrage of questions. As directed, he removes his shirt. One moment, the medics stop to gaze at the opaque sheaths covering his arms. The next, they are back to gabbing medical-talk amongst themselves.

Andorf's chest is shaved before being wiped with an alcohol solution. He sucks air between his teeth at the slight needle jab but more so at the painful chilled solution being forced through his veins. His thoughts drift as he turns his head away. Before he knows it, the medics are putting their tools away and exiting. One medic stays behind to hand him 'what to expect' information and do his best to explain what the many pages mean.

Andorf slips the shirt over his head and pulls the sleeves over the protective sheaths. As he begins to rise, he becomes light-headed. The world spins as he falls backwards.

Observation
ANDORF

Andorf awakens lying flat on his back. He flinches at the sight of a frazzled nurse hovering above. "What happened? Why am I here?"

The nurse leans close. She pulls a fancy device from her blouse pocket and gazes into his baby blues. "Do you remember anything about having an intravenous portal installed in your chest?"

Squinting at the bright light, Andorf circles a finger around the piece smack dab in the middle of his shaved chest.

"It appears you had a reaction to the anesthesia. The medics want to keep you in observation another forty-eight hours."

Andorf sits straight up in the flimsy hospital gown. "Forty-eight hours?" he yells, pulling at the gown's draw strings. "How long have I been in sick-bay?"

"Six hours, I suppose," the nurse says, much too calmly for Andorf's patience.

"Six hours?" Andorf slides off the cot. "I wasted four hours at the skin doctor appointment. Another four hours were spent on the skin procedure and another two getting the portal. Now you tell me I have wasted six hours in sickbay?" His eyes widen at sight of the nurse's timepiece. "Help me find my clothes. We have little time before the Galactic Drives go online."

The nurse takes hold of Andorf's hand. At sight of his glaring eyes, she releases her grip. "But I cannot let you go. You're suffering from a serious health condition. I think you should—"

"Hell with that! I'm getting out of here!"

"You must rest!"

"I shall have thirty-two years to catch up on my rest," Andorf says. "I need to be seated in my environmental chamber in less than four hours. Otherwise, the *Atlantis* will be traveling too fast for me to be teleported beyond the armada's realm. I will not be going back to Earth. There will be no chance of saving my late wife."

Jasmine suddenly appears. She covertly winks at Andorf. "I listed myself as your next of kin." She tosses Andorf his clothes, escorts the nurse out, and then disappears. Before Andorf can zip up his pants, Jasmine returns pushing a wheelchair. "Hurry up. Time's a wasting. We've got a wife and husband to save."

Andorf sits back as Jasmine wheels him toward the private elevator at the far end of the hallway. "I must return to my cabin and get a few things in order."

The wheelchair speeds around corners on two wheels. Approaching Andorf's A-deck cabin, Jasmine takes one corner too sharp. The wheelchair flips, sending Andorf spilling onto the floor. After a few minutes, Andorf is reseated but one of the chair wheels has been twisted off. So, with an arm over Jasmine's shoulder, he limps the final distance to his cabin.

Apologizing, Jasmine appears in a panic. "How will you ever get to Sarak's lab in time?"

Andorf smiles calmly. "I have a trick up my sleeve."

CHAPTER 52

Problems Uncovered
TURK

Turk barges into the *Aegean's* bridge yelling. He shoves Emin aside. "Why has the *S.S. Atlantis* suddenly broken from formation?"

Burak reviews the instrument console. "I've been noticing power draining off the starship's engines during the past four weeks but it hasn't been much of a problem until now." He winces at the admiral. "It's originating somewhere in the bowels of the starship."

"Unless I'm mistaken, that's the starship's electro-mechanical service area." Emin growls. "It must be the work of those bastard gypsies."

The navigator's head surfaces from behind his console. "I doubt gypsies are involved."

The admiral's eyes bounce between his son, Burak, and the navigator.

"What are you guys implying? Come on. Spit it out."

With Emin and the navigator tongue-tied, Burak looks about the bridge nervously. He clears his throat loudly before locking eyes with the admiral. "It's the crazed son of your little Goshi friend, Admiral. I suspect he's performing his mad experiments again."

Turk paces about the bridge deep in thought. "I recall when the young scientist had early experiments with the teleportal device. While correcting bugs, the *Atlantis'* navigational systems were often flakey, sometimes going completely offline." The admiral raises a brow. "Whatever could he be working on?"

Burak looks about the bridge as if choosing his words carefully. "Rumor has it Sarak's been dabbling in time travel."

"No! "Turk yells. "Sarak can't be doing that. He'll corrupt the timeline."

The navigator resurfaces. "I heard his father intends to return to Earth and save his late wife."

The admiral snarls. "Of course, the great Serin Gray."

"What happens if the Goshi runs into his other self? Or worse …" Emin gulps. "What if I meet my mother-in-law?"

Burak's eyes narrow. "I suspect Sarak's behind the delays in bringing our Galactic Drives online."

Eyes narrowing as well, Turk slams a fist onto the command console. "Sarak's mad experiments must be terminated. Burak, shuttle a handful of warriors to the *Atlantis*. Whatever Sarak is up to it must be shutdown. Shut it down now!"

Burak begins to exit but pauses at the opening and closing bridge door. "Sarak's lab door has been dead-bolted. It would take welders to bust through."

"Then gather up welders," Turk yells. "A—and warriors."

"Warriors will be useless," Barak adds. "He's got all those odd devices with colored wires running all over his lab. Our warriors won't know which wires needing to be to cut and which ones needing to be jumpered."

The admiral drives a fist into the console. "Dammit Burak, grab an electrician … an army of them if you must. Sarak must be stopped!"

CHAPTER 53

Mila's Concern
MILA

Alarms sound throughout as well as every starship in the armada. Captain Jobi's voice rings aloud. "Attention! Attention! This is not a drill. The armada is poised to exit this leg of the Murray Disturbance. Everyone must seek their designated safe spot. If you are in a public area, please find the nearest safe spot on one of many conveniently located informational displays scattered throughout the starship. Consider this your fifteen-minute warning. Again, this is NOT a drill."

Mila grimaces in thought of what changes have occurred during her extended absence. With announcements blasting out ship-wide speakers, she has little difficulty slipping covertly inside her cabin. In dimmed lighting, she looks about the room she has shared the past thirty-two years. As her eyes dilate, she spots too many of her father's things encroaching upon her side of the room. Mila soft-steps toward her father slumped over at his desk, appearing to be lost in deep thought. She bends over his shoulder and reads the last entries on the mini-screen before him.

<My final transcription, this first day of the thirty-second year in the Tenulian calendar. My son, and daughters, and I have poured our souls into our Kaantas. Those attempting to decipher them have labeled us as crazy fools, evil prophets of sorts. With life becoming a series of predictably repeating events, memories of my late wife have been eating at my soul like acid. I can no longer tolerate the pain. I will soon fulfill my promise to Serrin … to spend my last breaths with—>

Andorf stiffens at Mila's hands massaging his shoulders. He begins to cover the screen, but her eyes have already scanned his dictated words. "Siros, pause transcription."

Mila feels her father's tense muscles relax at the brisk motions of her warm, kneading hands. "I hate to keep rubbing this in, Daddy, but Serin's never returning. Nothing you say or do will ever change this fact. You cannot go back in time. You cannot save her. And Siros, there is but one 'r' in Serin."

Siros: Negative! I only respond to Captain Jobi Cates, Chief Engineer Silas Angora, and Goshi Andorf Johnson.

Andorf lifts his head. "Siros, accept Mila's corrections to my log, sign as Andorf Johnson, and then terminate the log."

Siros: Affirmative, Goshi Andorf Johnson.

After the corrected log closes, Andorf wrenches his neck to gaze up at his eldest. "I feel terrible. I allowed Sarak to send someone back in time … to a great distance. Doing so, I've unwittingly stolen half of the young man's life. How could I have done this to my artist friend?"

Mila chuckles. "All this grandiose talk of Sarak's time-leaping experiments. With papa Brutus gone, my *dear* brother is craving your attention. I assure you, this artist friend of yours is hiding. Sarak is merely humoring you. Being a Goshi, you should know this truth."

Andorf squints, defiantly. "Mila, I swear, if I did not love you so much, I would—"

"I'm only saying this because I don't care to lose you. Even if it *were* possible to time-leap back to Earth, you'd be what … ninety-five-years old when you arrived?"

"Ninety-three."

Mila rolls her eyes. "Think about the last time you saw Serin. You were what in your thirties? Expecting someone much younger, she'll never recognize you."

"Well, I—"

"And what about your memory? At that advanced age it would have more holes in it than a politician's promise. You would barely remember Serin or why you were even there."

Andorf smiles, coyly. "The memory issue has been addressed."

"What? How?"

For the second time, the captain's voice sounds throughout the *Atlantis*. "Attention! Attention! The armada is poised to exit this leg of the Murray Disturbance. Everyone must seek out their designated safe spot. If you are in a public area, please find the nearest safe spot on one of many conveniently located informational displays scattered throughout the *Atlantis*. This is your ten-minute warning."

"No worries, my child. You shall figure it out in another …" Andorf scans the timepiece wrapped around Mila's wrist. "Sixteen minutes give or take. Wait! What are you doing here? You are not due back from your assignment until tomorrow. It was noted in the morning Council minutes."

Eyes narrowing, Mila jerks her hands away. "Ah ha! You *were* behind the exploratory assignment."

"Whatever do you mean?"

"I kept telling myself it wasn't true, but everyone around me was telling me otherwise. With the Murray Disturbance boundary approaching and you being laid up in sickbay, the Council thought it wise for me to return home." Mila looks about the living area and spots the wheelchair tucked in the corner of the room. "What happened to you? Shouldn't you be in sickbay?"

"I am perfectly fine. Now, Mila, tell me about this guy you met on the extended tour. I heard the two of you have become quite an item."

"Raphe? We began hanging out at the tail end of my tour."

"This Raphe fella … does he have good bloodlines? I hope he is not that crazed Ezraban I have heard about with the terribly long serpent tongue."

Mila catches herself grinning, At sight of her father's focus on her reddening face, she redirects her thoughts. "Stop that, Daddy! Quit distracting me! Serin's gone. When will you ever accept this fact? You'll never be with her again."

Andorf wipes his dampening eyes. "Today marks the thirty-second anniversary of her death … the day your twin-siblings were born?"

Mila snarls. "How could I ever forget? I was there when it went down. Shall I wish my siblings happy birthday?" she says, begrudgingly.

"Mila!"

"As you've frequently told me as I was growing up, leaping millions of miles through time is impossible … that time and distance were nature's cruel hoaxes."

"In light of recent developments …" Andorf clears his throat. "I have reconsidered my stance."

Mila's brow narrows. "And what's with the long sleeves? You never wear long sleeves. Is something wrong with your arms?" As she reaches for one of Andorf's sleeves, he jerks his arm away. Mila's eyes widen at sight of the re-vealed sheath underneath. "What's that funny stuff covering your arm?"

Andorf clicks his tongue in a specific pattern and the cabin lighting further dims. To Mila's dismay, he rolls up one shirt sleeve.

"Daddy," Mila screeches. "You were in an accident while I was gone? Oh, I never should have left you alone for so long."

"No, Mila. There is no need to worry. What you see is the latest in protective skin masking. The breathable sheaths reflect ninety-nine percent of light's damaging ultra-violets. It protects the artificial skin beneath from premature peeling."

"Artificial skin? Premature peeling? I'm never again leaving you alone."

Andorf smiles widely. "These come with a full ninety-day warranty."

Mila gulps. "And what happens after that?"

"Colorful tattoos displaying critical events will begin to reveal themselves."

"What? Tattoos? Next, you'll tell me there's a second layer beneath that one."

Andorf rolls back a protective sheath on one of his arms. He takes her hand and rubs it across the artificial skin. "Feel this. Softer than a baby's bottom and tougher than nails."

Mila quickly retracts her hand and then stares at him dumbfounded. "How could you do this? It violates Tenulian rules, many of which you had some hand in creating."

The captain's voice again sounds throughout the *Atlantis*. "Attention! Attention! The armada is poised to exit this leg of the Murray Disturbance. Everyone must immediately seek shelter in their nearest designated safe spot. If you are in a public area, please find the nearest safe spot on one of many conveniently located informational displays scattered throughout the *Atlantis*. This is your five-minute warning."

Andorf eyes the corner of the room before turning back to his eldest. "Don't you see, Mila? When the tattoo mappings come into play, the memory problem will no longer be an issue."

"Huh? What? Look, I …," Mila says, stuttering in confusion at her father's grossly out-of-character behavior.

Andorf then lifts his shirt to expose a shaved chest. "Come check my chest portal. Nurse Jasmine tells me everyone over fifty will soon be wearing these."

"What? Nurse Jasmine? Wasn't she that wacko I threw out of our cabin months back?"

Andorf shrugs his shoulders.

At her father's insistence, Mila thumbs over the portal cover before pulling back her hand. Her face sours. "You've gone too far this time. Nurse or no nurse, turning into a cyborg is never an option. Come, Daddy," she says, grabbing his arm. "It's time we pay someone a little visit."

"Enough talk of men in white coats," Andorf yells, whipping his arm loose. "Just hear me out, Mila! There is method to what appears as madness."

"But, Daddy—"

"Sit!" Andorf yells, pointing at a chair.

Mila obliges. Sitting impatiently, she eggs him on with both hands.

"Our descendants will require guidance long after I am gone."

"Quit talking about your death," Mila says. "You're barely sixty. Ship medics say with luck I'll be stuck with you another thirty years." She looks at away, mumbling, "If I don't kill you first."

"Everyone must become intimately familiar with the four Kaantas."

Mila's jaw drops. "Wait! Four Kaantas? Are you implying Sarak has one out there too?"

"Indeed. He drew a mighty fine mural on the *Atlantis'* B-deck wall for all to see."

"But—but."

Andorf stands and steps around Mila. He gazes back at her. "I found the amendments you and Ayla made to my original Kaanta quite interesting. Even captains Albie and Waters thought they were quite ..." Andorf clears his throat. "Impressive."

Mila smirks.

"But you two need not have gone through such trouble. Ship engineers insist there is more than ample lead engine shielding. There is no chance fluoride gas will contaminate the starship before it explodes, as I had once believed."

Mila purses her lips.

"You see, the day Serin passed during childbirth, Jasmine was the attending nurse. She had a terrible fight with her husband and skipped breakfast. She also had a pet squirrel named Aquino. If only I had mentioned any of those things, there is good chance Jasmine would have believed me and have granted the vital blood transfusion which would have saved Serin's life."

Again, Mila stares bewildered.

Andorf rubs the overgrown growth on his chin. "Don't you see, Mila? Thirty-two years is all I need. If I could go back and mention Aquino, the fight with her husband, or her missing breakfast, Serin's life may be spared. Tattoos are my maps, a Kaanta so to speak."

Speechless, Mila scans the living area and points. "And what about that filthy 'Andorf for Mayor' yard sign over there in my corner. Is this some kind of joke? Dirt … more damn dirt. Just what I need right now."

"Hey! I turned down a perfectly good Benghazi berdoli for that sign. See the dirt on the sign post? It is from the apartment courtyard back home. I have been told uncontaminated Earth dirt is worth a small fortune."

"And why is there an 'X' taped on the floor?"

Andorf smiles. "You will find out shortly."

"Everything circles back to the crazy notion of rescuing your late wife, doesn't it? No! I forbid you to do this!" Mila yells, shaking her head. "I'm never leaving you alone again. I'm staying right here until—"

As before, alarming sounds precede captain Jobi's message. It is the same verbiage as before but this instance giving a desperate one-minute warning.

Grabbing a packet of forms off his desk, Andorf dashes toward his designated safe seat. Mila chases after. She straps into an adjacent seat. "No! Don't even think about it. This time you're not getting away so easily."

Staring at the 'X', Andorf smiles. With the cabin beginning to resonate in low-frequency vibrations, Andorf winks at his daughter. "Showtime."

The shaking elevates to much greater intensity than during any previous Murray Disturbance. Mila winces at everything around her furiously shaking in their own resonant frequencies. Andorf suddenly bails from his safe seat and darts across the room. Grasping the yard sign in one hand and packet of forms in the other, he stands atop the X-mark.

Mila takes hold of security rings dangling above her head. She grasps them so tight, her hands become white-knuckled. For a brief moment her hands are translucent. As the tremors subside, she releases her grip. Scanning the cabin, she realizes her father has once again given her the slip.

"Damn! Double damn! Daddy's done it again. He's used another one of those Murray Disturbances to be elsewhere."

Rising, Mila takes a moment to review how everything in the living area around her has been secured down. *Since* when *has father gotten so well-organized? I've been gone what, eight weeks, and …?*

Sniffing the aroma of the spent, cherry-smelling schooner lying on its side beneath Andorf's desk, she shuffles desk papers. A thick folder magically surfaces from the heap. Inside, she discovers rough sketches labeled with thirty, sixty, and ninety-day notations and notes pertaining to which appendage and skin layer of where each tattoo is to be applied. The top outline is a hand-drawn scene of an old man labeled Chester, selling wares to a young man labeled Andorf. She fans through each stencil down to the last, depicting the same old man with a cane, reaching out to a long-haired girl. The same girl with long hair is noted on many of the stencils.

"Serin," Mila says, huffing out an extended breath. Her hand covers her mouth as she begins to piece together puzzle parts purposely laid out before her. *The nurse … the one who visited … she was dropping hints … hints of how to convince her to help father save his beloved Serin through a vital transfusion.*

She pushes away from the desk and stares off into space.

Skin that peels away at specific intervals … layers of time-released tattooed events. What's it got to do with that filthy yard sign? Since when has dirt become valuable?

The many bread crumbs her father left behind suddenly coalesce. Mila's face pales. She turns about and dashes out the cabin door. *If Daddy's gone to where I think he has, he's got a good twenty-minute lead on me. I've got to hurry. There's little time to stop him.*

CHAPTER 54
Ayla's Panic
AYLA

Carrying a bundle, Ayla hurriedly enters the *S.S. Aegean's* bridge. Totally unannounced and lacking pretext, she parks Misty smack dab in the middle of the Admiral-In-Training's buddy seat. "You must watch Misty, Emin. I won't be gone long."

"Hanin!" her husband yells, turning red-faced in front of the snickering bridge crew. "You cannot be doing this. I'm in the middle of—"

"Something awful is about to happen. I feel it in my soul."

"But … but—"

"Sarak has altered course. He's about to teleport father back in time to ancient Earth."

Listening to her parents argue, Misty's head volleys between them.

The navigator winces. "Earth? Who'd ever want to go back to that wretched, uncivilized world? Everything I've heard about the place with its authoritarian empires spells terrible."

Emin spits on the floor. "To go to Earth, you'd have to be cr—"

Smiling back at Emin with Misty cradled safely in his arms, Ayla rushes out the bridge door. She heads for the nearest teleportal, hoping to stop her twin brother before it's too late.

CHAPTER 55

Fade Away
SARAK

Unaware of trouble brewing in the main stairwell above, Sarak fine-tunes his complex equipment. The moment his father materializes in the lab, he shoves a full schooner into the sixty-one-year-old's outstretched hand.

"I was beginning to think you stood me up, Father. Here's the last of your protein bomb." Sarak scans the timepiece dangling from a lanyard around his neck. "We must hurry. The Galactic Drives are scheduled to fire-up in sooner than I thought. Turk advanced the timeline. Say, what happened to your hair?"

Andorf sets the folder and yard sign aside to slurp the thick, cherry-flavored concoction through a pipette. Finger-brushing his thinning hair, he stares wild-eyed at his Sarak. "Timing the Murray Disturbance required an expedient exit." He smiles at Sarak. "Oh yes, Mila and I wish you a happy thirty-second birthday."

"I wish you'd quit using spatial anomalies as personal transport. No one really knows when or to what effect they'll strike. Why, you could end up wedged inside the starship's walls. Worse yet, you could be cast into space like the late captain Thom."

Burping, Andorf chokes down the last of the elixir which should sustain him while frozen in an ambient state. Steps away from Sarak, he casts his overused 'you should know better' glare. "For your information, the bridge's front portal windows shattered that fateful day. Yes, I remember it vividly. It was when our good captain was sucked into space … the day I lost my beloved wife."

"Mother," Sarak mumbles.

"Did you know, your sisters have been plotting to put me away … for my own good they tell me. But you of all people know I have not gone completely insane, do you not?"

"Well, I don't know," Sarak says, rubbing his chin. "If tattoos and skin grafts weren't enough, your recent escapade with professional ladies left everyone talking."

"Ladies?" Andorf raises a brow. "Oh, you heard."

Sarak nods. "More than a few citizens watched you pull up your pants on a hasty retreat from a vixen's den." Sarak stares hard at his father. "I heard one naked woman actually chased after you while screaming 'Nanook.'" Sarak's eyes widen. "Who is Nanook and why was she asking for dessert?"

"It is a long story for another time, but know this. I went there with the intention of setting up a trade for our inker friend. I got blind-sided by their brothel."

"Father!"

"All right. All right." The Goshi laughs. "I am only human. Like you and every healthy heterosexual male, I have my needs."

"I only hope I'm as fit as you when I'm in *my* sixties." Sarak snorts an abbreviated laugh before leaning closer. "So, tell me, Nanook, one man to another, what's it like being with three voluptuous vixens at the same time?"

Andorf turns his reddened face away, wincing at the latest nickname. He paces about the lab, looking about as if not knowing where to begin.

"What started out innocent quickly escalated. Before I knew it, arms and legs were flying every which way. At one point, I could not tell which limb belonged to whom, including those of my own. Believe me, Son, it would not be a situation you would have wanted to fall into."

"Are you kidding me? Since your little escapade, women have been cornering me in hallways, asking if I'm as flagorous as my stud-muffin father? What the hell is flagorous?"

Mumbling, Andorf shrugs his shoulders. "What the hell is a stud-muffin?"

"And they've been knocking on my cabin door at all hours of the night. My wife's patience is running thin. She's beyond frustrated. Tell me, what am I supposed to do."

Again, Andorf shrugs.

A buzzer sounds. Sarak loudly clears his throat. "We've got little time. Let's get this over with … before my sanity returns."

Andorf glances at the cluster of industrial power cables feeding the environmental chamber and then at the racks full of complex equipment. Flashing nixie-like numbers draw him closer. He stares at each row of numbers, as if trying to make sense of it all. "So, Sarak, this fancy apparatus of yours, are you absolutely sure it can teleport me back to Earth, thirty-two years in the past?"

"There are no absolutes as you've often reminded me. But you mustn't worry. You'll be perfectly safe, sealed inside the improved eco-friendly environmental chamber. I've constructed this around a pair of food pastry cabinets. You know, those roll-around cabinets used in the kitchens?"

Andorf rolls his eyes.

"Incorporating them in travel chambers has worked flawlessly dozens of times. Although never beyond the confines of the *Atlantis*," Sarak adds beneath his breath.

"By the way, Sarak, you can uncross those fingers you are hiding behind your back."

Sarak redirects his father's attention to the primary control panel. "Now, you were inquiring about the time-leaping mechanics."

Andorf stares at the console with its long streams of meaningless numbers seeming to be standing between him and his lost love. He shuffles his feet anxiously in anticipation. "Will I really be safe in this contraption? Show me using both hands."

"Do you think I'd risk sending my own father millions of miles away in something untested?" Sarak walks off, beginning to blabber to himself while reviewing the crisp, new butterfly tattoo spanning the back of his hand. *Artemis begged me to send him thirty-two years into the past in a similar enclosure. For father's sake, I hope the inker survived his journey.*

Andorf scratches his head in amazement at the equipment appearing to be stitched together with spaghetti-like wiring in hap-hazard fashion. He steps around the rear, daring not to touch any piece which could break apart in his clumsy hands. His finger reaches inside one of the racks to tap a component vibrating inside the cabinet.

"Hey! Don't touch that!" Sarak yells, chasing after him. "It's delicate equipment. You don't want to damage anything this late in the game."

Andorf backs away from the equipment. He removes the lanyard with his ID and hangs it over one of Sarak's workbenches. He smiles at Sarak. "I no longer need those."

Sarak picks up the yard sign with the dirt-encrusted post and reviews the specimen. "I can't believe you have so much uncontaminated Earth dirt. There must be three or four ounces here."

The Goshi grins. "I've been told by more than one person at the swap-meet, it is worth a small fortune."

Sarak scrapes a few ounces of dirt into an empty beaker before placing the beaker in a chamber within one of the racks. "Before we proceed, are you absolutely sure you want to go through with this?"

Andorf nods.

"If by some miracle you do make it back to Earth in one piece, your ninety-three-year-old brain will be scrambled. Until those colorful tattoos appear, you may not remember who you are or what the hell you're supposed to do."

Andorf raises a brow. "For how long, Son?"

"At least several days … perhaps weeks … maybe longer."

The Goshi nods again.

"You'll be lost, confused, without a friend in the world. And—and most likely the last thing you hear when I lock you in the environmental chamber will most likely be who you permanently become."

"So," Andorf snickers. "If the last thing I hear when you seal me inside is say … flapjacks, I shall arrive lying flat on my back, buttered up and craving warm maple syrup?"

Sarak winces. "One thing is certain. When you awaken, you'll be absolutely famished. I'm giving you a little a snack, along with fresh clothes. Also, these scraps of colored paper with numbers I found in Uncle Greg's closet. Perhaps you can use them to barter for proper sustenance."

"Yes, thank you, Son. Having Earth money and fresh clothes will make things easier." Andorf unfolds the wad of twenties before stuffing them in his folder.

"Keep in mind, it will take hours to peel out of the plasti-derm cocoon you are about to apply."

"If I am truly having a deja-vu moment and we have done this before, I may find an old man exactly my age at the other end ready to greet me. I am also looking forward to meeting up with my inker friend."

Sarak tightens his brow. "Stranger things have been known to occur."

Andorf burps and then smacks his lips at the cherry after taste of the nutrient-packed drink. "Better set my arrival time to 7AM, Sarak. I won't want to miss breakfast. You know, breakfast is the most important meal of the day."

"As you have told me many times." Sarak flashes a hermetically-sealed Claxton fruitcake in his father's face. "It's the only non-perishable food item I could find, if you can call it such. A friend's maternal grandmother gave me this fruit loaf. It's been handed down through ten generations so I suspect it will survive humanity's last breath. The cake loaf should be good and fermented by the time you open it so you may be starting your journey sporting a good buzz."

After stripping down to his briefs, Andorf secures the thin plasti-derm protective wrap around his arms and legs before stepping beneath a blowing column of hot air, piped in from gravity generators next door. "How long did you say it takes to peel out of this plasti-derm? I cannot imagine anything worse than a cranky ninety-three-year-old making a dreadful fashion statement."

"At least several hours."

"Oh, yes." Andorf winces. "Your sister by now has pieced things together the bread crumbs I left behind. I suspect she is currently screaming a path down the main stairwell to reach this lab."

"Bread crumbs," Sarak mumbles. Suddenly, his mouth contorts. Sarak's head quickly spins around. "Sister? Wh—which sister is screaming her way down here? I can handle Ayla but if it's Mila …" Sarak throws his hands out, shaking as if shivering down to his bones.

Half-smiling, Andorf rotates inside the plasti-derm machine. "Take a wild guess."

"No! Not Mila! You know how wicked she is. She'll be barging in here, doing whatever she can to terminate our project in a whip-snappy fashion."

"You think I do not know this? I've lived with the girl thirty-two years. She has not only taken control of *my* affairs but those of the Council as well." Andorf grins. "Fortunately for us, Mila is fearful of floating steps. She always takes the main stairwell. This last Murray Disturbance granted me a good twenty-minute lead."

Freezing mid-thought, Sarak inspects his timepiece and cringes. "Wait! You've already been here fifteen minutes. "Hurry up with the shrink-sealing. If Mila's on her way, we don't have much time."

*

"Out of my way," Mila yells, darting around those seeming to linger without purpose other than to impede her progress as she descends the starship's main stairwell. She often wonders why the narrow passage was not marked with lines dividing the steps into lanes.

There's a disaster brewing and no one will get the hell out of my way. Why can't I be more like daddy and brush them aside with a whisk of my hands?

*

As Andorf rotates beneath the column of blowing heat, the plasti-derm molds around every part of him, leaving a few pockets for the access portal and breathing tubes. He gasps at it snugs tight around his neck.

"Enough of the damn heat, Father. You may want to actually remove that wrap when you arrive."

Andorf exits the hot air column. "You know, Ayla may actually beat her sister here. She too is dead set against us doing this."

"What? Ayla is on her way too?" Sarak yells. "What else could go wrong?"

The overhead lights flicker. Relays in the floor-to-ceiling racks click several times. Sarak sighs at sight of the control circuitry coming back online.

"Hurry, Father! The Galactic Drives are cycling through their initialization sequences."

"Guess I should not mention nurse Jasmine," Andorf mumbles as he hobbles over to inspect the heavy lead-lined vault with the self-contained travel chamber wedged inside. "There must be several thousand pounds of lead lining this thing."

Sarak ushers him into the chamber's opening. "Try seven-and-a-half-tons. It'll take every last ounce of lead to teleport you back thirty-two years."

"Where did you ever find so much lead?" Andorf says. "I thought it was a rare commodity aboard starships."

"I called in my last favors with the techs across the hallway. They also helped me form the soft edges into a smooth shell."

Andorf hesitantly climbs inside the environmental chamber. "I see you have not granted me much leg room. It's pretty cramped in here with my folder and the spare clothes."

"With you traveling through space, I had to super-insulate this one. Then there's the proton generator powering the chamber and the gyroscopic adjusters which should keep the chamber vertically aligned. A I mentioned before, you wouldn't want to arrive on Earth upside down. But you needn't worry. You'll be hibernating until arrival, so comfort won't really much matter. Now are you absolutely sure about this, Father? You'll be giving up thirty-two years of your life."

Andorf peers at the photo of his beloved Serin pasted inside the chamber. "Gladly."

"Once I inject you with this compound there's no turning back, no changing your mind. Like Rip Van Winkle, you'll be entering a long, deep sleep."

"And how will I awaken upon my arrival?"

"Your lower spine will tingle with electrical sensations which will escalate until you are awake and moving about. It's not enough energy to be harmful, but you'll be feeling it sometime afterwards. Now, this is your last chance to back out."

At Andorf's nod, Sarak extracts a 100ml syringe from his top pocket. He injects enough milky solution to drop a full-sized horse into his father's chest portal and then snaps the plasti-derm flap shut. He runs his fingers around its perimeter, enabling the thermo-sensitive glue to seal the fabric cover.

"I am still struggling with how you obtained so much lead, Son. Did you not say the vault's shell weighs seven-and-a-half-tons? According to the admiral, that is exactly how much missing lead is required to protect the *Atlantis* from secondary engine emissions."

Sarak grins mischievously. "The techs ensured me that the primary slipstream engines are so reliable, the secondary engines will never engage. And besides, with the Galactic Drives coming online, we'll never need the lead shielding. It was just sitting there wasting away. Now crouch down, Father. Try to make yourself comfortable." Sarak slips a mask over Andorf's head, connects the harness and breather hose, and then seals it to the neck collar.

Retracting both legs, Andorf squeezes inside the chamber. He drowsily gives Sarak both thumbs up.

Sarak tosses the hermetically-sealed Claxton fruitcake into his father's lap. "And don't worry, Father. Anything you left behind, will be left in your chest of drawers."

"Chester Drawers," Andorf chants. His head suddenly jerks. His hands flail as the environmental door shuts.

Sarak hears his father mumbling but cannot make out exactly what he is saying. "I know … Led Zepplin was the greatest," Sarak says, nodding his head. "I wish I was back on Earth a hundred years ago. Yes, they could destroy every secondary band." Pushing hard, he latches the heavy door shut, sealing Andorf and his fate inside the cramped environmental chamber.

Sarak punches in a code, presses the engage button, and then covers his ears at the piercing whine of control circuits doing their best to sync up with the Galactic Drives. He watches one long number string slowly increment, while another slowly decrements.

Both sets of long number strings freeze at their target values. As the Galactic Drives engage, the numbers update too rapidly for Sarak to read any but the lesser-significant numbers. He steps away from the seven-and-a-half-ton lead vault as it begins to dance awkwardly about the floor like Mariachi dancers learning new steps. Moments later, the vault THUNKs to an abruptly halt.

The room goes eerily quiet. The young scientist's eyes widen at the sight of both sets of number strings frozen. He FWAPs one side of the cabinet and the long number strings take off counting, as well as the high-pitched whine of the control circuitry.

Nausea suddenly overcomes the experimenter. He covers his mouth and runs for the sink. In a long heave, he expels his breakfast. Wiping his mouth on a damp rag, second thoughts quickly set in. Sarak stares back at the lead box, now covered in thickening layers of frost.

"Oh, my, father! What have I done?"

CHAPTER 56

That Little Green Light
AYLA

Ayla pushes through the heavy door of Sarak's lab. Covering both ears and yelling, she leers at her twin brother through crazed eyes. "What's that blasted noise? It's tinnier than Emin's Tacquay Heap music."

Sarak swallows in relief. "Ayla? I was expecting—"

The lab door again swings open. Mila bursts inside, huffing out of breath. She too yells while covering her ears. "Me? You were expecting me, Sarak? What the hell's that damn noise?"

Sarak dashes toward the rear of his lab. Reaching inside one of the floor-to-ceiling racks, he TWANGs the vibrating piece with an index finger. The irritating high-pitched noise momentarily ceases.

Ayla's raging eyes redirect toward her sister. "Still taking the stairs?"

Grabbing hold of a workbench, Mila catches her breath.

"Father's rubbing cream has me hearing everyone's thoughts," Ayla says. "Something's broke loose in my head. Whatever I do, I can't make it stop."

Mila smirks. "Welcome to *my* world, Sister."

"So, Sarak, where's father?" Ayla yells above the reoccurring high-pitched whine. "I need to tell him what he can do with these visions of his."

"Yeah, where's Daddy? Where are you hiding him?"

Sarak's apparent indifference as he again TWANGs the errant piece draws both girls like a magnet to the rear of the lab. "Father's not here. He's been—"

"Wait!" Ayla says, "What are you doing back here, Mila? I thought father—?"

"Sent me away for ten weeks?" Mila yells. "I know all about him instigating the bogus fact-finding tour. He was getting rid of me while he—"

"Got tattoos." Sarak adds, grinning at Mila. "I heard you were dating some guy with a serpent tongue. How's that going?"

Face reddening, Mila turns away.

Ayla steps in front of her to face Sarak. "What? Father's got tattoos? I knew of the artificial skin, but when did he get tattoos?"

"Beneath the layered skin on his arms and legs, father has eight tattoos."

"We should have had him committed, Mila, when we had the—" Ayla sneezes and then grabs a small cloth from a pants pocket to wipe her runny nose.

Mila leers back. "Catching a cold, are we?"

"It's from wading through damp caves. Did you know, captain Jean-Claude of the *Mayflower* offered to take me under his wing, teach me about fine art?" Ayla sneezes again. "I can't afford to be sick. How could father do this to me?"

"Oh yeah? Take a look at this." Mila pulls at her blouse. "Those three-legged creatures from Daddy's visions poked holes in my blouse … my favorite blouse."

Sarak chuckles. "Well, look at *my* best shirt. I've scrubbed and scrubbed but these chalky bird stains won't come out."

Hiding smirks, the girls scope out everything in the lab, from the buckets of indistinguishable items to Sarak's collection of dented containers and shriveled up fruits from failed experiments appearing like shrunken heads. Both grimace at the lead-wrapped vault.

Sarak turns his head but cannot escape the girls' following faces, cornering him as he tries to walk away.

"Where'd you say father went?" Ayla asks, scrutinizing his face. "My gosh, Sarak. What have you done to yourself? I see deep cracks in your face. Like the stains on your shirt, you look like shit."

"And what's become of your hair?" Mila says, examining her brother. "It's grayer than Daddy's."

"My time-leaping experiments using inanimate objects weren't going well. I needed live specimens but I couldn't very well just ask anyone for help."

Ayla slugs her twin's shoulder. "How many times, Sarak? How many times have you leapt through time?"

Mila wedges between the siblings. "Why didn't you stop when you caught yourself aging?"

"I really didn't think much about it at first." Sarak grits his teeth. "What's a few lines on a guy's face anyway? A few grey hairs appeared … then many more. The further I leapt, the deeper the lines in my face and the thinner my greying hair became. You must believe me. I wanted to stop but time-leaping is so damn addicting. It was only when father's inker friend …"

"I'm tired of hearing about this damn inker." Mila's eyes fixate on the lead-wrapped vault as she paces about the lab. "We know Daddy came in here. Fess up big brother. Where are you hiding him?"

Ayla sneers. "I sensed father entering this lab fifteen—" Following Sarak's pointing fingers, she runs toward the vault. She grabs its frosty door handle, tugs hard. The heavy door refuses to open. Mila grabs the handle as well. The girls pull as hard as they can but the door refuses to budge. They pull harder, giving it their collective all. With a CLINK, the frosty handle snaps off in their hands.

Sarak winces at the CLANK of the broken handle striking the floor and at sight of the screaming sisters rubbing their frostbitten hands. He directs them to stand beneath the hot-air column while he gathers a handful of tools. He then climbs atop a ladder with a four-foot crow bar, pries behind the top of the door and along both sides.

Sighting Sarak's determined hands, the girls' eyes widen. They exchange horrid looks as he slips both hands into insulated gloves. Sarak works the crow bar along the door's perimeter seal to no avail. He steps down and returns to the ladder holding a ten-foot pipe, again advising the girls to move away.

"Here's a little trick papa Brutus taught me as a child," he says, slipping the pipe over the crow bar. "With enough force and leverage, something always breaks."

Sarak inserts the business end of the extended rigging between the seal and frame. With a firm pry, the seal emits cracking sounds. Still, the door refuses to budge. He tries again. After a third pry, in as many places, the heavy lead door works partially-free of its seal. The door finally breaks loose. It's bottom strikes the concrete floor in a BONK only to lean vertically against the vault opening.

Sarak moves the six-foot ladder. His gloved hands push hard against the door. The door leans and finally falls, hitting the floor in a dull THUD. Everything in the lab shudders as a thick fog pours out of the empty lead shell. All surfaces within the lab become coated in a thin frost layer. The lab's temperature drops faster than the test fruits rolling off Sarak's workbenches.

The girls stare, seemingly hypnotized by the glow of two flashing sets of long number strings on the display, one string rapidly incrementing and the other string decrementing just as quickly.

Ayla is first to ask, "What do all these numbers mean?"

Sarak explains how the incrementing numbers indicate relative distance between the *Atlantis* and the traveler's position and how the decreasing number represents the time remaining until the traveler's expected arrival.

Mila shrugs her shoulders. "But what's that got to do with Daddy?"

"If my experiment proves successful, father is currently Earthbound, speeding thirty-two years into the past. Like the three of us stepping through time. He is doing likewise, only much faster and in reverse."

Ayla's jaw drops. Her eyes home in on Sarak. "I hope you're proud of yourself, Sarak. I never got to say goodbye to father."

"Neither did I," Mila yells. "What'd Daddy say? Did he give you final instructions? How are we to get by without—?" She slaps a hand over her mouth. "Oh … I'm having one of Daddy's deja-vu moments. I've said this very thing before." Her eyes widen at the others. "Don't you guys feel it in your gut? This has happened to all of us before."

Ayla shrugs her shoulders.

Sarak changes the subject. "According to his inker friend, father mentioned cravings for coffee. He also desired some fancy French pastries called beignets."

Mila's eyes narrow. She pushes Ayla aside to corner the young scientist. "Oh, I warned you, Sarak, but no … you wouldn't listen. I told you what I'd do if you sent Daddy away!" Forming scissors with two fingers, she throws them in Sarak's face. But this time she cannot get her fingers to make the suggestive cutting motion as she had threatened him with so many times in the past. Her hand flattens at his whisking hand.

Sarak snarls at big sister's scowling face. "I fear you no more, bitch."

Mila slams a fist onto the workbench. "Damn it, Sarak, how could you let Daddy talk you into doing such a stupid thing? You knew how gullible he is when it came to your mother."

Ayla cringes. "Father's sixty-one. Do you realize how old he'll be when he arrives back on Earth?"

Sarak smiles. "Yep. Ninety-three."

Mila begins to hyperventilate. She again leans against the workbench. "There'll be no one his age," she says, panting out the words. "I won't be there to help him. How will he ever survive without me?"

"That's assuming father even gets there, let alone alive," Ayla says. "And why the hell were you helping him, Sarak? We've been through all this. I thought the three of us were in agreement."

Distancing himself from the irate sisters, Sarak begins to stutter. "I—I had a change of heart when …" he clears his throat. "I dislocated my shoulder. After a few squirts of Uncle Greg's analgesic rubbing cream, I was hallucinating." He pauses to see the girls rolling their eyes and placing their hands on their hips.

"Next you'll be telling me there's a fourth Kaanta out there," Ayla says.

Sarak smiles proudly. "Yep. My artwork decorates the *Atlantis'* B-deck. I was, deep into sketching out wild visions, when I envisioned father as an old man at the Cos, so happy to be reunited with mother. Did you know, Ayla, you could pass as mother's identical twin?" Tipping his head as if begging their absent forgiveness, he takes a deep breath. "Dammit, you two! Don't you see? I saw father's destiny. It was in my vision."

"Daddy put those visions in our heads," Mila says. "Like how he astro-projected us to planet Nero."

Ayla steps close and firmly grasps her brother's forearm. "Let's assume father does make it back to save mother. What happens then? Does everything change, like in those time-travel movies?"

Mila winces. "What if it's like the sequels, where each instance they screw with the time-line they corrupt it even worse?"

For a moment, all cringe.

"I suspect, when father arrives on Earth his brain will be terribly scrambled," Sarak says. "The last thing he heard will echo in his head over the next thirty-two years. It shall be the one decisive thing which defines his identity … the person he permanently becomes."

"You were here when Daddy departed, Sarak. What was the last thing you said to him?"

Sarak shrugs his shoulders.

"Think harder!" Ayla yells. "Father's life depends on it."

Sarak scratches his thinning hairline. "Well … I was closing the lead door, sealing him into the vault. I saw him flailing his arms, heard him ranting something from beneath his air mask. I agreed Led Zepplin was the greatest but he seemed awful worried about things being left behind. I assured him I'd put whatever he forgot in his chest of drawers."

"Ha! Chester Drawers," Ayla says. "That's who father becomes."

Mila's hand cups her chin. "Hmm. Chester Drawers ... I vaguely recall Daddy mentioning an old man ... yes, his name was Chester."

Sarak's eyes widen. "Chester was the cranky old coffee vendor of whom father often spoke."

"You know, he'll be arrested for treason the moment he steps onto Earth soil," Ayla says. "The Canine Empire had a history of rounding up anyone they considered a threat, roughing them up, and then executing them on the spot. They'll hang him in the back alleys of Yestermore."

Mila cringes. "Daddy will never get his coffee."

"Or his fancy French pastry." Ayla wipes her dripping nose. "Let alone see mother again."

Sarak casts his hands outward, waves both in appeasing circular motions. "Whoa! Calm down, you two. Think anyone would recognize father as a feeble ninety-three-year-old man going by the name of Chester Drawers?" He grabs Andorf's ID off his workbench and flashes it at the siblings. "Don't you see? Father's got the perfect cover. The crimes you're both worried about him committing like hijacking this starship will have yet to occur."

Mila lunges at Sarak, hands going straight for his throat. "I ought to kill you, Sarak. Give me one reason not to finish you off right here and now."

Squeezing between them, Ayla struggles to pry Mila's hands off her twin brother's throat. "If anyone kills him, Sister, it's going to be me."

Sarak gasps as he catches his breath. Mila's hands again reach for his throat. Ayla again jumps in to stop her.

Locked in a three-way battle stance, the siblings freeze at the sound of the lab's heavy door opening. Their heads turn toward the sound.

Breathing hard and mouth flapping, nurse Jasmine boldly invades the hostile territory. "I hate to interrupt your little family feud, kids, but has anyone seen Andorf? I've scoured the *Atlantis* from stem to stern and cannot find him anywhere. The starship directory has him this lab."

Slipping free of the huddle, Sarak backs away. Ayla's eyes narrow upon the nurse. "This is a private lab. What gives you the right to barge in here?"

Sarak half-way grins. "I've been working with Jasmine during this project. I've granted her lab access."

Mila's eyes narrow as well. "And who gave you have access to passenger files?"

Jasmine stares at the sisters, still embraced in a battle position behind Sarak. "Consider it a job perk." Jasmine peers into the empty lead-wrapped vault. She gazes at Andorf's badge dangling from Sarak's hand and then looks up at the overhead fans and around the lab at the traces of a thinning fog. "So, Andorf actually went through with it. You sent your father back to old Earth, didn't you, Sarak?"

The girls release each other to straighten their clothing. Their attention shifts from Sarak to the woman who apparently had a grave influence on their father's decision.

Jasmine gazes long and hard at one sibling and then the next, as though sensing them dissecting her thoughts. "Stop it! Stop it!" she yells, grabbing her head with both hands. "My head's about to explode. Everyone quit picking at my brain."

Sarak steps in Jasmine's direction. "You came here with the intent of reminding my father to save your late husband."

Mila squints in despise of the nurse she has distrusted since the day they met. "Dougie … Dougie was his name."

"Dougie was refueling the doomed *S.S. Inca* during the tragic Titan Incident," Ayla adds.

Jasmine's jaw drops. "Ah ha. I knew it. You're *all* Goshis, every last one of you!" She stares at Mila quite confused. "But I don't understand how are you doing this, Mila? Andorf's not your biological father."

Ayla winks at Mila. "What would you expect? She's lived with a master Goshi most of her life."

"I see," Jasmine says, catching the sisters' eye interactions. "Now back to Andorf …"

One of the graphical displays in Sarak's equipment rack begins to flicker, drawing everyone's attention. All gather around to watch the destination display rehome from City Park to a little French bakery, nestled deep within the commercial district, a mile off course.

Sarak gulps at three pairs of eyes staring him down. "The device apparently has a few glitches. But no worries. It's nothing that should affect father," he mumbles.

Taking a swing, Ayla slugs Sarak's shoulder. "Uncross those fingers behind your back, brother. We know there's as much chutzpah as there is science in your crazy experiments."

Jasmine appears confused. "Chutzpah?"

Mila snarls. "It means our *dear* brother exhibits shameless audacity."

Nodding her head, Jasmine walks about the lab. Spotting the spent schooner, she takes a whiff and then peers at Sarak. "Your father's last drink, I presume?"

"Yep."

Jasmine swirls the cherry-colored liquid remnant. She withdraws the straw and blows the thick remnants into her belt-mounted scanalyzer.

She waits. Everyone waits.

When the scanalyzer buzzes, Jasmine grins. "It appears your father's drink was packed with proteins. A series of these time-delayed drinks could possibly sustain him in a hibernation state over thirty years. Congratulations, Sarak, we've mastered the sustenance issue."

"All the signs were there," Ayla says, lightly toe-kicking the lead-lined vault. "First father's fanatical Kaanta … then his obsession with seeing mother. I should have put him away when I had the chance."

"Don't tell me the Goshi fooled each of you with his insanity act?" Jasmine says. "Who else in the armada knew we'd be speaking Tenulian? And name anyone who calculates Murray Disturbances and their effects in his head right down to the second. Believe me, I know. I've witnessed him doing such things."

Mila smirks. "Daddy used that last disturbance to slip past me."

"And Sarak," Jasmine continues. "I bet he was familiar with your racks filled with fancy equipment, like he'd seen it all before."

Eyes widening, Sarak reluctantly nods, recalling how easily his father had homed the display onto City Park. "Why, yes. he acted as though this was not his first time."

Jasmine's eyes sweep across at the siblings. "Don't you see? Your father was pushing your buttons, toying with you. The sly man had everyone fooled, including myself. To him, this was another full-dress rehearsal. And you know he'll keep doing this until …"

Ayla sighs. "He never loses her."

Mila suddenly chokes up in tears. "I was barely five, a stowaway aboard the *Atlantis* when Daddy found me. Speakers were blasting from everywhere, demanding he return to his cabin. Scooping me in his arms, he smiled at me as no man has done before. I recall him kicking the cabin door open and finding your mother, weak and drained, sprawled across the floor in a pool of blood. Left behind and shivering in fear beneath a bed, I watched him rush out the cabin door, cradling Serin in his arms. Never having seen anyone so caring, I ran after him all the way to sick bay. He did everything he could to save your mother before breaking down sobbing when she passed."

Mila pauses, to wipe her damp eyes. "He and I cried for weeks on end. I thought the pain would never subside. And you two were babies, so demanding of his attention. For Daddy's sake, I dealt with my jealously and we became a family of four, five including Binky the rabbit."

"Six including papa Brutus," Sarak adds.

Mila lifts her chin. "You two moved out, had your families, but I stayed. I've been the one taking care of Daddy these past thirty-two years."

Sarak glances at the panel displaying one number rapidly incrementing and the other decrementing just as quickly. He gulps. "I'm beginning to have doubts about whether father will succeed on his quest to save mother. You see, the inker was interrupted by Q-nots and never got the critical instructions applied to the back of his hands. Father will be lost when tattoos on his limbs eventually reveal themselves."

Ayla sneezes and then wipes her runny nose. "But how will we ever know? What proof will we have father even made it back to old Earth alive?"

Mila stomps on the floor. With narrowing eyes and crinkled brow, she sequentially addresses the others, one pointed rant at a time. "—You,

Ayla! You started all this by wearing your mother's clothes and her flowered perfume. You had Daddy believing his beloved wife had returned. What the hell else was he to think after discovering you lying face down on my bed? It was *you* who pushed him over the edge."

She whips her head around. "And some great son you turned out to be, Sarak, sending Daddy back to Earth without regard for anyone else. How could you do this, knowing even your teleportals aren't one-hundred percent reliable?"

"We all have accidents once in a while," Sarak grumbles. "Nothing is infallible."

"And you, Jasmine. What kind of nurse baits someone's hope with intent of saving her long-dead husband? Quit telling the big lie. You've lost Donnie. Get over it!"

"Dougie. My husband's name was Dougie."

"All right, Dougie. It's time to accept defeat. Move on with your life and quit dragging everyone down with you. All of you should be ashamed of yourselves … playing off Daddy's emotions like you did." Mila stomps her feet. "Because of you three, I'll never see Daddy ever again."

Sarak steps forward. "You can't blame any of us. Father's obsession flared up months ago when his old friend returned. Sven drilled the notion of being with mother into his head. If anyone is to blame, it should be old man Sven."

Ayla tips her head to one side, appearing quite confused. "Sven? As in Uncle Sven? Are you telling us the crazy old coot who believed he was a Swede came back after all this time just to have a chat with father?"

Sarak nods.

Mila takes a deep breath, as if to keep herself from hyperventilating. Folding her arms, she joins the others at the rack console as they stare, hypnotized by the long busy streams of numbers, one incrementing and the other counting down to zero. "Well, I know Daddy best. I lived with him most of my life. I say we grant him his final wish, to be reunited with his beloved Serin. It's all he's ever wanted since—say, Sarak, what's with that little green light over there? Why isn't it glowing bright like those others?"

Sarak's face squinches. "Ignore that light. It's only worked once. I believe the circuit may be blown."

The women encircle Sarak. Ayla's eyes narrow upon him. "What is it you aren't telling us, Sarak?"

Mila grunts. "Yeah, little brother, what's going on?"

"Spit it out," Jasmine snarls.

Breathing hard and perspiring, Sarak flinches at being surrounding by the sisters and nurse who are staring him down. Flexing at finger jabs to his ribs, he steps away. "Th—that green door indicator has only illuminated once and … even then, it was but only for a moment. Theoretically … if the object reaches its desired target—"

Mila grabs Sarak's arm as the others close ranks around him. She grabs hold of his face and pulls it inches of her own. "What the hell do objects and targets have to do with Daddy?"

"Spell it out," Ayla yells.

Jasmine growls. "In plain Tenulian."

Cornered, with nowhere to run, Sarak lowers his head as if feeling shamed. He hesitates until three sets of fingers again poke hard into his ribs. Stuttering and pausing between words, he dares not peer up at the angry threesome. "I—it means the environmental chamber door—the one housing father has opened. B—but the chamber could have intersected something like a Murray Disturbance and been thrown off target in another direction. Or it could have taken hits from any number of spatial objects between here and Earth." Sarak clenches his teeth. "The door could blow off, exposing him to the frigid vacuum of space."

"And still, you sent him off in some untested environmental chamber," Mila yells. "Didn't you have enough time to build something more of a battle cruiser?"

Ayla's brow narrows. "From what I've learned, Earth was an extremely hostile place. I'd never want to live there … certainly not under the domination of the seven authoritarian empires." She glares at Mila. "Father could have spent his last years enjoying his great-grandkids."

Being single and childless, Mila growls at her sister's latest volley.

Sarak gulps. "I know father's chance of surviving to the ripe old age of ninety-three would have increased exponentially if only he had chosen to remain aboard the *Atlantis*." He offers a grim look at the others. "But, there's always a slim possibility he succeeds. Everything would change. He and mother would both be alive in their early sixties. Jasmine would not be with us as we never would have met her since birth. And Mila would be living on her own. Hell, everything we know at this very moment, would instantly change and then—"

"Then what, Sarak?" Mila says.

Ayla winces. "Yeah, what happens next? Are we about to break some forbidden space-time continuum? Is reality about to—?"

The lab door bursts open. At Burak's direction, six electricians armed with tools ravage through Sarak's lab. Before anyone can stop them, random wires throughout the lab have been sliced. Sparks fly everywhere. The Goshis cast their hands out, sending the intruders falling to the floor.

The overhead lights suddenly dim. The control circuitry's whining noise ceases. All eyes are drawn to the pair of long numerical strings, one frozen on a very large number, and the other displaying all zeros. A bell at the far side of the lab rings out like school recess. The dull green lamp illuminates, bathing all in bright green light. Twenty seconds later, the light extinguishes.

With his heart racing, Sarak gazes wild-eyed at Ayla in the otherwise vacant lab. "Do you know what this means? We're about to meet our—"

Footsteps sound in the hallway, growing louder with each step. When the heavy lab door opens, the room fills with a sweet scent of wild mountain flowers. Ayla spins about. Her eyes widen at the sight of the long-haired woman standing before her.

"Mother?"

The lab door again swings open. Sixty-one-year-old Andorf approaches Serin to slip an arm around his beloved's waist. He then gazes at the twins. "Why are you both down here in Sarak's lab? You are missing your birthday celebration." He leans into the twins. "I hear Mila and captain Murray both have tributes to your papa Brutus."

Serin extends an arm. "Come. We mustn't keep everyone waiting."

AFTER THOUGHTS

As the result of Andorf saving Serin's life, the tragedy at Titan Station in the previous novel never occurred. Serin was instrumental in handling terms of the revised refueling negotiation. All forty-six armada starships departed the outpost with fuel tanks filled to capacity. Although Brutus and Captain Murray Barnwell escaped their crushing fate, Brutus's destiny remains inside replicator #6. Needless to say, Murray remains the Atlantis' captain.

Binky and Gregory passed on as described in the current story. Nurse Jasmine was never again seen after delivering Serin's twins. Raised by Andorf and Serin, Mila moved out to be on her own soon after turning twenty-one.

Tales of Andorf's travels back to Earth thirty-two years in the past are described in the fourth novel, *The Howling Winds of Yestermore*. Nothing appears to go right for the ninety-three-year-old, leaving everyone wondering whether he can pull off this caper. Returning to old Earth, how troubles in his quest, navigating around Brutus, Serin, Chester, and his younger self. But how will he know the right time to interact with them and how? It all boils down to one final moment.

Look for

The Howling Winds Of Yestermore

Gary McConville
Lagomorph Publishing LLC
http://www.lagopub.com

The author may be contacted at:
http://www.garymcconville.com

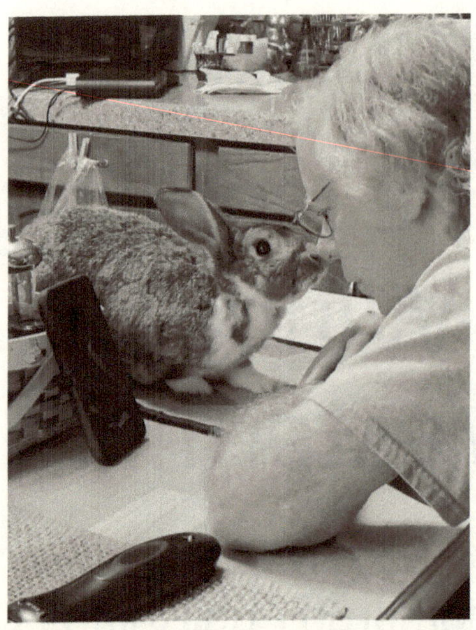

Gary lives with his wife, cats, and house rabbits. Each estranged rescued pet carries unspoken tales of past lives. His hobbies include amateur (ham) radio and working on electronic projects.

Book 1 – A Stiff Wind Blows

Book 2 – Winds Of Darkness

Book 3 – Winds Of The Goshi

Book 4 – The Howling Winds Of Yestermore